HEARTWARMING

Sweet Mountain Rancher

—

Loree Lough

H HARLEQUIN® HEARTWARMING™

Recycling programs
for this product may
not exist in your area.

ISBN-13: 978-0-373-36742-9

Sweet Mountain Rancher

Copyright © 2015 by Loree Lough

Printed in U.S.A.

Nate slid the envelope over to Eden.

"I don't know what to say."

He lifted her chin. "Say okay. And that you'll find a safe place to keep it until you need it for a contractor, new appliances and whatnot."

"A safe place?" Eden sighed. "Is there such a thing these days?"

"Would you feel more comfortable if I held on to the money? Say the word and name the amount you need, and I'll be right over to deliver it." He grinned. "Probably at mealtime."

"*Thank you* doesn't begin to cover what I feel." Eden focused on something beyond his left shoulder. Nate couldn't pinpoint the change in her expression. Anger? Fear? Disgust?

"No thanks necessary. I like those kids." *And I like you.* "I'm glad I can help out a little."

"A little?" Eden laughed. "I took a writing class a few years ago," she said, "and the instructor stressed two things over and over."

"Oh?"

"One—don't undervalue your contributions."

She leaned in close, real close.

"And what's number two?"

"Show," she whispered, "don't tell."

Eden pressed her lips to his, a lingering, heart-pounding kiss that left him breathless, wanting more.

When it ended, he looked into those striking storm-gray eyes and found a word to describe the subtle shift in her mood, and it hurt like a roundhouse punch to the gut: *obligated.*

Dear Reader,

At one time or another, we've all recited the adage, "You can't judge a book by its cover" and the ol' Will Rogers quote, "You'll never get a second chance to make a first impression." Put the two together and we'd sound a little like my secondary character Shamus Magee: "You'll never get a second chance to judge a book by its cover." Not even Eden Quinn, who relies on his grandfatherly insights, knows if Shamus's mixed metaphors are deliberate or just a facet of his quirky personality. She has a surrogate mom of sorts, too: Cora Michaels, who teaches Eden that sometimes even the best mothers raise not-so-good kids. It's a particularly tough lesson for Eden, whose life and career are dedicated to helping troubled teen boys...

Surrounded by a loving, tight-knit family, Nate Marshall doesn't need surrogate relatives. His raised-as-brothers cousins, Sam and Zach, know when things aren't right and have no trouble doling out much-needed advice—whether Nate thinks he needs it or not!

As an avid reader, you've no doubt figured out that secondary characters are integral to a story's design...and the main characters' development. Secondaries serve as sounding boards, advisors, even comic relief, and their interactions with the main characters allow readers to see deep into the minds and hearts of a book's stars, too.

After you've finished reading *Sweet Mountain Rancher*, I'd love to hear which secondaries were your favorites!

Meanwhile, here's hoping your life is filled with caring, helpful "secondaries"!

Wishing you only the best,

Loree Lough

Loree Lough once sang for her supper. Traveling by way of bus and train, she entertained folks in pubs and lounges across the USA and Canada. Her favorite memories of "days on the road" are the hours spent singing to soldiers recovering from battle wounds in VA hospitals. Now and then she polishes up her Yamaha guitar to croon a tune or two, but mostly she writes. Her past Harlequin Heartwarming novel, *Saving Alyssa*, brought the total number of Loree's books-in-print to one hundred (fifteen bearing the Harlequin logo). Loree's work has earned numerous industry accolades, movie options and four- and five-star reviews, but what she treasures most are her Readers' Choice awards.

Loree and her real-life hero split their time between Baltimore's suburbs and a cabin in the Allegheny Mountains, where she continues to perfect her "identify the critter tracks" skills. A writer who believes in giving back, Loree donates a generous portion of her annual income to charity (see the Giving Back page of her website, loreelough.com, for details). She loves hearing from her readers and answers every letter personally. You can connect with her on Facebook, Twitter and Pinterest.

Books by Loree Lough

Harlequin Heartwarming

Saving Alyssa
Devoted to Drew
Raising Connor
Once a Marine

Visit the Author Profile page
at Harlequin.com for more titles.

This story is dedicated to all the good-hearted people who see to the needs of helpless kids when their loved ones can't...or won't. There's a special place in heaven for all of you!

Acknowledgments

A huge and heartfelt thank-you to those of you who took time from your busy schedules to answer my lengthy list of questions involving the foster care system, halfway houses and shelters that provide for kids in need. I admire the dedication that pushes you far, far above and beyond the bounds of your assigned duties—even when facing seemingly insurmountable odds. Though I respect and understand that in order to protect the kids in your care you must remain anonymous, I will remember your names and your deeds with fondness and gratitude!

CHAPTER ONE

NATE RESTED GLOVED hands on the gatepost and watched the long green van pull up to the barn. Over the past few days, he'd spoken several times with Eden Quinn, who'd called to ask if she could bring the teen boys in her care to the Double M for a weekend of communing with nature.

Right off the bat, he translated "boys in her care" to mean juvenile delinquents, and issued a matter-of-fact *no*. If they weren't trouble, they'd be home with their parents or guardians instead of some county-run facility. Nate had to hand it to her, though, because after she repeated her spiel three different ways, he gave in. It was Memorial Day weekend, after all, and the ranch hands had scattered to the four winds, leaving him and Carl to hold down the fort. Once he'd taken the boys' measure, he'd decide whether or not he could trust them alone in the bunkhouse. But no need to worry about that just yet, since it wasn't likely they'd last until dark. In his experience, city folk shied away from work—

the good old-fashioned hard work that involved powerful animals and manure.

As the van came to a stop, Nate thumbed his tan Stetson to the back of his head. The boys, staring out the windows, did their best to look older and tougher than their years. To date, his only experience with young'uns of *any* kind involved his cousins' kids, all happy, well-adjusted and under the age of ten. Nabbing sweets without permission was the worst crime any of them had committed. Something told him this hard-edged bunch was long past lifting cookies before dinner, and he hoped he hadn't made a gigantic mistake inviting them to the family's ranch.

The noonday sun, gleaming from the windshield, blocked his view of the driver. After seeing the boys' sour expressions, he half expected someone who resembled Nurse Ratched to exit the vehicle. Instead, a petite woman in a plaid shirt and snug jeans hopped down from the driver's seat and slid the side door open with a strength that belied her size.

"Okay, guys, everybody out!"

Nate recognized the husky-yet-feminine voice from their phone calls. He'd been way off base, thinking she'd look like a burly prison guard. He guessed her age at twenty-four, tops. But she had to be older than that if she'd passed muster with the state officials who'd hired her.

One by one, the teens exited the van and stared gap-jawed at the Rockies' Front Range. As Eden walked toward him, he noticed her high-topped sneakers that would probably fit his eight-year-old niece. Nate grinned to himself, wondering how feet that small kept her upright…and how long the shoes would stay white.

"Hi," she said, extending a hand, "I'm Eden Quinn."

The strength of her handshake, like everything else about her, surprised him. She pumped his arm up and down as if she expected water to trickle from his fingertips.

"Nate Marshall said I should meet him here at noon. If you'll just tell me where to find him—"

"I'm Nate," he said, releasing her hand. "Good to meet you." He'd uttered the phrase, but couldn't remember ever meaning it more.

Eden tucked her fingertips into the back pockets of her jeans. "I expected you'd be, well, older."

"Ditto," he said, grinning.

Eden rested a hand on the nearest teen's shoulder. "This is my right-hand man, Kirk Simons, and these are our boys."

Nate followed Eden and Kirk down the line, shaking each boy's hand as she introduced them.

"Is that a Stetson?" one asked.

Nate smiled. "Yep."

"Cool."

At the other end of the line, Eden clasped her hands together and faced Nate. "So where do we start?"

He searched each boy's face to single out the troublemakers. One or two gave him pause, but none showed any signs of blatant mutiny. He hoped the same would be true when the green van drove back down the driveway.

"Leave your gear in the van for now," he said. "Let's head on into the barn. Once we're saddled up, I'll give you the nickel tour of the Double M."

"Saddle up? None of us ever rode a horse before."

The kid looked sixteen, maybe seventeen, and spoke with an authority that seemed out of place, given the fact that he lived in a place like Latimer House.

"Just follow my lead and you'll be fine," Nate assured him.

"Can we pick any horse we want?"

Eden had told him the boys were fifteen to seventeen. This one, Nate decided, must have a growth hormone problem.

"Why don't we let Mr. Marshall choose this time," Kirk said. "He'll know better how to match you up with a horse that isn't a runner, or worse, one that isn't of a mind to move at all."

The suggestion satisfied them, and like mustangs, the boys charged ahead, laughing like four-year-olds as they raced toward the barn.

"Hey, fellas," he called after them, "hold it down, or you'll spook 'em."

Instantly, they quieted and slowed their pace. This might not be such a bad weekend after all. If they survived the ride—and what he had in mind for them next.

As the assistant joined the boys, Eden fell into step beside him. "This is really nice of you, Nate. Not many people are willing to give kids like these a chance. I hope you'll consider inviting them back. At your convenience, of course. Because being out here in the fresh air, learning about horses and cattle..." She exhaled a happy sigh. "I just know they're going to love this!"

Since losing Miranda, Nate had made a habit of saying no. But there stood Eden, blinking up at him with long-lashed gray eyes. He couldn't say, "Let's see how the rest of the weekend goes," because yet again, his brain had seized on the "kids like these" part of her comment. What had they done to earn the title?

"I wasn't the best-behaved young'un myself." He hoped the admission would invite an explanation.

"That's true of most of us, don't you think?"

Nate noticed that Eden had to half-run to keep up with his long-legged stride. Slowing his pace, he said, "So how did you hear about the Double M?"

"Oh, I didn't tell you when we spoke on the phone?"

She had, but he wanted to see her face as she repeated it.

"We have a mutual friend. Shamus Magee. He suggested this might be a good change of pace for these city-born-and-raised boys of mine."

His grandfather often referred to Shamus as "good people," and that was good enough for Nate.

"And I asked for you, specifically," she continued, "instead of your dad or one of your uncles."

"Why?"

"I read all about you in *Sports Illustrated.* You know, the issue where they featured major leaguers who…"

She trailed off, telling Nate she didn't know how to broach the subject of the accident that ended his pitching career—and killed his fiancée—two years ago.

"Does the shoulder still bother you much?"

"I can predict the weather now," he said, grinning, "but that's about it." It wasn't, despite months of grueling physical therapy. And the head shrinker that'd helped him come to terms with his Miranda issues. But he had no intention of dredging up bad memories with someone he'd just met—and would likely never see again.

"They'd never admit it," she said, using her chin as a pointer, "but they were more excited about meeting a baseball star than spending the weekend at a ranch." She paused for a step or two, then added, "Think you'll ever go back? To baseball, I mean?"

"No. Too much damage." He reflexively rotated the shoulder and winced at the slight twinge. "But it doesn't keep me from doing things around here, so…"

He'd never seen eyes the color of a storm sky before. Funny that instead of cold or danger, they hinted at warmth and sweetness. He hadn't felt anything—*anything*—for a woman since the accident, and didn't know how to react to his interest in her. Nate tugged his hat lower on his forehead. Unfortunately, it did nothing to block his peripheral vision.

"And anyway, that was then, and this is now."

She leaned forward slightly, looked up into his face. "Ah, so you're one of those guys who isn't comfortable with compliments?"

Nate only shrugged.

"The boys were fascinated when I told them about your baseball history." She glanced toward the barn. "Something tells me when they get to know you better, they'll have an even bigger case of hero worship."

Hero worship. The words made him cringe. Before every game, fans from four to ninety-four lined the fence beside the outfield, waving programs, caps, even paper napkins in the hope of acquiring a signature. He'd taken a lot of heat from teammates when a kid in the autograph line slapped the label on him. "We're not heroes," he'd blurted, thinking of his cousin Zach, who'd served multiple tours of duty in Afghanistan, and his cousin Sam, a firefighter in Nashville. "Fans oughta look to soldiers, firefighters and cops as their heroes, not a bunch of overpaid athletes like us." The beating he took from the media had taught him to let his teammates do the talking from that point on, but it hadn't changed his mind on the subject.

"I hope they know what a bunch of garbage that is…and how to recognize a bona fide hero when they see one."

Confusion drew her eyebrows together, and he pretended not to notice by focusing on the boys, who stood just inside the barn. A few still looked bored, but most seemed excited about saddling up. And then there was the smallest one, with that deadpan expression. He'd have to keep an eye on that one.

Using Patches as his example, Nate showed

the teens how to approach a horse and where to stand, and after saddling each horse, he explained how their attitudes would put the animals at ease—or rile them. Before long, the group was ambling single file on the bridle path that ringed the Double M pond before meandering into the woods beyond the corral, doing their best to stay upright and in control of their mounts. "I'm just so proud I could cry!" Eden said, bringing her horse alongside his. "They'll remember this for the rest of their lives. I can't thank you enough, Nate. You don't know how much good you've already done them."

He was too busy wondering what her hair looked like under that Baltimore Orioles baseball cap to answer. Was it long and thick? Or did it just seem that way because of the curly bangs poking out from under the bill?

She quirked an eyebrow, proof that she'd caught him staring.

"What's with the hat? You're not a Colorado Rockies fan?" With any luck, she'd believe it had been the Orioles logo that had captured his attention, not her pretty face.

"I was born in Baltimore, and my dad held season tickets. He took me and my brother to nearly every home game." On the heels of a wistful sigh, she added, "I sure do miss him…"

"How long ago did you lose him?"

She waved, as if the question was an annoying mosquito. "My folks were killed nearly fifteen years ago."

Her tone told him something more sinister than an accident had been responsible for their deaths. But how her parents had died was none of his business. Maybe he'd ask Shamus.

"Afterward, we came to live with my dad's parents, here in Denver. After graduation, my brother went back east for a while. Joined the Baltimore County police force. But a year or so ago, Stuart signed on with the Boulder PD." Smirking, she drew quote marks in the air. "To keep an eye on me, he said."

A good idea, considering what she did for a living. "How old were you guys when you moved here?"

"I was twelve, Stuart was nine."

Nate could only shake his head. At that age, he'd spent half his time shirking chores and the other half thinking up excuses when his parents caught him at it. The tension continued through his teen years, but these days, he considered them close friends. Nate glanced ahead at the boys, who had lost or been taken from their parents and now looked to Eden as their surrogate mother.

She leaned forward to whisper something in her horse's ear. This may have been the boys' first time in the saddle, but it definitely wasn't Eden's. "So your dad was a native Coloradan?"

"Yes, but he joined the army right out of college and they stationed him at Fort Meade, where Mom was a clerk in the records office." She looked over at him. "What about you? Did you move to Maryland when the team signed you?"

"No, I was already out there, attending the University of Maryland."

"Oh, that's right. I remember reading about that in the article. You were majoring in animal husbandry and playing for the school's baseball team when a scout saw you."

Nate snickered quietly. "You remember more about that fluff piece than I do."

"I'd hardly call it fluff. But it says a lot about you, that you don't buy into your own publicity." Eden winked. "Gotta admire a guy who's comfortable in his own skin."

Miranda had majored in communications and minored in psychology, so he'd heard enough psychobabble to choke Patches. Her insistence on analyzing his every word, action and reaction had been the main bone of contention between them. If she hadn't taken her eyes off the road to rant at him about his indecisiveness…

"Long, long way between then and now," he ground out. And to smother any platitudes she might spout, Nate said, "Did you and your brother spend summers back east?"

Eden was silent for several moments. "No. My mom's parents visited once, about five years after…" She shrugged. "We raced around doing so many touristy things, there wasn't time to re-connect. We saw them a time or two after that, and then their health declined."

She fell quiet again. "Stuart looks a lot like my mom, and I inherited her mannerisms. It's nobody's fault that we reminded our grandpar-ents of their only child, but it explains why it was tough for them to be around us." Another shrug. "Listen to me, droning on and on about the past. What a bore!"

He laughed with her, although he found her anything but boring. Nate nodded toward her charges. "Takes a courageous woman to take on a challenge like that."

She glanced ahead on the trail, where the boys joked and talked as if they didn't have a care in the world. And for the moment at least, they didn't.

"Oh, believe me, I haven't reached all of them," she said softly. "Yet."

He might have asked what she meant, if he hadn't noticed one of the boys leaning too far right in the saddle.

Eden saw it, too. "Uh-oh. Thomas won't take it well if he falls."

Man, what he wouldn't give to know what *that* meant!

"Don't worry. Nobody will fall. Not on my watch."

Nate rode up the line, knowing Thomas's mount would automatically match his own horse's pace. "Thirsty?" he asked, holding out a bottle of water.

"No way. If I let go of this handle, I'll end up in the pond."

He didn't bother correcting the boy. "Use your knees, everyone," he said loudly enough for the others to hear. "That'll let your horse know you're the boss and help you keep your balance."

Something about Thomas unnerved him. That almost-smirk on his face, for starters… like he was up to no good. The feeling stayed with him for the rest of the afternoon, as he showed the boys how to remove and stow saddles, blankets, bits and harnesses, taught them how to brush the horses' coats, and lectured them on the dangers of overfeeding or overwatering the horses following a long ride.

He put them to work mucking the back stalls, and when they finished that, he pointed to the pitchforks and shovels hanging on the wall.

"Wheelbarrows are out back. Fill 'em up and roll 'em out there," he instructed, pointing at the steaming mound near the tree line.

Last, Nate asked for help moving sacks of feed from the grain shed to the barn. And the whole time, he made it his business to know where Thomas was.

Eden pitched in and pulled more than her fair share of the load. They were all red-faced and sweating by the time they were finished.

"Good job, y'all," Nate told them. "Go ahead and grab your gear, and meet me at the bunkhouse so I can explain how we do things around here."

Kirk led them toward the driveway as, too tired to complain or ask what he meant, the boys muttered about achy muscles and blisters on their palms. He'd expected to lose them after the first wheelbarrow tipped. Surprisingly, they stuck it out. Even Thomas.

Eden started to join them in their slog toward the van, too, but he stopped her. "They're liable to be sore in places they didn't even know they had," he said, smiling down at her. "Any aspirin in your pack?"

"Yes," she said, laughing as she headed toward the van. "But if they feel anything like I do right now, they'll need some strong liniment, too."

Later, as the boys played rock-paper-scissors for their turn at the showers, he led her to a small room at the back of the cabin. Hardly bigger than a closet, the room held a narrow cot, a coat rack, a small desk and chair, and a shelf that held quilts and pillows.

"Foreman's quarters," he explained. "The walls are thin, so it doesn't offer much in the way of privacy, but it's clean." He nodded toward the foot of the bed. "Everyone's got fresh linens, but the nights can get cold this time of year, so if anyone needs extra blankets, help yourselves."

She pressed her fingertips into one of the pillows. "Fat and fluffy," she said with a wink. "Just the way I like 'em."

"Think the guys will be okay with these rugged accommodations?"

She glanced at the boys, who were snickering and exchanging good-natured shoves as they flapped sheets and shook pillows into their pillowcases.

"This place is like Buckingham Palace compared to where some of them lived before Latimer House. And you worked them hard. I have a feeling they'll be dead to the world long before dark." Eden started for the door. "Walk with me?"

Outside, she removed the baseball cap, freeing a mass of curls that spilled down her back like a cinnamony waterfall.

"Two of them were homeless. Living in alleys and under bridges before the cops picked them up." She harrumphed. "And trust me, they were better off there than under their parents' roofs. Every time I think about the things they must have seen and survived…"

He remembered Thomas's dark, darting eyes. What had the boy experienced to inspire that look of fear and apprehension…and simmering anger?

"I'm guessing you're not allowed to get specific about their pasts."

"You're right. But you'd be less than normal if you *didn't* wonder how they all ended up with me." She crossed both arms over her chest. "Let me put it this way: Kids who end up in places like Latimer House usually have fairly long records. Nothing overtly violent, mind you, but repeated offenses, like arson, breaking and entering, shoplifting, assault, even loitering and curfew violations. With no parental supervision, they were well on their way to a prison cell. Latimer House is the end of the line. One more goof-up, and it's off to juvie."

"What about foster care?"

A sad smile lifted one corner of her mouth. "There's nowhere else in the system for boys with their histories. Besides, the number of kids waiting for placement in foster homes far out-weighs the number of families willing to take them in."

"Why would the state put that many troubled teens in the care of one itty-bitty counselor?"

Eyes narrowed slightly, she arched her left brow. "I'm sure you aren't insinuating that I'm unqualified or incapable of doing my job. Because that would be insulting."

Experience had taught him that when he didn't know what to say, silence trumped words, every time.

She took a step closer. "Just so you know, I'm a psychologist, not a counselor. Basically, I can identify a disorder and provide treatment—I have a PhD—while a counselor's goal is to help patients make their own decisions regarding treatment. Clearly, these kids are in no position to do that."

Eden propped a fist on her hip. "Every hour of every day is a challenge, but I'm fully qualified to handle it. I appreciate your concern, but trust me, it's unwarranted."

He'd obviously hit a nerve, and right now those big gray eyes looked anything but warm and sweet.

"Hey, Eden?"

"Be right there, DeShawn. I'll be back in a few minutes," she told Nate.

Hopefully not to pick up where she'd left off. She jogged across the yard to talk with a boy who towered over her and outweighed her by at least fifty pounds.

Something peculiar caught Nate's attention as Eden and DeShawn chatted beside the bunkhouse: Thomas, alone in the doorway, aiming a baleful glare at no one in particular. Suddenly, he wished he hadn't invited the group to the Double M. Any one of those kids could come back, now that they'd made the trip.

Had his inability to say no put his parents, his sister, Hank, aunts and uncles, cousins and their children in unknown danger?

CHAPTER TWO

DURING THE FIRST half of the hour-long drive back to Denver, the boys talked nonstop about the weekend.

"I thought mucking stalls was bad," DeShawn said, "until Nate made us shovel up the mess and move it to that stinking mountain over by the woods."

"Wouldn't have been so bad if you hadn't tipped the wheelbarrow over...*on your shoes*," Kirk teased.

"Seriously, dude," Wade said. "You're lucky Nate found a pair of running shoes that fit you."

"Yeah, but now I owe some ranch hand I never even met for a new pair. And I ain't got that kinda money."

"Don't have," Eden corrected. "But didn't I hear Nate say you shouldn't worry about that?"

"Man's not gonna keep his word about us comin' back over the Fourth if he keeps having to shell out for stuff we messed up."

"It was just one pair of old shoes. And even Nate said the man rarely wore them," Eden said.

"Yeah, maybe," DeShawn said, "but just wait till he finds—"

In the rearview, Eden saw Thomas smack De-Shawn on the shoulder and aim an angry glare in his direction.

Once they arrived home, Eden would take the smaller boy aside and find out what DeShawn was talking about. Knowing Thomas, it could be anything from a broken lamp to something stolen from one of the ranch hands bureaus... or worse.

Thomas had never been particularly easy to control, but since his father called, demanding his parental rights, things had gone from bad to worse. Thomas didn't have access to the man who'd first neglected, then deserted him. Before moving to Latimer House, Thomas had vented his anger by starting fires; these days, for the most part, he took out his frustrations on the other boys.

"Did anyone think to write down Nate's chili recipe?" she asked, hoping to distract them.

"Nate said he'd email it to me since I did most of the work," Travis said.

"Did not," Cody grumbled.

"Whatever."

When Denver cops found Travis shivering and nearly unconscious in his hut of corrugated metal and cardboard, he had fleas and lice, multiple bruises and cigarette burns on his back, chest and forearms. And even after two operations to repair shattered bones in his left hand, he still had trouble manipulating the thumb. State psychologists who evaluated him in the hospital predicted he'd run away. Often. That he'd have a hard time adjusting to life in a house populated by ten other boys his age. That Eden should prepare for tirades, acts of aggression, destructive behavior. On his second night at Latimer House, he proved them right by flying off the handle because she'd served cheese pizza instead of his favorite, pepperoni. Eden sent the other boys upstairs out of earshot, and in a calm, quiet voice let it be known that she'd earned a black belt in karate. "Please don't test me," she'd told him. Travis took her at her word and ate the pizza without further complaint. And from that day to this, he'd been her best ally, quickly calming disputes between his housemates and helping Eden every chance he got.

It was no surprise that he'd imitated Nate's walk, his cowboy drawl, even the way he stood, feet shoulder-width apart and arms crossed over his chest. Halfway through the weekend, Thomas noticed all this and called him a copycat. The old Travis might have thrown a punch, or at the very least, bellowed at the smaller boy. But eighteen months at Latimer House had changed him, and he took his cue from Nate, who shrugged and smiled as if to say, "So what?"

There was a lot to like about the man, including his rugged good looks. No wonder he'd made *Baltimore Magazine*'s "Bachelor of the Year" list twice, and appeared in dozens of other news stories partnered with beautiful models and popular entertainers. Clearly, he preferred tall, blonde, buxom women. *That leaves you out*, she thought, smirking. But even on the off-chance he occasionally made an exception and dated short, skinny, dark-haired women, Eden didn't have time for a relationship. Especially not with a guy who might withdraw once he learned more about the boys' problems, most of which could be traced back to abandonment issues. After just one weekend, it was clear they were fascinated by Nate's no-nonsense approach to discipline and teaching. And who could blame them? His warm, inviting demeanor had almost tempted *her* to spill the beans about her weird and depressing past.

Eden could blame the near confession on his soft-spoken drawl. The understanding glow in his bright blue eyes. More than likely, though, her inexperience with men, which consisted of half a dozen onetime movie dates in high school and college. Until she met Jake…

Young and foolish, she'd been so swept off

her feet by his hardy good looks that it was easy to confuse his constant doting for love. All too soon, Jake's involvement in every facet of her life began to seem less like caring and more like control. It wasn't until Stuart recounted the events of a domestic violence case that she remembered something her psych professor had said: "Some people try to be tall by cutting off the heads of others." The breakup had been messy, but Eden was determined to keep her head, literally and figuratively.

Somewhere out there, she told herself, was a special someone who'd share her dreams, achievements, even regrets. A man of character, like her dad and grandfather, from whom she could draw strength when life struck a hard blow, yet comfortable enough in his own skin to lean on *her* when the need arose. A man like Nate Marshall?

Eden sighed. No, not Nate Marshall. Even if he'd shown interest in her as anything other than the manager of Latimer House—and he had *not*—she couldn't afford a single misstep. Since taking over when the last administrator quit, she'd been under intense scrutiny from state and city agencies. If she messed up, she could find another job. But if the boys got off track, they may never find their way back. Protecting them, providing for them, was the sole reason she put in eighteen hours a day.

Instead of hiring someone to teach history and literature to boys who'd been expelled—multiple times—from public school, Eden saved money by teaching the classes herself. She could have hired outside help for household chores and yard maintenance, but doing the work made it possible to afford extras—internet access and satellite TV—without bowing to some bottom-line-obsessed bureaucrat who didn't give a hoot about providing the boys with something akin to normal family life. Field trips, such as the one to the Double M, were but another step toward that goal.

Arranging private tours of galleries, museums, dozens of vocational and technical facilities they might attend hadn't been easy, mostly because Eden believed the administrators had the right to know that her kids' hardscrabble lives might mean they wouldn't always behave like Little Lord Fauntleroys. Most seemed sincere when they said things like "Boys will be boys" and "How bad could they be?" But even the most well-intentioned had trouble disguising shock, impatience, even full-blown disgust when the boys tested them with crude language or outrageous manners.

Nate Marshall was not one of those people. The boys could distinguish between phony acceptance and genuine interest, so when he issued clear-cut rules about everything from pushing and shoving to foul language, they listened. And when he told them that respect had to be earned, not doled out like candy, she could see by their solemn expressions that he'd earned theirs.

He wasn't a man who took shortcuts, either. That first night, he brought the boys into the kitchen of his two-story log cabin, showed them where to find pots and pans, his corn bread recipe and the ingredients, and instructed them to work together, because supper was in their hands. He didn't complain about the noise or the mess they'd made preparing his famous five-alarm chili. Instead, he laughed and joked during the meal, and let it be known it was their responsibility to clean up after themselves.

He'd taken the same approach in the bunkhouse, where it had at first looked as though their duffel bags exploded, raining jeans, T-shirts and socks everywhere. Without warnings or threats, he simply stated that until the place was shipshape, no one would saddle up again.

As they'd piled into the van, everyone but Thomas had thanked Nate—with no prompting from Eden—and asked how soon they might come back. Much to her delight and theirs, he'd invited them to the Marshalls' annual July Fourth festivities.

"I'm starved," Travis said once they arrived home. "Okay if I make a grilled cheese sandwich?"

"Biology test tomorrow," Kirk reminded him.

"I know, I know." He addressed the group. "Anybody else want one?"

Only Thomas—the one who could use a little more meat on his bones—remained quiet.

"All right," Kirk said, "but that means lights out the minute you get upstairs."

Eden wondered which of the teens would volunteer to clean up, to put off bedtime a few minutes more.

"I'll do the dishes," Thomas said.

"But you ain't even eatin'," Wade pointed out.

"Aren't," Eden said. "Let's use paper plates. And I'll clean up the griddle."

Several of the boys distributed napkins, plates, and paper cups of milk. The others formed an assembly line, one buttering bread, another slapping on sliced cheese, while Travis tended the stove.

Eden thought back a few months, to when a similar event would have incited arguments and shoving matches that led to threats and balled-up fists. Time—and Kirk's steady presence—helped her deescalate the brawls, and slowly they began to put into practice the lessons she'd taught about negotiations and compromises that allowed them to live in harmony.

They devoured two dozen sandwiches, all while discussing what Nate had taught them… and wondering aloud what more they might learn on their next trip to the Double M. It was so good to see them looking forward to something that Eden found herself fighting tears.

"Hey," Wade said, "what you cryin' about, Eden?"

"My eyes are as tired as the rest of me," she said. "And speaking of tired, it's time for you guys to head upstairs."

"Biology exam," Kirk repeated.

Groaning, the boys disposed of their plates. They each said good-night before heading for their rooms.

Half an hour later, when Eden closed the door to her own room, she expected to lie awake, worrying about where she'd find the money to fix the roof, the leaky washing machine and on-its-last-legs dryer. Instead, memories of Nate's interactions with the boys lulled her to sleep.

She woke feeling rested and upbeat, until the boys gathered at the table, devouring oatmeal or crunchy cereal as they picked up where they'd left off last night. Listening as they recounted the trip to the Double M…and their perceptions of Nate.

"I like him," Travis said, "'cause he ain't all full of himself." He glanced at Eden and quickly added, "Isn't."

"Yeah, but all grown-ups seem real at first," DeShawn observed. "Takes a while before the phony wears off and the *real* hangs out."

Eden started to disagree, but what if he'd been correct? Jake had seemed too good to be true at first, too; what if Nate's friendly behavior had been nothing more than a polite facade? Every one of the teens had experienced some level of abandonment...

Once their plates and bowls were stacked in the sink, they grumbled all the way to the science lab, well aware that after the exam, Kirk intended to walk them through their last assignment of the year: frog dissection.

Dishes done, Eden joined them, standing at the back of the classroom as her able assistant handled their protests with his usual aplomb. The young counselor had completed several degrees, and could surely earn far money more teaching or counseling elsewhere. Instead, he'd chosen to dedicate himself to the boys of Latimer House, teaching math, science and history, as well as fixing broken doorknobs and leaky faucets. Eden was the first to admit that without him, the place might have fallen down around them—literally and figuratively—months ago.

The doorbell pealed and Eden hurried to respond to the impatient, unscheduled visitor. Brett Michaels stood on the porch. Eden's nerves prickled with dread as the landlord swaggered into the foyer.

She forced a smile. "Brett. Hi. What brings you here so early on a weekday morning?"

As usual, he didn't answer her question. "You look lovely, as always." He nodded toward the classrooms. "Amazing, considering what you do for a living."

Eden ignored the snide remark. "There's fresh coffee in the kitchen…"

"Sounds great," he said, following her.

Something about his attitude heightened her tension. Back in November, the purpose of a similar early-morning visit had been to raise the rent a hundred dollars a month. She'd managed, barely, by trading her new car for the big clunking van, and by directing a portion of her county-paid salary toward other Latimer bills. Adding those saved dollars to minuscule funds raised by local churches and a handful of regular donors, she'd made every payment. Eden didn't know what other corners she could cut if he wanted more.

"Almost fresh from the oven," she said, peeling the plastic wrap from a chipped ceramic plate of chocolate chip cookies.

"My favorite. But you knew that, didn't you." He sat at the Formica and chrome table donated by Kirk's parents. Winking, Brett added, "If I didn't know better, I'd say you were sweet on me."

Not a chance. Eden grabbed a mug from the drainboard and filled it. "Now, now, we both know I'm not your type."

For the first time since they'd met, Brett looked genuinely surprised. "And what, exactly, do you think my type *is*?"

The same kind of woman Nate is attracted to, she thought, frowning slightly. Eden searched her mind for a polite way to say "stuck up," and noticed a crack in the ceiling. Brett followed her line of vision, from the light fixture above the table to the corner beside the back door. He sipped his coffee, pretending not to see it.

"She'd need a degree from Barnard," Eden said finally. "Or Brown, and memberships at Valverde Yacht Club and Castle Pines Golf Club." Laughing quietly, she added, "For starters."

"Is that how you see me? As some guy who's only interested in social networking?"

To be honest, Eden thought, *yes*.

"But, I've always thought you and I would make a great team."

Just what she needed—another control freak. The only thing she and Brett had in common was Latimer House. And a fondness for chocolate chip cookies.

"We haven't seen you around here in months." She shoved the plate closer to his elbow. "What have you been up to these days?"

He helped himself to another treat. "Funny you should ask."

Something told her she wouldn't find anything funny in what he was about to say.

"I got an interesting offer last week," he said around a bite. "One that could prove profitable."

She sensed a big *if* coming and put her hands in her lap so he couldn't see them shaking. Maybe she could buy a moment or two to prepare herself for the bad news. "Haven't heard from your mom lately, either. Guess that means she's still on her world cruise?"

"Never better," Brett said. "Talked to her yesterday, as a matter of fact. She sends her love."

"Wait, you talked about *me* during a ship-to-shore phone call?"

"Sort of."

His tendency to sidestep straight answers reminded her yet again of Jake, and Eden didn't like it one bit. "She asked what my plans were for today, and I mentioned that I needed to pay you a visit. She said that as soon as she's unpacked, she wants to tell you all about her trip over lunch." He grunted. "For your sake, somewhere other than Tables."

Cora Michaels loved it there, and often commented on the quaint Kearney Street location, the restaurant's white picket fence and eclectic collection of mismatched tables and chairs. Eden would happily have met Cora at the interstate rest stop if she'd suggested it; Brett's mother was a lovely woman...and one of Latimer's most generous donors. At their last meeting, Cora confided that if it hadn't been for Duke's firm hand—and his willingness to adopt her sullen, unruly only child—Brett would have ended up in a place like Latimer House.

But why had Brett told Cora that he needed to visit today?

"How soon will she get home?"

"Who knows? She was supposed to get back last week. Now it's next week." He shook his head. "If I didn't know better, I'd say she's taken up with another old geezer."

Eden laughed. "How old are *you* that *geezer* is the first word that popped into your mind?"

He took another sip of coffee and met her eyes over the mug's rim. "Maybe someday you'll share your secret coffee recipe."

"It's no big secret. I don't follow instructions."

He raised his eyebrows as he put down the mug. "Beg pardon?"

"On the coffee can. The instructions say to use a rounded scoop. For every cup. Too strong. Way too strong, and in my opinion, I think it's because they want you to use up the grounds faster." Nervousness was to blame for her stubby fingernails, and fear tended to make her talk too fast. Waiting for Brett to deliver his bad news was making her feel both. Eden took a deep breath and willed herself to calm down because if history repeated itself, she'd start stuttering next.

"So I use half as much, er, many. Coffee grounds per pot, that is."

"Makes sense," he said, dusting crumbs from his fingers.

He sounded bored. Uninterested. Distracted, no doubt, by the awful message he'd come to deliver.

"So about this proposal I was telling you about…"

She squeezed her hands together so tightly, her knuckles ached.

"I thought it only fair to run it by you, give you a chance to make a counteroffer before I sign anything."

"A counteroffer?" Could he hear her pounding heart from his side of the table?

"Yes. Someone wants to buy Latimer House."

"You're joking."

Brett bypassed her comment. "Not as a rehab center for young criminals, of course. The buyer wants to rehab the house and live here."

Yet again, she ignored his unkind reference to her boys. "And you think *I* can present you with a better offer?"

"Well, that's the general idea. But—"

"Oh, now I know you're joking," she said. "My savings account balance doesn't even have a comma in it anymore!" *Thanks to you*, she finished silently.

Brett chuckled. "Always the kidder." His expression went stony and professional as he leaned back in the chair. "But you didn't let me finish."

In truth, her bank statement did show a comma—and a few digits preceding it—thanks to the small estate she'd inherited from her grandparents. Their house on the other side of town wasn't as big as this one, but it would do...if Brett forced her hand. Denver officials would no doubt demand an inspection before issuing a permit to house the boys at Pinewood, and sadly, the tenants hadn't left it in very good condition. Eden had no idea what it might cost to bring it up to code.

Brett knocked on the table. "Earth to Eden..."

"Sorry. You were saying?"

"Are you okay? You look a little green around the gills."

Green. As in money. "How much did your buyer offer for Latimer House?"

When Brett named his price, her heart rate doubled.

"Oh my," she whispered. "How soon do you need an answer?"

He shrugged. "How much time do you need?"

Why this constant game of cat and mouse! Couldn't the man answer just one question straight-out?

"How much time do I *have*?"

Brett's face softened slightly. "For anyone else, I'd say sixty days. But because I like you, I'll stretch it to ninety."

Her gaze darted to the calendar on the wall behind him. He might as well have said ninety minutes. Plus, his timing couldn't have been worse. Most of the boys were making steady progress, changing from angry, mistrustful teens into productive, hopeful young men. This place, along with the steadfast work of Kirk and the handful of volunteers—psychology students, mostly—who helped run it, had given the kids stability and taught them that some adults, at least, could be trusted to act in their best interests. If Brett sold the place right out from under them? She shuddered.

Brett got to his feet. "Give the offer some

thought and get back to me, one way or the other. Just don't wait too long, okay?"

Eden stood, too, wrapped half a dozen cookies in a paper napkin and handed them to him.

"Gee, thanks," he said, tucking them into his jacket pocket before making his way to the foyer.

As soon as he drove away, Eden went back to the kitchen and slid her to-do list from under the napkin holder. "Go to Pinewood," she wrote across the top. Maybe Shamus had exaggerated when he'd described the mess her tenants had left behind. The visit would have to wait until tomorrow, though, because after teaching two classes and preparing tonight's supper, there wouldn't be time to drive to the other side of town. She pictured the clothesline she'd rigged in the basement to aid the limping dryer, and every clean-but-wrinkly shirt and pair of jeans that awaited her steam iron.

On her way to the classrooms at the back of the house, Eden peeked into the hall mirror. The boys were shrewd, and one look at her troubled expression would make them worry, too. She smiled and fluffed her hair, and felt a strange connection to Scarlett O'Hara.

Because for the first time, Eden truly understood the quote, "I'll worry about it tomorrow."

CHAPTER THREE

THE MINUTE EDEN pulled up to Pinewood, her heart sank.

She parked the van near the deep wraparound porch and hoped the interior of her grandparents' three-story farmhouse was in better shape than the exterior.

It was not.

A slow tour of the house where she and Stuart had spent so many happy years proved that weathered clapboards and lopsided shutters were the least of her worries.

Last time she'd been here—to deliver the lease to a nice young family—the chandelier had painted a thousand minuscule rainbows on the tin ceiling. Now, years of cooking grease and cobwebs clung to each crystal teardrop. A fresh coat of paint would hide the scrapes and fingerprints that discolored the walls, but repairing the gouged, dull oak floors would require hours of backbreaking labor. Things were worse in the kitchen, where cabinet doors hung askew and floor tiles showed hairline cracks.

There were glaring, empty spaces where the stove and fridge once stood. And in both bathrooms, missing faucets and broken medicine cabinets, dumped unceremoniously into the claw-foot tubs, made her tremble with anger.

Eden sat on the bottom step of the wide staircase and held her head in her hands.

"Hey, half-pint."

She looked up. "Hi, Shamus. It's good to see you."

The elderly neighbor drew her into a grandfatherly hug, then held her at arm's length. "I suppose you've taken the grand tour."

She nodded.

"Bet you thought ol' MaGee was exaggerating, didn't you?"

"Not exactly. But I did hope you had overstated things a bit."

Scowling, he shook his head. "Don't know how they sleep at night, leaving Pinewood in such sorry shape, 'specially after all you did for 'em." He studied her face."

How did she feel? Worried. Sad. Embarrassed, because Gramps had been right: "You think with your heart instead of your head," he'd said, time and again. "Someday, that good-natured personality of yours is going to hurt you."

The way Eden saw it, poor judgment, not temperament, had hurt her. She was almost as much to blame for this mess as the Hansons. All the signs were there: Unkempt children. Unmowed lawn. Undone household chores. Late payments—and for the past six months, no payments at all. She'd bought into every one of their excuses. Harold lost his job. Lois's car was rear-ended, putting her out of work, too. The oldest boy cracked a tooth eating walnuts. The youngest girl broke her toe trying to stop the playground merry-go-round. "Just give us a month," they'd said, "and we'll get back on track." She'd suspected all along that they saw her as a pushover, but she couldn't evict them midwinter, or midsummer, for that matter.

"Desperate people do desperate things, I guess," she said at last.

He eyed her warily. "You don't believe that any more than I do. The Hansons are deadbeats, plain and simple." His tone softened. "You can fool some of the people some of the time, but you can't pull the wool over this old man's eyes."

Since childhood, she'd wondered whether Shamus's mixed metaphors were inadvertent, or a quirky attempt at humor.

"In your shoes, I woulda booted 'em to the curb after they missed the second payment."

"Please," she said. "You aren't hard-hearted enough to put asthmatic, anemic kids into the street." Eden hadn't wanted to do it, either, even after they'd fallen so behind.

"Quit lookin' so guilty. You did what you had to do. You couldn't keep paying the taxes, insurance, county fees—without sinking yourself." He snorted. "You should have let me handle them, instead of Joe Templeton."

She'd let the owner of the property management firm get away with a lot, too. "Well, what's done is done, I guess."

"You're well within your rights to take the lot of 'em to court. My grandson just got his law degree. Right now, he's playing gopher to some big shot at a downtown legal firm, and he's itchin' to sink his teeth into a case of his own. Bet he'd give you a real good price, just for the privilege of flexing his law muscles against those deadbeats *and* that lousy excuse for a property manager."

The way things were going, she probably couldn't even afford Shamus's inexperienced grandson.

"Want me to talk to Ricky for you?"

"Ricky...not that little blond kid who used to picked Gran's roses as presents for Maggie?" Eden pictured his sweet-tempered wife.

Shamus beamed. "One and the same."

"Wow. Hard to believe he's old enough to have completed law school."

"Now, now," he said, "you can't change the subject on a fella with tunnel vision. I'll email his contact info to you, and tell him to expect your call."

"I appreciate the offer, but…" Even if she could scrape up a few extra dollars to pay Ricky's fees, Eden didn't relish the idea of getting entangled in what would likely be a lengthy, unpleasant lawsuit. "Let me do some research first. Get some estimates. Find out what it will cost to bring Pinewood up to code. Double-check my contract with the property managers. Because I'd hate to waste Ricky's time." *Or my quickly vanishing savings.*

Shamus had been a fixture at Pinewood for as long as she could remember. After her grandfather's fatal heart attack, the elderly widower stepped in to help her grandmother with minor repairs and acted as a sounding board when she needed to purchase not-so-minor things such as replacement windows, the new roof, a car. And since Eden's grandmother passed, Shamus had become the self-appointed guardian of the house and grounds. It was comforting to have a substitute grandparent of sorts, but Eden didn't want to take advantage of his good nature. That's why she'd hired Joe Templeton.

Shamus frowned. "Bring it up to code? Does

that mean you're thinking of moving another tenant in here?"

"Not exactly…" Eden explained the tight spot Brett's proposal had put her in.

"Aha, I get it now. If this old place can pass all the inspectors' tests, you want to move the Latimer House boys in here."

"Only as a last resort. Their lives have already been too chaotic. I hate to uproot them just when they're settling in and doing so well."

"Let me give you a little something to think about, half-pint. When soldiers get the order to pack up and move from one base to another, or some corporate type accepts a transfer to a new city, their families go with them. Whole kit and caboodle. The kids might not like it, at least not at first, but they adjust. Same as you and Stewie did when you came here from Baltimore."

Eden had to admit, he made a lot of sense. Still…

"You homeschool those boys, so it isn't like they'll need to transfer into a new district. Something else to think about. I can help out if you're shorthanded. Teach the boys to use power tools, maybe even put 'em to work on a big vegetable patch out back."

Shamus would love that. With his only son and every grandchild but Ricky out in California, he spent a lot of time alone. It might be a great arrangement for everyone concerned—if moving became necessary. If she could convince city authorities to allow her to relocate the boys. If she managed to come up with the money to make the house safe and comfortable for them.

If...the biggest little word in the English language.

Shamus leaned against the newel post. "Can I ask you a question, half-pint?"

"Sure, as long as it isn't 'how do you expect to find a man, settle down and have kids of your own while you're in charge of those ruffians?'"

He laughed quietly. "I imagine you've heard that one a time or two."

"Or three."

He saluted her. "On my honor," he said, smiling, "I will never ask you that question." His expression grew serious. "So whatever happened with that police report I made the day those deadbeats moved out and took half of *your* stuff with 'em?"

This was the first she'd heard of any police report, and she said so.

"Would've sworn I told you when I called to say they were leaving." Shamus shook his head. "By the time a squad car rolled up, the crooks were long gone, along with your light fixtures, cabinets, appliances..." He shook a bony arthritic finger. "You better believe I told those officers everything I saw. Showed 'em the pictures I took with my cell phone, too. One cop wrote down your phone number, promised to call you to see if you wanted to press charges. When I didn't hear from you, I figured you'd gone soft on 'em, again, and were too embarrassed to admit it."

"Probably just as well that no one from the department called."

"Let me guess…because they'd throw those criminals in the slammer, and their kids would end up in foster care?"

"In separate houses, no doubt."

"Yeah, that'd be a shame. Isn't their fault they were born to a couple of losers. Still…" Shamus started for the door. "Soon as I get home, I'll email Ricky. Anything particular you want me to tell him?"

"Would you mind holding off on that, actually? I have a lot of research to do and a lot to think about, remember." She squeezed his forearm. "Okay?"

"If nothing else, you're proof that giraffes don't change their stripes." Chuckling, he shook his head again. "Remember what your grandpa said? Your heart has always been bigger than your head—a good thing, so long as it doesn't hurt *you*." He stepped outside, pausing on the porch. "Don't wait too long to get the wheels of justice rolling, though. Call me when you change your mind."

"I will. And thanks, Shamus. Why don't you stop by next time you're on our side of town, have supper with us. I know the boys would love seeing you."

"Might just do that." He shuffled down the walk. "Probably the only way I'll find out what's going on with this place," he mumbled, jerking a thumb over one shoulder. Then, in a louder voice, "You have every right to be reimbursed for the time, trouble and money it'll cost to replace everything they took, you know. And you don't need to feel guilty about it, either!"

"When you're right, you're right," she said, but he was already out of earshot.

Eden returned to her seat on the bottom step and dialed Joe Templeton. After the obligatory greetings, she asked when he'd last visited the property.

"Not since I delivered the eviction notice. Why? Is there a problem?"

"Not *a* problem," she said through clenched teeth. "Lots of problems. If I made a list, I'd get writer's cramp. Or carpal tunnel. Or both."

"Gee, Eden, I'm sorry to hear that, but—"

"I'm coming back over here in the morning, and I'm bringing my camera. I'd like you to be here when I document this…" She looked around and ground her molars together. "This mess."

"I, ah…"

His phone hit the desk with a *thunk* and Eden heard him riffling papers. "What time did you have in mind?"

"Seven." At that hour, he couldn't use the old "other meeting" excuse. "That'll give us time to evaluate things without taking too big a bite out of the rest of your day." And speaking of eating, Joe didn't know it yet, but he was going to explain how he'd allowed this to happen—and why he hadn't notified her about it earlier—over coffee and eggs at Breakfast King.

"Oh, and, Joe? Bring your camera, too."

"Okay, but why?"

"We're compiling photographic evidence for a possible lawsuit, that's why, and two cameras are better than one."

She listened patiently as Joe explained how unlikely it was that they could find the Hansons, let alone get them to stay in one place long enough to file suit.

"Besides," he said, "you know the old adage, 'can't squeeze blood from a—'"

"I thought you might say something like that."

"Anyone who'd all but destroy the place they called home can't be expected to do the right thing and reimburse me for the damage done," Eden said.

With the wisdom of Gramps and Shamus ringing in her ears, Eden said, "See you tomorrow, seven sharp. And don't forget the camera. I've had too many pictures go missing to trust my cell phone."

"See you in the morning, then," he said, hanging up.

She'd paid Joe a handsome monthly fee to oversee Pinewoods, and he'd let her down, bigtime. Admittedly, that was partly her fault. If she hadn't been so concerned that spur-of-the-moment inspections might hurt his feelings, she might have nipped things in the bud before they became problems. Starting tomorrow, she'd lead with her head instead of her heart.

"Better watch it, Quinn," she said, locking the front door behind her, "because this exercising-your-rights stuff feels good enough to be habit-forming!"

CHAPTER FOUR

JOE SLOUCHED AGAINST the tufted red Naugahyde booth at Breakfast King, scrolling through the pictures Eden had taken at Pinewood. "I'll bet this happened when they dragged the stove out the door," he said, pointing at an image that showed a deep gouge in the kitchen's door frame. His dark brows furrowed as he studied photos of curtain rods hanging from single screws and cabinet shelves that slanted at awkward angles. He turned off the camera and slid it to her side of the caramel Formica tabletop.

"Saying I'm sorry doesn't begin to cut it," he said. "I feel awful that the Hansons stuck you with that mess."

Eden folded her napkin back and forth, back and forth, and fanned herself with the resulting paper accordion. "I'm sure you've faced situations like this before. Any idea what we're looking at in repair costs?"

Joe shook his head as the waitress delivered their coffee.

"Thousands," he said when the woman walked away. "Easily."

Eden waited for him to empty two milks and three sugar packets into his mug before continuing. "So how does this work? Will you hire a contractor?"

He nearly dropped his spoon. "Me? Whoa. You expect *me* to foot the whole bill?"

Eden smoothed out her paper accordion. "In retrospect, I should have paid more attention to the Hansons. It's my property, after all." She met his eyes. "But as we discussed when I hired you, the nature of my job makes it difficult, at best, to get away. You told me not to give that another thought, because absentee landlords make up the bulk of your client list, and that it was your job to do periodic spot checks, to make sure tenants are living up to the conditions outlined by the lease. And that if they didn't, we'd come to an agreement about repairs, in order to avoid arbitration." She paused long enough for her words to sink in. "Remember?"

"Of course I remember." Nodding, Joe stared into his mug. "I spent most of the night on the computer, trying to hunt down the Hansons." He looked up. "Unfortunately, I didn't have a bit of luck."

She drew an invisible figure eight on the tabletop. "In other words, since you can't find them, we can't file a lawsuit."

He winced slightly at the word. "Oh, if I kept looking, I could find them. Eventually. I used to be FBI, remember. But what's the point?"

If he quoted the old "can't squeeze blood from a turnip" cliché again, Eden didn't know what she'd do. She pointed at her purse beside her on the seat. "I brought our contract, just in case we needed to refer to it."

Smiling slightly, he nodded again. "Why am I not surprised." Joe picked up his mug, put it right back down again. "Okay. I admit it. Somehow, we completely overlooked your property. I could make excuses, like it's on the opposite side of town, or my regular guy quit and there wasn't anyone in the office capable of doing the job. I'm embarrassed to admit that we screwed up big-time, but—"

His phone rang, and one glance at the screen was enough to cut his sentence short.

"Sorry, it's my kid's school. I have to take this." He stood. "When the waitress gets here with our food, ask her to bring me some tomato juice, will ya?"

Eden went back to pleating the napkin. Her landlord wanted an answer. More accurately, he wanted to sell Latimer House, the sooner the better. A lot depended on whether or not Joe would do the right thing. She felt like a passenger in a leaky dinghy, sinking slowly, while a big storm loomed on the horizon.

"You're up and at 'em early…"

Eden jumped, and then looked up into Nate's smiling blue eyes. "I could say the same thing."

"Had some early-morning appointments. Thought I'd grab a cup of coffee before heading back to the Double M." He pointed over her left shoulder. "I've been sitting right over there."

She glanced at the red counter stools behind her. He'd been near enough to hear everything she and Joe had discussed.

He slid into Joe's seat. "I'm surprised you didn't hear me back there, shuffling the pages of yesterday's *Denver Post*. Bet I read the same article four times, trying to tune out what you guys were saying."

"Oh, good grief. I'm so embarrassed."

"Why?" Nate harrumphed. "That guy should be embarrassed, not you."

The waitress delivered breakfast. "Coffee, sir?"

"Sure. Why not."

When she left, Nate pointed at Joe's food. "I saw your pal leave. Seems a shame to let perfectly good flapjacks go to waste."

"See, that's why I hate sitting with my back to the door."

The waitress brought over his coffee and topped off Eden's mug. "Thanks, hon," he said.

"Hon? I haven't heard that since I left Baltimore."

"Yeah, it's one of the few things I picked up out there that I can't seem to put down."

Eden smiled. "I always loved the way everybody used the term. Made the city seem so much friendlier."

"Speaking of friendly, think your pal is off wheeling and dealing to spare himself a lawsuit?"

The idea made her laugh. "I bet he's halfway to his office by now."

"Well, good riddance to bad rubbish, I always say."

"And I haven't heard that one since grade school."

Nate shrugged one shoulder. "It's just as true today."

"I don't know if it's fair to lump him in with the trash just yet."

Nate returned her halfhearted smile. "So what's your next move?"

Move. What a peculiar choice of word, considering what she and the boys might be doing in the very near future. She sighed. "It'd be easy to blame Joe for everything the tenants did to Pinewood, but there's no escaping the fact that the house was—and is—my responsibility. I should have checked on things myself."

"Still, he had contractual obligations. What if you lived in Chicago or San Francisco? Or Baltimore?" He grinned. "I really like that name, by the way. Pinewood has a homey ring to it."

"That's what my grandfather thought." Eden had no sooner finished the sentence when her cell phone pinged. "Well, speak of the devil," she said, opening the text.

Sorry to stick you w/tab. Son fell @ school, broke a tooth. Here's my offer: Templeton Prop. Mgmt. will replace missing appliances, light fixtures, faucets, vanities. You make cosmetic repairs. If agreeable, call & I'll recommend contractors.

She repeated the message to Nate, trying her best to sound lighthearted.

She could almost read Nate's mind: Joe had all but ignored Pinewood; what made her think she could trust him now? If the answer affected her alone, it wouldn't matter nearly as much. But the boys had put their trust in *her*. Why hadn't she seen this coming, and done something to prevent it?

"Hard to believe a few measly words could solve so many problems, isn't it?" she said, sliding the phone into her purse.

"Uh-huh."

She took a sip of her coffee.

"Do you believe the guy this time?" Nate asked.

This time? Even a near stranger understood that Joe's word was less than stellar.

"Aw, don't pay any attention to me," he added. "Ask anybody. I tend to rain on parades."

"No, you made a valid point. To be honest, I don't have a clue if he was sincere or not, or if something like a text message would stand up in court if he wasn't."

"I know a couple good contractors. How about I make a few calls for you? We can meet them at your grandparents' house—your house—and see which one can give you the most for your money. And if that snake slithers out of his promise to share the costs, I'll front you the money for repairs."

"What? I can't ask you to do that!"

"You're not asking. I'm offering." He grinned and, using Joe's fork, speared a bite of sausage. "I like your boys, so we'll consider it a donation to Latimer House."

She could tell that he meant every word, but she couldn't take his money. Eden never had a problem accepting checks from Cora Michaels and other regular donors. What made Nate's contribution feel so...different?

"I appreciate the offer, really I do, but I just can't—"

"Fine. I get it." He held up a hand, preempting her rejection. "Who knows? Maybe ol' Joe will do the right thing."

There was an awful lot riding on that *maybe*.

That leaky dinghy seemed deeper in the water now, and despite the sunshine on the other side of the windows, she sensed that storm was closing in fast.

NATE POSITIONED THE Phillips head drill bit into the crosshairs of a loose screw, wincing when it slipped and gouged his left thumb. "Nearly bored a hole clean through it," he mumbled. "My own fault for letting my mind wander."

On the other side of the stall gate, Patches bobbed his dark-maned head, as if in agreement.

"Okay, smart guy. I'd like to see how well you'd concentrate with a pretty filly running around in your head."

The Paint only snorted and went back to munching contentedly from his eye-level hayrack.

"Nobody likes a smart aleck, y'know," Nate said, moving the tool to the next loose screw in the hinge.

Fellow ranchers had accused him of spoiling his horses. "You treat them nags better'n I treat my wife!" Phil Nicks often joked. But Nate wouldn't have it any other way. He'd personally drawn up the blueprints for the new barn that housed ten stalls, each with wrought iron gates, rails and yoke openings, swivel grain and water doors, and windows set high enough that the horses could stick their heads out to watch the goings-on outside. An insulating wall-to-wall rubber mattress system covered the floors, and oscillating fans helped circulate the air. Since the flicker of fluorescent bulbs made some of the horses jumpy, he used nothing but incandescents, purchased by the truckload when the government banned them in favor of swirled compact fluorescent, LED and halogen bulbs. Finally, at one end of the barn, he'd installed a wash bay, and across from that, a tack storage cubicle outfitted with saddle and bridle holders and swing-arm blanket racks.

"If ever you take a wife," Phil had said at the last hoedown, "you'd better keep her out of this place, or she'll expect the same kind of pamperin'!"

"Take a wife?" Nate's dad countered. "How's that supposed to happen when this son of mine hasn't said yes to a woman in years?"

"Hasn't said yes to much of *anything* in years!" his mom added.

They'd been right, and Nate still hadn't figured out if his Just Say No policy was a good thing or a bad thing.

Instantly, Eden's pretty face came to mind. Eden, who earned the respect of boys big enough to snap her like a twig, though none seemed to have a mind to. Nate admired her, too, for all she'd accomplished with her charges and for what she'd sacrificed to guarantee them a stable home and a secure future. He hoped the boys were mature enough to realize how fortunate they were to have her in their corner.

When he'd overheard her tell Joe what the state paid to keep Latimer House functioning, he'd nearly choked on his coffee. With such a paltry amount, how did they expect her to do more than pay the rent and keep the lights on? It didn't take a genius to figure out that using her own money was the only way to afford gas for the van, food and clothing for growing boys, and something other than the TV to keep them entertained and occupied.

A good thing or a bad thing? he wondered again.

She'd looked sad, scared and humiliated when he'd offered to front the cash for repairs at her grandparents' place. For the past two years, he'd lived by two simple rules: "do unto others," and his own "just say no." How weird, he thought, that by following one, he'd violated the other.

Least he could do was give her a call and apologize for putting her on the spot.

He was about to dial her number when his foreman's name appeared on the screen.

"Hey, Carl," he said, picking up. "What's up?"

"Found another one of your dad's horses out in the south pasture. I sent Ivan and Seth out there to pick up the carcass. No sense encouraging more of the same."

"Good thinking." Nate ran a hand through his hair, wondering which horse it had been and how to break the news to his father. "What do you reckon, bear or cougar?"

"Cougar, most likely. Bear would have left a far bigger mess."

Carl was right. Bears were greedy, sloppy assassins that often began feeding before their quarry was dead. Cats, even when near-starved, preferred to kill with a bite to the back of the neck. And because the opportunistic felines didn't like feeding out in the open, they tended to drag uneaten carcasses as far as possible from the kill site and cover them with grass, pine needles or dirt, preserving the meat for a future meal and reducing the chance that another predator might sniff it out and steal it.

"My guess is this cat was forced into new territory by a bigger, better fighter," Carl said.

"Either that," Nate said, "or those so-called

animal experts captured and tried to relocate it, and now it's scoping out new hunting ground."

"Well, we got plenty of pictures, in case Colorado Parks and Wildlife demands proof if we have to take drastic measures."

"Good, good," Nate said. "You boys keep your wits about you and rifles and sidearms at the ready, you hear?"

"Don't worry, boss. We're like that credit card company—'Never leave the bunkhouse without 'em.'"

CHAPTER FIVE

"I CAN'T TELL you how much I appreciate this."

Stuart returned his dog-eared magazine to the stack on the bank's waiting room table. "Hey, anything for my big sister. Even putting on my uniform eight hours before my shift starts." Yawning, he leaned forward and rested his elbows on his knees. "So tell me again why I'm here?"

"Moral support. No one would say no to me with a police officer present. Not even a banker!"

"I hate to break it to you, but disrespect isn't against the law." He winced slightly. "Neither is turning down a borrower who has no collateral."

When it had come time to split their grandparents' assets, they'd flipped a coin. Stuart called tails, giving him ownership of the condo in Vail.

"I have Pinewood," she countered. Eden pictured their grandparents' house and groaned. "Then again, point taken." She took a deep, shaky breath. "Do I look as petrified as I feel? Be honest, I can take it."

Stuart studied her face for a moment. "Just

remember what Gramps taught us—always re-peat a question in your head before answering it out loud. And sit on your hands."

"He never said… Oh, I get it," she said. "So Mr. Judson won't see them shaking."

"Or those raggedy cuticles."

Eden gave Stuart's shoulder a playful poke. "Thanks, Stewie. *That's* the way to show sup-port."

"Hey, what do you expect from a sleep-deprived, overworked, underpaid cop?"

The door beside them opened, startling them both.

"Well, well, well, if it isn't the Quinn kids," the banker said, extending a meaty hand. "Good to see you. How long has it been? Ten, fifteen years?"

"Too long," the siblings harmonized as he ushered them into his plush office.

Mr. Judson's black leather chair squealed when he filled it with his considerable bulk. He spent a few moments catching up, asking what they'd been doing in the years since los-ing their grandparents. He was semiretired, he told them, and spent as much time as possible skiing in Aspen or sailing at Tahoe. And then he sat back and smoothed the nonexistent hair on his shiny head.

"Now," he said, flashing a salesman-like smile, "what can I do for the two of you?"

Eden sat up straighter. "As I told the receptionist when I made the appointment, I'd like to discuss a loan."

Frowning, he adjusted his black-framed glasses. "Yes, yes she did make note of that." He grabbed a sleek silver pen from the marble holder on his desk and glanced at Stuart before meeting Eden's eyes. "My goodness, dear girl. How much do you need that you felt it necessary to bring a gun-toting companion?"

While he laughed at his own joke, Eden remembered Stuart's advice and repeated the question internally. "Twenty thousand," she said, tucking her fingertips under her thighs.

The gleaming ballpoint went *click-click* as Judson raised one bushy eyebrow. "More than I expected. What, exactly, is the loan for?"

Eden kept her explanation brief and to the point: Pinewood's tenants had left behind a lot of damage, which had to be repaired before it would pass a city inspection in the event the sale of Latimer House forced her and the boys to relocate.

"For the most part," she concluded, "the money will buy paint and replace missing appliances and light fixtures."

Click-click. "With twenty grand, you can buy a lot of lamps."

Judson slid open a desk drawer and removed a manila folder labeled Quinn.

"I had a feeling Pinewood might have prompted this meeting, so I drove by the house on my way home last evening. And the minute I arrived this morning, I perused your file." Removing his glasses, he opened the folder. "As I recall, your grandfather's will specified that upon his death, his life insurance was to pay off the mortgage, so that your grandmother would never have to worry about keeping a roof over her head."

"And we abided by his wishes to the letter," Stuart said. "So your point is…?"

The banker ignored Stuart's impatient tone. "I understand you hired Templeton Property Management to oversee the house and grounds?"

"Yes…"

"That's odd. He made no mention of damage to the house or grounds."

"You spoke with him?"

"Well, of course I spoke with him. It's my job to gather all the facts to look out for our investors' and depositors' best interests."

I'll bet Joe didn't tell you what he promised— in writing! "And did Joe provide any helpful facts?"

"No, not really." Judson smirked. "He didn't say much of anything, except that you threatened to sue him." *Click-click.*

Eden's pre-meeting jitters had turned into full-blown panic. "I didn't threaten to sue. Exactly."

"If we *can* arrange a loan—and at this stage, I can't promise that—what collateral can you present? Property? Vehicles? Investments? Savings?"

Since every penny to her name was right here in his bank, Judson already knew the answers. Eden decided his questions were rhetorical, and felt no obligation to reply.

Click-click. "Says here that numerous complaints were registered against the boys who reside at Latimer House. Litter, noise ordinance violations, lack of attention to the home's exterior…" He met Eden's eyes. "If you were to move the youngsters to Pinewood—if you can bring it up to the city's code requirements, that is—what assurances can you offer that the boys won't cause the same problems in your grandparents' neighborhood? Continued bad behavior will impact property values, you know, and since the house is your collateral…"

"How did all of that end up in the Pinewood file?" Eden glanced at Stuart, who merely shrugged.

"Stuff like that is part of the public record," Stuart said. "Just a matter of typing some basic information into the state's court records files, and voila."

So Judson had *looked* for reasons to turn her down, even before hearing how much she wanted to borrow? But why?

"First of all," Eden said, "lack of proper supervision by the former administrator was to blame for everything on your list. And since your research is so thorough, you're no doubt also aware that since I took over, the house has been well-maintained, and there hasn't been a single complaint."

"True, but…" Judson tapped the file entry. "With kids like that, you can't guarantee continued good behavior. Uprooting those boys, in and of itself, could spark a rebellion and who knows what else." *Click-click.* "I personally approved the mortgage on your grandparents' home, so it pains me that I can't help you out now."

Not can't, Eden silently corrected. *Won't.* "It isn't fair to judge the boys based solely on what happened in the past, or to punish them for their parents' mistakes, or for the former director's neglect, for that matter."

Judson closed the file and got to his feet, a not-so-subtle indication that the meeting was over.

"It was good seeing you both, truly."

Stunned and disappointed, Eden felt her mouth go dry. Returning his half-baked compliment or offering her hand seemed beyond hypocritical, but she did it anyway.

"Wish I could say the same," Stuart growled, taking her elbow. "Sorry we wasted one another's time."

Halfway across the parking lot, he said, "If I had the money, I'd give it to you in a heartbeat."

"I know." She side-bumped him. "Ya big softie."

He feigned pain and rubbed his biceps. "Sheesh! Have you been working out?"

"Oh, right. Like I have the time and money for a gym membership or exercise equipment." Instantly, she regretted her brusque tone. "Sorry, little brother. You're not to blame for any of this mess. I should have barked at that tightwad, instead of taking my frustrations out on you."

He stood between his pickup truck and her van. "Meet me at Tom's. My treat."

"Your treat? I thought I promised breakfast would be *my* treat."

"You don't have money for a gym membership, remember?"

"Ah, I see. It's pity food."

He produced a ten-dollar bill. "Found this last night in the precinct parking lot." He returned her halfhearted grin. "Do you know how to get there from here?"

"I was a little beside myself for a minute in

there," she said, "but I think I can find my way to our favorite diner."

Thanks to their crazy work schedules, getting together was a challenge, so they met at Tom's once a month to catch up. Eden considered passing on his offer, but she didn't want to go home just yet. One look at her worried face and the boys would want to know what was wrong. They would also know if she was lying, so she needed time to collect herself.

"I'll follow you over there," she said. "But just so you know, I'm not in my usual chatty mood."

Stuart unlocked his pickup truck. "You won't hear me complaining. You talked enough when we were kids—and ever since—to tide me over till retirement."

She opened the driver's door, grimacing when the rusty hinge groaned. "I hear they're looking for comics over at the Bug Theater. In case you ever decide to switch careers, that is, wise guy."

He slid behind the steering wheel. "I'll keep that in mind, if you'll be my straight man."

During the short drive, Eden thanked her lucky stars for that brother of hers. He'd made it easier to cope with the brutal loss of their parents. Made it easier to adjust to relocating from Baltimore to Denver after the funeral, too. They'd always been close, but over the years, they'd also become best friends.

Friends. She steered into Tom's parking lot, wondering why the word brought Nate to mind. Had his offer to finance repairs at Pinewood been genuine? Or was he cut from the same cloth as Jake, whose every action had been carefully calculated to ensure complete control?

NATE'S SISTER LEANED around their cousin and his new wife. "Just look at you," she said, "hoggin' the biscuit basket, again."

Zach and Summer sat back to give the siblings a direct line of sight to each other.

"Poor Henrietta," Nate said, "never has figured out the difference between biscuits and rolls."

Her wadded-up napkin flew past the newlyweds and landed in Nate's mashed potatoes.

"How many times do I have to tell you, it's Hank, not Henrietta."

"You may be Hank on the barrel-racing circuit," he told her, calmly buttering his roll, "but you'll always be Henrietta to me."

"Nate," his mother scolded, "don't taunt your sister. You know as well as anyone that her name change is legal."

"Legal or not," his dad muttered, "I'm sticking with my initial opinion— it's ridiculous. The name Henrietta was good enough for your grandmother, and I'll never understand why it isn't good enough for you."

Hank sighed. "Dad, please. We've been over this a dozen times. It was a business decision, pure and simple. The name gives me a psychological edge over my competition. No one would fear a barrel racer named Henrietta."

She'd probably taken this guilt trip often enough to earn frequent-flyer miles, and Nate felt bad about stirring things up again, especially over Sunday dinner at Aunt Ellen and Uncle John's house.

"You still planning to change it back once you're married with kids?" he asked. With a little luck, she'd agree, at least for the moment, and put an end to the whole name-change discussion.

Zach laughed. "Don't do it, cousin! I can hardly wait to introduce our young'un to Auntie Hank," he said, patting Summer's round belly. "Sooner or later, you'll have to quit the rodeo circuit and settle down. I can almost hear your kids' kids calling you Granny Hank. It has a nice ring to it, don't you think?"

"*Your* grandmother might not agree."

If their father noticed Hank's second heavy sigh, he hid it well. Nate heard it, though, and he didn't need to look up to know she'd branded him with a blistering glare. After dessert, he'd take her aside and apologize. She'd always had a fiery temper, and if things ran true to course, she'd make him prove how sorry he was...with dinner at Shanahan's, her favorite restaurant. Hank sure did know how to get her way.

"I thought you gave up sucking your thumb when you were three, Nate."

It took a second to figure out what his mother was talking about. Laughing quietly, Nate put down the butter knife and wiped his glistening thumb on a napkin.

"I know that googly-eyed look," Hank said, smirking. "I'd bet my Greeley Stampede barrel champion buckle on it. He was off in la-la land, daydreaming about some woman."

Time and again, he'd told well-intentioned family members that he wasn't ready for another relationship, not with the cultured young women who volunteered with his mom and aunt or the flirty rodeo gals Hank tried to set him up with. His sister knew the reasons better than any of them, so her wisecrack made no sense.

Zach piped up. "You know, Hank, I think you're on to something here." Leaning around Summer, he added, "All right, dude. Out with it. Who is she?"

Nate's ears and cheeks went hot, and he hoped they hadn't turned bright red. Why hadn't any of the other Marshall men been cursed with the tendency to blush like schoolgirls?

Don't overreact, or you'll play right into their hands. "There is no 'she.'"

His mom's eyebrows disappeared behind dark, silver-streaked bangs. "Oh, my," she said, drawing out the word. "This one must be a real doozie if he feels the need to hide her."

Et tu, Mom?

He could easily take the spotlight off himself by directing the conversation back to the Hank v. Henrietta thread, but throwing his sister under the bus wouldn't solve anything. "If there isn't a 'she,' then it stands to reason there's no one to hide, right?"

They weren't convinced. He could tell by their sly grins and winks.

"Sheesh. Guy can't even butter his thumb around here without everybody jumping to conclusions."

While they laughed, Nate decided to keep them distracted by reporting the latest ranch news.

"Carl found another horse yesterday." He kept the description vague, as much for his nieces' and nephews' sake as his dad's. "We got plenty of pictures. Near as we can tell, it was a cougar attack."

His mom gasped softly. "Oh, I hope you're

mistaken. There hasn't been a cat sighting since…" Maeve faced her husband. "How long has it been, Royce?"

"Five, six years? I'd have to check my log books." He looked grim. Concerned. "Are you sure, son?"

"Positive."

"So the boys found tracks, eh?" Zach said.

"Not at first. The ground's pretty dry. But once we found one sign, plenty more showed up. We have pictures of those, too."

"What about rumen and bones?" his dad asked. "Right near the kill sight, or scattered all around?"

"Close by for the most part. No blood trail, either, so it's pretty clear the cat didn't feel pressured to move the carcass. It left plenty behind, though, which tells me its meal was interrupted."

"Any idea by what?"

"Could have been anything, Hank. Another cat. Bear. Heck, one of the other horses could have spooked it."

She nodded. "True. Cougars are pretty skittish."

"Honestly," his mom interrupted. "Can't the four of you wait until later to discuss this? You're frightening the children."

Nate looked at the wide-eyed faces of his cousins' kids. At their mothers' faces, too. Sally and Nora agreed with his mom, and he could hardly blame them. Even though he'd been far younger than any of them when he got his first up-close-and-personal eyeful of what a determined predator was capable of doing to livestock. The experience taught him the importance of caution and alertness. He turned to their parents. "If you're okay with it, I'd like to take them out there soon," he said, pointing toward the fields. "Teach them how to keep their eyes open and their ears perked." Nate met each child's eyes. "You're ranch-raised, same as the rest of us, and spend a whole lot of time outside. There are all kinds of dangerous critters out there. But you already knew that, right?"

They nodded their agreement.

"Things are scariest when you don't know anything about them. Once you have the facts—"

"Well, now," Hank said, "aren't you just a big ol' ball of warm and fuzzy today."

He got to his feet. "I'd rather give them a couple of scary dreams tonight, *Henrietta*, than have something terrible happen out there later."

Tossing his napkin onto his chair, Nate faced his aunt. "Dinner was great as always. Thanks."

"You're leaving?" his mother said. "Before dessert? When I made your favorite?"

Not even hot-from-the-oven apple pie could tempt him to stay. Nate didn't know what to blame for his agitated state of mind. With any luck, a few gulps of fresh mountain air would cure what ailed him.

"Thought I spotted a loose gate, couple of leaning fence posts in the main corral," he said with another nod toward the window. "That sky looks pretty threatening. I'm gonna check 'em out before the storm rolls in."

He made a beeline for his pickup and drove straight to the barn. If he didn't waste time, he could saddle Patches and get those gates secured before the storm hit. And there wasn't a doubt in his mind that they were in for a big one. The clouds hung low and dark, and there was a certain bite in the spring air. The wind rolled across the north pasture, laying the new ryegrass fields almost flat. They needed a gentle soaking, not the hard-pounding downpour that was about to hit. Patches sensed it, too. Normally, he'd nibble contentedly at the blades of grass growing alongside the fence. Today, he whimpered, stamping his front hooves and testing the strength of his tether.

"Easy, boy," Nate said. "I'm almost through here, and if you quit kickin' up a fuss, I'll give you a good rubdown and add some oats to your feed."

Good thing you started at the corral, he thought, disconnecting the come-along from the now-taut barbed wire. He stowed it in the burlap sack that hung from his saddle horn, untethered Patches, and climbed into the saddle as the first fat drops began thumping the brim of his Stetson. The air quickly filled with the thick, musky scent of plant oils, bacterial spores and ozone. Nate found it rather pleasant. Patches did not. But the horse, true to form, obeyed his master's every directive.

The rain was falling in earnest now, hitting the hard ground like wet bullets. It was tough to see more than a few yards ahead, but Nate held tight to the reins to make sure Patches didn't panic, rocket forward and step into a gopher hole.

"Easy, boy," he said again, holding the steady pace even as the gusts rustled the grass and bent the trees to the breaking point. A violent boom rolled across the fields, startling Patches and Nate, too, and seconds later, lightning sliced the sooty sky.

Once they reached the barn, man and horse exhaled relieved sighs and shook off the rain. Now Nate wished he'd eaten some pie; when this deluge let up, the pan would no doubt be empty.

Patches nickered and bobbed his head. "You're right," Nate said. "Fifteen minutes more and we'd be out in the middle of this bedlam, instead of warm and dry in here." Plus, the broken latch and leaning gatepost would have blown over. It took only one curious cow to notice the opening for a couple of dozen to follow, and it would require days to round them all up.

If that cat didn't get them first.

Based on the size of the paw prints, Nate and the ranch hands had decided it was likely a female. They all agreed she had a right to hunt and prowl the territory. But with elk and deer so plentiful in the Rockies, they knew something was wrong. Very wrong. Choosing easy pickings such as tame horses and cows could mean she'd been wounded. She might be pregnant, or have a litter of cubs hidden nearby. Cubs that would learn many lessons in killing from their stealthy mother.

Nate stowed Patches's combs and brushes in the tack room and walked to the window, where the rain clouded his view of the Front Range. But he didn't need to see the mountains to know they were there. He'd been living in their shadow since birth, and could point them out with his eyes closed: Grays Peak and Mount Evans, Longs Peak and Mount Bierstadt, and one of the world's highest, Pikes Peak. Several years ago, Nate had been able to cross an item off his bucket list when he'd reached its summit. Up there, it seemed he could see the whole world. The sight made him pity Lieutenant Zebulon Montgomery Pike, who, after a four-month trek, spied the mountain on the horizon and knew even before arriving that he'd never reach its pinnacle.

"Wonder how many cougars old Zeb saw?" he asked Patches.

The horse snorted again, as if to say, "I'm busy eating the treat you gave me and can't be bothered with such trivial matters."

Nate's mood began to lift. It wasn't so bad, being stuck out here in the barn. He'd spared no expense to equip it with every creature comfort for the horses. In the loft, he'd even constructed a sparsely furnished bedroom and a closet-sized bathroom, and installed grates in the floor to allow heat to rise from the propane-fueled furnace. On the rare occasion one of his mares had difficulty foaling, he wanted to remain nearby, and the space had served its purpose well.

Seated on the corner of his cot, Nate toed off his work boots and changed into dry jeans and a flannel shirt. Everything, even the socks, smelled like mothballs, but the scent was far preferable to the stale, fusty odor of mold or mildew. Back in the main area of the barn, he filled the aluminum coffeepot with water and grounds and set it to boil on the two-burner hotplate. He kept a stash of energy bars in the metal box atop the minifridge, and unless one of the ranch hands had raided it, he'd have one for supper. Not his first choice, but unless he was seriously mistaken, this storm had no intention of letting up anytime soon. He'd take granola over hitting the hay on an empty stomach.

The horses didn't seem to mind having their nosy, two-legged Pa meander the barn, as evidenced by soft snorts, blows and nickers. There might be a cougar on the prowl, but for the moment, all was well at the Double M.

Sated by his makeshift meal, which he washed down with strong black coffee, Nate lay back on the cot and closed his eyes. Rain pelting the barn's metal roof made him drowsy.

He remembered the year when he, Zach and Sam had ridden to the Double M's north boundary to round up two runaway calves. They'd been in high school, and felt proud and manly, being out there on their own. They'd searched until they ran out of daylight, then set up camp and bedded down under the starry sky. Nate was the first to wake up, and after stoking the fire, he'd gone looking for sticks and twigs to get it hot enough to brew their coffee and heat up the bacon biscuits Zach's mom had packed them. Nate didn't know what made him look up, but when he did, the breath froze in his lungs. A huge male cougar stood on a rocky outcropping nearby, head high and powerful shoulder muscles undulating under thick, reddish-brown fur. Nate had reached for his revolver, realizing too late that he'd left it near his bedroll. Thankfully, in the blink of an eye, the cat had disappeared, leaving Nate to wonder if he'd imagined the whole thing.

His cell phone rang, startling him so badly he sat straight up on the cot. He didn't recognize the number and answered with a terse "Yeah?"

A slight pause, and then, "Oh. I'm so sorry to disturb you. I must have dialed the wrong number."

Eden. "It's not the wrong number," he said, softening his tone. "This lousy storm has me stuck out here in the barn. Guess I drifted off and the phone surprised me."

"Sorry," she said again. "If I hang up, you can pick right up where you left off."

Was she kidding? Go back to that pins-and-needles cougar memory, when he could talk with an angel?

"I wasn't asleep," he admitted. "This cougar stuff has us all a little edgy." And so did his reference to her as an angel.

"Cougar stuff?"

He gave her an abbreviated version, leaving out some of the gorier details to avoid scaring her. "I'm sure it's holed up somewhere in this weather, though, so for the time being, it's not a concern."

Liar. Anyone with a functioning brain would be worried, especially after finding that mutilated horse. But she hadn't called to listen to his woes. Just as well. He wasn't big on chitchat, either.

"So...what's up?"

"The boys and I have been talking," she said hesitantly, "and we'd like you to come for supper. Tomorrow night, if you're available. I'm making their favorite. Spaghetti and meatballs."

He'd planned to attend a town hall meeting the next night to discuss possible solutions to traffic problems caused by cattle getting loose. His father and uncles refused to go, citing the fact that their livestock rarely got out, and when the cows did stray, they never went too far for too long. He wouldn't be missing out on anything he hadn't heard before anyway.

"Just so happens spaghetti and meatballs is one of my favorites, too. What time do you want me there?"

"Well, we sit down at five thirty, but you're welcome to get here anytime after four. I'll put you to work chopping vegetables for the salad."

An hour and a half, alone in the kitchen with Eden Quinn? Sure beat listening to city folk moan and groan about cow poo on the highway!

"What can I bring? Dessert? Garlic bread?"

"Just your appetite."

He could hear the smile in her voice, and it brightened his gloomy mood. "See you tomorrow, then. If this storm doesn't wash out the road."

"It wouldn't dare," she said before hanging up.

Nate stared at his phone for a second or two before hitting End. A few days had passed since he'd offered to help her out financially. More than enough time for her to look into other options. He wondered if sometime between dessert and drying the last spaghetti plate she'd tell him how many hoops she'd jumped through to solve the housing problem on her own. He checked his watch. By his estimate, he didn't have much time to figure out how to convince her it was a no-strings offer. He'd known her just long enough to understand that Eden was a proud, independent woman who'd do just about anything for those kids. Truth was, he wouldn't mind a *few* strings, provided they kept her close by, at least until he got to know her better. She might have more baggage than an airport carousel, and common sense warned him to keep a safe distance, at least until he found out why, every now and then, her big gray eyes clouded with an emotion he couldn't define.

EVEN BEFORE HE climbed out of his pickup, Nate felt calm. He took note of flowers planted on both sides of the brick path that made the short

walk to the front porch of Latimer House colorful and welcoming. He rang the bell, and while
waiting for someone to answer, he took in the
row of mismatched rocking chairs lining the
white clapboard facade. Nate counted six before the wide wooden door opened.

"Hey, Nate!" Carlos said. "I'm glad you're
early!" He stepped aside as Nate entered the
foyer. "We had a bet, and I won."

Grinning, Nate inhaled the mouthwatering
aroma of spaghetti sauce as Latimer's youngest
resident led the way down a long hall lined with
photographs. "DeShawn said you'd be here at
exactly five thirty, 'cause you seem like a right-
on-time kinda guy. Wade said five fifteen."

By the time they'd reached the kitchen, Carlos had run down a short list of his roommates'
predicted arrival times.

"And what time did Eden think I'd get here?"

"Five after four," she answered without turning from the sink.

Nate glanced at the schoolhouse clock on the
wall above her as Carlos pulled out one of the
benches at the long trestle table. 4:06. Exactly.

"Have a seat," the kid said. "I'll get you some
iced tea." Halfway to the fridge, he glanced over
his shoulder. "Unless you like lemonade better."

Nate sat at the end of the bench. "Tea is fine.
Thanks."

Eden dried her hands on the blue-and-white-checked towel that matched the curtains. "So how was traffic?"

"Two fender benders. Road construction. Some fool getting a ticket who didn't bother to pull onto the shoulder."

She checked the clock, too. "And yet you arrived at almost the precise moment Carlos and I predicted."

"Well, you said something about me helping with the salad, so..."

"Thanks to you," Carlos said, handing him his drink, "I don't have to help with the dishes."

Nate held out the glass, as if offering a toast. "Happy to be of service."

"Yeah, but I still have towels to put away." He took the stairs two at a time. "And my reading assignment to finish."

"Reading assignment?" Nate asked Eden. "I thought school was out."

"It is. But I don't want them falling behind over the summer, so I make them read every day, right after breakfast and again before supper."

She lifted the lid on a battered old pot. "The added plus is that they come to the table nice and calm." She gave the sauce a quick stir and returned the big wooden spoon to the saucer beside the pan. "Peace and quiet is good for the digestion."

"Ah. A two-birds-with-one-stone kinda gal, are you?"

"Few things I hate more than wasting time," she said, pouring herself some iced tea. "I could be the multitasking poster girl."

Nate nodded toward the cutting board on the counter. "Looks like you've already done my job."

"I had a few extra minutes to kill, pun intended."

"Two birds with one stone," he repeated, and when she smiled, Nate felt a flush creeping up his neck. He put the tumbler to his lips and hoped the icy beverage would stop it in its tracks.

"My grandfather liked to say everything happens for a reason." Her gaze zeroed in on the Band-Aid on the back of his hand. "That looks like a cut that should stay dry."

When she locked those big, worried eyes on his, Nate wondered if his ears were glowing red. Because it sure felt as if they were.

"What did you do to yourself?"

"Aw, it's nothing, really." Nate laid the injured hand on his thigh, blocking it from her sight. "Scraped it up yesterday, trying to get some barbed wire restrung before that storm hit."

"It rained like crazy here. Got windy enough

that I had to take down the flags out front, for fear those flimsy aluminum poles would bend."

His stomach growled, and he tried to hide it by rattling the ice cubes in his glass.

"How bad was it at the Double M? The skies west of here got really, *really* dark."

And there it was again, that concerned expression that lifted her delicate brows.

"Spooked the horses and drove all the cows into the pine grove—worst place for them, what with the lightning and all—but for the most part, it was all bark, no bite."

"A relief for you all, I'm sure."

He'd never been any good at small talk. Clearly, it wasn't one of her talents, either. He added it to the plus side of his "Things About Eden" list. Nate didn't know which surprised him more, that he'd been subconsciously compiling a list, or the fact that the pluses far outnumbered the minuses. He hoped the boys would join them before he said something truly stupid. There hadn't been a dull moment during meals with them at the Double M, and he'd been looking forward to more of the same tonight.

"Hey, Eden," Travis called from the hallway. "Look who's here."

Cora Michaels strode into the kitchen on strappy gold sandals that click-clacked across

the hardwood floor. He hadn't seen her in
months, and wondered what she was doing here.

"Just look at you," she said, wrapping Eden
in a motherly hug. Bangle bracelets jangling,
Cora held her at arm's length. "Okay, out with
it. What's your secret? Every time I see you, you
look younger and prettier than the time before."

Eden's nervous laughter told Nate she wasn't
accustomed to compliments. At least, not about
her appearance.

Cora hip-bumped Nate, her not-so-subtle hint
that he should make room for her on the bench.
"What smells so heavenly?" she asked, scoot-
ing in close.

Eden got up and poured her a glass of tea.
"Spaghetti. Can you stay for supper?"

Turning to Nate, Cora winked and pretended
to hide her response behind her hand. "I thought
she'd never ask." Giving him a playful elbow
jab, she added, "See, it pays for an old widow
to know when all of her friends serve supper."
Turning slightly, she met his eyes. "How have
you been, handsome?"

"Good. Real good."

"And the rest of those Marshall boys? Oh,
when I think of all the mischief you kids got
into, I can't help but laugh."

"Except for the time one of Zach's July Fourth

rockets landed in the front seat of your convertible. I don't recall much laughing that day."

"Oh, my. I'd nearly forgotten about that." She giggled. "Duke bought seat covers and went right back to the banquet table." A wistful sigh punctuated the memory. "I hated missing last year's shindig. With any luck, I'll be at this one."

"That's good to hear." Her attendance at the annual barbecue had been sketchy since Duke's passing, and it was Nate's guess that Cora didn't know what to talk about once her always-a-candidate husband was gone. At the conclusion of last year's event, Nate had overheard his mother and aunts gossiping about Cora. They didn't know whether to blame depression or loneliness for the fact that she'd traded her shoulder-length blond bob for a sleek gray boy cut. The only hairdo Nate could name was the ponytail, worn by Hank and her barrel-racing friends.

"So how was your world cruise?" Eden opened two boxes of spaghetti noodles. "You took lots of great pictures, I hope, especially of those sunny Mediterranean islands."

She answered with a dismissive wave before peeking into the sauce pot. "I do declare, Eden Quinn, I know a restaurant chef or two who'd pay handsomely for this recipe."

Dumping the pasta into boiling water, Eden

harrumphed. "Unless it's enough to pay off this house, I might as well hold on to it."

"Oh, sweetie. I'm so sorry. I heard what Brett is planning. Believe me, if I thought for a minute that hard-hearted son of mine would listen, I'd talk him out of selling the place. Although, the way I understand it, the buyer approached him. Not that the information does you much good."

Nate had never been impressed by the one-liners that accompanied Brett's boisterous glad-handing.

Eden stirred the pasta. "Cora is one of our best supporters," Eden told Nate. "More than once, her contributions have kept the proverbial wolves from the door."

All except the wolf who called Cora *Mom*, Nate thought.

Travis, Latimer's oldest resident, sauntered into the room. "Aw, man," he said to Nate, "I didn't expect to see you so soon."

"Good to see you, too… I think."

"No, what I mean is, thanks to you I'll probably get stuck with dishes tonight." He groaned. "Or worse, I'll have to empty all the trash cans and drag the big one to the curb."

"Sorry, buddy. If I'd known…" Nate didn't finish. No matter what time he'd arrived, one of the boys would have gotten stuck with what they saw as obnoxious chores.

"Hey. What happened to your hand? Horse bite?"

The question reminded Nate of the boys' visit to the Double M, when Ben asked permission to feed "his" horse a sugar cube. Before Nate could tell him to balance it on a flat, open palm, Ben held it out...between his thumb and forefinger. Embarrassed, Ben had hidden the swollen, bruised digits until Cody pointed them out.

"Same one that bit Ben?"

"Wasn't a horse bite," he said. "And that only happened because—"

"I know, I know," Cody said. "It wouldn't have happened if Ben used his head for something other than to hold up his eyeglasses."

"Now, now," Eden inserted. "If Ben is guilty of anything, it's impatience. He should have waited for Nate to show him the proper way to feed sugar cubes to horses."

Travis snorted. "Everybody knows you don't go sticking your fingers into an animal's mouth. Dogs, cats, hamsters...heck, even a canary will peck ya if you're not careful."

"Well, Ben knows better now," Nate said. "And so do the rest of you."

"So what *did* happen to your hand?" Travis wanted to know.

Nate flexed his fingers. "Got into a brawl with some pigheaded barbed wire, and the wire won."

"Oh, Eden," Cora cooed, bracelets jangling as she clasped many-ringed hands under her chin. "Isn't he just *adorable*! You really ought to snap him up before…" She faced Nate and narrowed her eyes. "Say. Just exactly why isn't a good-lookin', successful fella like you hitched?"

A moment of prickly silence ticked by, and then Kirk joined them in the kitchen.

"Man," he said, rubbing his palms together, "this place smells like an Italian restaurant. When do we eat?" His gaze traveled the room, from Eden's wide-eyed face to Cora's amused grin.

"What?" he said, glancing over one shoulder. "Do I have toilet paper stuck to my shoe or something?"

Travis snickered behind one hand. "No. Wasn't you who made everybody clam up. That happened 'cause Miss Cora wanted to know why Nate isn't marr—"

"Things are just about ready for the table," Eden interrupted. "Why don't we eat early tonight, and I'll throw a pizza in the oven later."

Nate sent Eden a grateful smile.

"Sounds good to me," Travis said. "I'm starved! I'll round up the others." He started for the hall, but paused in the doorway. "Unless you need me to set the table."

Nate stood. "Since I didn't get to help you

with the salad, how about if I take care of that?" he asked Eden.

She blinked up at him for a second or two, and when she turned her attention back to Travis, he was reminded of the slight chill he always felt when the sun slid behind a cloud.

"Thanks, Nate." And to Travis, "Give me a few minutes to slide the garlic bread under the broiler. And make sure the boys wash their hands, okay?"

"Gotcha." He pointed at himself, then at Nate. "You and me," he mouthed. "Later."

Nate wondered what the teen wanted to talk with him about.

"The dishes don't match," Eden said, pulling open a drawer. "And neither does the silverware, but the boys don't seem to mind."

If she hadn't mentioned it, he probably wouldn't have noticed. Nate stood at the sink to scrub his hands, wondering why she thought stuff like that mattered to him. He smiled to himself. Maybe because she cared what he thought? He considered asking her out, then quickly dismissed it. Even if she could find the time, could he find the patience to cope with the razzing his family would give him?

Cora waited until Travis was out of earshot to sidle up to him. "So what's this I hear about a bunch of your horses being attacked by a pack of cougars?"

"Two horses, one cougar." The only person he'd told about the latest attack had been an agent with Colorado Parks and Wildlife. "How did you hear about that?"

"My Duke spent the last fifteen years of his life knee-deep in politics." She winked again. "I know people, sweetie. Lots of people in high places."

Interesting, Nate thought, but her reply hadn't answered his question. He had a feeling that pressing her for details would be a waste of breath. Still, the fact that word had gotten around unsettled him. Humans tended to panic and do stupid, dangerous things when threatened. Things that could get innocent animals— or people—shot.

From the corner of his eye, Nate saw Eden grab two pot holders from a hook near the stove, no doubt to strain the pasta. "Let me do that," he said. Nate poured the pasta into the colander, then dumped the noodles into the sauce.

"There must be a little Italian in your DNA," Eden said, setting a trivet on the table. "We're the only ones I know who mix it all up instead of ladling sauce onto the noodles."

Nate opened the fridge and peered inside. "My mom is half-Italian."

"No kidding? So's mine."

"You'd have gorgeous kids," Cora said, wiggling her eyebrows.

Eden's eyes widened as he opened and closed cabinet doors.

"Can I help you find something?"

"Parmesan."

That's when he noticed that everything in the fridge was alphabetized. Stepping back and fighting a grin, Nate glanced at her spice rack. Sure enough, every tiny jar had been stored in alphabetical order.

She caught him inspecting the shelves. "My brother says this is proof that I'm way too fussy, but the truth is, I'm in a perpetual hurry. Order and organization helps me find things quickly."

Nate got that. What he didn't get was how she'd secured the cooperation of the boys.

He carried the big pot to the table. "How long did it take you to teach the kids to put things back where they found them?"

"I didn't, unless you call learning by example a lesson." Opening another cabinet, Eden removed drinking glasses. "When each boy first arrived here, he displayed typical teenage attitude, but even the toughest of them softens after a week or two. By that time, the new kid considers everybody else family, and he's happy to go along with a few simple rules. Even the unwritten ones."

"Eden has a list," Cora explained, pointing at the bulletin board near the door. "There's another one just like it on the back of every bedroom and bathroom door." She began to read aloud. "'One—up at seven, lights out by eleven except on weekends. Two—homework must be completed before electronics are turned on. Three—boys who are late for classes or meals can expect extra homework and chores. Four—you are part of a caring family now. Show your respect by picking up after yourself.'"

Nate put a glass next to each plate. "I'm impressed, but not surprised."

Cora returned to her place at the end of the bench. "Because of their backgrounds, you mean?"

Plastic ice bin in hand, Eden proceeded to drop cubes into each tumbler. "How about if you two table this discussion—pun intended—for a time when there's no chance one of the boys might overhear you."

"Okay by me," Nate said.

Cora rolled her eyes. "Oh, stop trying to butter her up. And don't encourage her, either. Eden is the fuddy-duddiest young woman I've ever met. Why, I can't remember the last time she did anything for herself, or just for fun."

"Emphasis on *time*," Eden said. "The one thing there's always too little of around here."

"Still." The older woman pointed at Nate. "Don't you agree that it isn't fair for someone her age to work and worry so much?"

She'd have a whole lot less to worry about if not for your son, Nate thought.

"You know what they say," Cora continued. "'All work and no play makes Eden old before her time.'"

Laughing, Eden said, "You remind me of Shamus."

"How so?"

"He loves mixing metaphors, too."

"What do you mean, *too*? I never mix…" She squinted. "Wait a minute. You don't mean to say you're comparing me to that old geezer who lived next door to your grandparents?"

"He still lives there. And Shamus is anything but a geezer. I wish I had half his energy."

Cora waved her close and gave her another hug. "Oh, now, I didn't mean anything by that." Winking over Eden's shoulder, she mouthed to Nate: "Miss Sensitive."

Eden straightened and put a hand on Cora's shoulder. "I'm glad you're home, you world traveler, you. Looks to me like you could use some R & R. And a little TLC. And about a week's worth of sleep and hearty meals."

A knock at the back door silenced any re-tort Cora might have made, but Nate was pretty sure he saw a tear glistening in the corner of the older woman's eye. He didn't see how sensitivity like Eden's could be a bad thing, and he'd take it over Miranda's "You're a grown-up. Suck it up!" any day.

"Oh, my," Cora said when Eden opened the door. "What are *you* doing here?"

Brett Michaels frowned. "You said—"

Her frown matched her son's. "Well, as long as you're here, you might as well come give your ol' mama a hug."

Brett Michaels closed the space between them in three long strides, bent at the waist and wrapped his arms around her. "You're not old."

Cora pushed him away. "Aren't *you* the mas-ter of subtlety?"

Eden filled the sudden silence with, "What brings you here this evening, Brett?"

"She… I…" He faced Cora, then looked back at Eden. "When Mom said you invited me to dinner, I thought maybe it was to tell me you'd figured out a way to buy the place."

"Brett Lee Michaels, I said nothing of the kind, and you know it as well as I do!" Cora faced Eden, too. "I simply told him that I planned to stop by." She sniffed, chin high and shoulders squared. "And that if you asked me to eat with you and the boys, I would." Aiming a bony forefinger in her son's direction, she added, "See what happens when you only half listen to what people say?"

Michaels held up both hands and shrugged. If Eden saw the gesture as a plea for help, it went unanswered, for she'd put her back to him to slide the garlic bread into a napkin-lined wicker basket. "Nate, would you mind checking on the boys? I'd hate for their spaghetti to get cold."

"Be happy to." Her request made Nate feel like part of the household. *Better watch it, Marshall*, he thought, following the sound of boyish laughter down the hall. Because what if her only intent had been to put Michaels in his place? With any luck, the guy would be gone by the time Nate returned to the kitchen.

The kids were huddled around some sort of video game when he walked into the family room. Cody was the first to notice him.

"Hey, Nate!"

"Hey yourself, kiddo. Eden says dinner is served. Better get in there before everything's cold." He glanced around the room. "Where's Thomas?"

"With his dad. And he ain't none too happy about it, either."

"Why not?"

"Maybe 'cause the loser tried to sell him a couple of times," Cody said.

"And left him alone in all sorts of weird places, like bars and pool halls," Carlos added.

Travis nodded. "Every time Thomas sees the dude, he totally freaks out. He'll get home after dark, all mean and mad."

Ben agreed. "And he'll be impossible to live with for days."

"Yeah, well, like Eden says, ain't nothin' we can do but deal with it. Same as last time," Travis said.

Eden loved these kids as if they were her own. The only way she'd allow Thomas to leave Latimer House with a man like that was if the law required it.

"Better get washed up," Nate advised.

"Yeah," Carlos said to the others. "You know how Eden feels about dirty hands at the table."

The boys pushed and shoved all the way down the hall. All but Cody, that is, who hung back with Nate.

"Just so you know, we call it supper around here. Eden says dinner is for Sundays and big holidays, like Thanksgiving and Christmas."

"Y'know, I don't know why I called it dinner. My family has always called it supper, too, for the same reasons."

"Must be nice, having lots of relatives around all the time."

"Yeah, but like any bunch of people who share a house, there were times when it seemed the only thing we did was tussle."

"Tussle?" the boy asked.

"Pushing, shoving, poking, wrestling. Good-natured stuff, mostly, but once in a while, somebody came out of the huddle with a black eye or a swollen lip." Nate grinned, remembering plenty of brotherly camaraderie, too. The mail-order missile they'd built and launched—right into the roof of Aunt Ellen's potting shed. The chemistry experiment that stunk up Zach's house so badly, the whole family had to move in with their grandparents for a week. The misfired baseball that shattered the windshield of his dad's vintage muscle car, and put him on the road to a major-league career. Their pranks and mischief often inspired friends and relatives to say things such as "What's to become of those Marshall boys?" and "Hide the good china…here come those Marshall boys!"

"Only one around here who tussles anymore is Thomas." The boy shook his head. "It's like he has no clue how small he is."

During the Memorial Day weekend at the ranch, Eden had told him that she nearly lost her job for refusing to fill the doctor's prescription for growth hormones. Lucky for her, she'd sought a second opinion, and a third, both of whom listed serious side effects, such as recurring ear infections or changes in vision, joint pain, depression, even damage to major organs. "Thomas and I had a heart-to-heart," she'd told Nate, "and he assured me he's okay being a little lighter and smaller than the other boys. So why risk his health for a few inches and a couple of pounds!"

"Thomas doesn't mess with me, though," Cody said. "I don't know why, but I'm glad."

"Maybe it's because he trusts you more than the others."

Cody nodded, a slight smile lighting his face as he considered the possibility.

"Yo, Codes. What you grinnin' about?" DeShawn asked when they entered the kitchen.

"Oh, I'm just wondering how many meatballs you'll pound down tonight."

The boys made room for Cody on the bench, and as he sat, Travis said, "Yeah. Last time, you ate *four*."

"Ain't my fault Eden makes the best meatballs ever."

"Isn't," she corrected. "And thank you."

"Yeah, you moron," DeShawn teased. "It's isn't, not ain't." And before Eden had a chance to chastise him for the slur, he added, "The *best* biggest meatballs ever."

Carlos sprinkled cheese into his palm and licked it clean. "Bet you've never had a meatball the size of a tennis ball, have you, Nate?"

"Carlos, aren't you a little old to eat cheese that way?"

"Sorry, Eden."

Nate saw that the kids had left an opening for him at the far end of the table, right beside Eden. She met his eyes long enough to correct his assumption: The boys hadn't left the seat beside her empty. *She* had.

"I set an extra place for you right here beside me, son," Cora told Brett.

All heads turned to see how Michaels would react to the obvious shun. The man seemed none too pleased as he slid onto the last space on the bench, between his mom and Chuckie.

The eye contact between Eden and Michaels lasted a blink. Two, at most. Yet the intensity reminded Nate of every boxing match he'd ever watched, where the challenger hoped to cow the champ with a fierce, determined glare.

"Who's gonna say the blessing?" Travis asked.

"You are," DeShawn said.

Another instant of silence preceded the to-the-point prayer. Long enough for Nate to decide that, first chance, he'd find a way to ask Eden about her peculiar relationship with Michaels.

CHAPTER SIX

FIRST THING MONDAY MORNING, Nate drove into Denver for a meeting with Colorado Parks and Wildlife.

There wasn't much the agent could do about the cougar attacks. Her advice on how to discourage the cats—and other predators—echoed what every rancher learned as a child: cougars, unpredictable and stealthy, were at the top of the food chain, and it didn't take long for them to become as comfortable in cities and suburbs as they were in the wild, content to hunker down behind shrubbery until an unsuspecting quarry strolled by. It was precisely why the youngest Marshalls were never allowed outside alone, and why only a bare minimum of decorative bushes grew near the house, walks and drive. It was also why every Marshall over the age of twelve carried a firearm—and knew the proper way to use it.

The agent was supportive. Sympathetic, even. Raised on a nearby ranch, she understood the loss of two horses cost more than money. Still, it was more than a little frustrating that the agency, with access to countless studies conducted by animal experts, couldn't tell him anything he didn't already know…except that two neighboring ranchers had experienced similar problems.

The information was unsettling, to say the least. A cougar's territory might span nearly a hundred miles. For one cat to have killed four times in just over a month, in an area of only two thousand acres?

Fat chance, Nate thought, climbing into his truck. CPW's hands might well be tied, but his weren't. Soon as he got home, Nate intended to call a meeting with the Marshall men and their neighbors. Between them, they should be able to come up with a plan that would ensure the protection of their families, livestock and property.

As he prepared to merge onto the I-70 ramp, Nate noticed a big green van parked on Colfax. Eden's? He turned at the corner, instead, and discovered that sure enough, he'd seen the Latimer House vehicle parked outside the Division of Community Relations building. Nate glanced at his watch. Nearly lunchtime. She'd been on his mind for days…and nights. What could it hurt to wait a few minutes, see if Eden wanted to join him for a bite to eat? He was fairly certain that she'd invited him for supper the other night to ask if his loan offer was still open. But since Cora's and Brett's sudden appearances had made it impossible to discuss it, lunch might provide the perfect opportunity.

He pictured her in the Latimer kitchen, cheeks flushed from standing over steaming pots, smiling and laughing at the boys' antics, gently chiding them if they forgot their manners. When Michaels had tried to insert his two cents into every conversation, she'd listened...and politely dismissed him. The memory made him grin. Who but Eden could reject a person *nicely*?

As if on cue, she pushed through the big glass door and stepped into the sunshine. He was in such a hurry to exit the truck and catch up with her before she drove off that he forgot to unbuckle his seat belt. Then he bent back his thumb trying to yank the keys from the ignition. He'd consider himself lucky if she didn't see him as some crazed stalker.

Eden turned at the slam of his driver's door, and much to his delight, she appeared pleased to see him.

"Well, hi. What are you doing all the way out here in the big city?"

"Filed a report with Colorado Parks and Wildlife about that cougar."

"Oh, right. There haven't been any more attacks, I hope."

"No, thankfully." He paused, pointing to the building behind her. "Starting the paperwork to move the kids to Pinewood?"

"Yeah, I filled out a short stack of forms," she said on a sigh. "As I expected, they won't approve the move until their inspectors have checked the place out."

Nate didn't like seeing her this way. A woman as bighearted and selfless as Eden should never have to worry about anything. He'd help—if she'd let him. "I skipped breakfast and I'm starved," he said. "How about keeping me company while I grab a quick bite at Barry's?"

Eden glanced at her watch. "Well, I suppose there's time for a quick bite. But you can't have it at Barry's. They don't open until three."

"Is that so?"

"I worked there a few years ago."

"Okay. Then how about Rooster & Moon? I've never been there, but I hear it's good."

"I've never been, either. I'm game if you are. Meet you there?"

"Great," he said, meaning it. "If I get there first, I'll grab us a table."

"I'd prefer a booth, if they have one."

He'd *build* her a booth if they didn't, Nate thought, heading back to his truck and easing into traffic.

She arrived at Rooster's just a minute or two

behind him. They parked side by side in the lot to the left of the building, and walked in side by side, too. An inch, two inches at most, and he could wrap his hand around hers.

"Oh, look," she said, "they have sidewalk dining." Eden smiled at him. "It's such a pretty day. What do you think about eating outside?"

"I think it sounds perfect." Miranda called it alfresco, but to his knowledge, she'd never experienced an out-of-doors meal in her life. Oh, she had her reasons: too hot, too humid, too many bugs, or too chilly, too windy, too damp for her TV-coiffed hairdos. But Eden? Eden pulled that frayed Orioles cap out of her purse and stuffed her curls under it. She let him lead the way to an empty table alongside the wrought iron railing, and allowed him to pull out her chair, too. In Miranda's world, any display of chivalry was an insult to her womanly independence and intellect. He was the first to admit how smart and capable his fiancée had been, and never understood how being treated gently, tenderly—like a lady—diminished her in any way. It was one of many things that made him admit, months before the accident, that the relationship was doomed. And yet, for a reason he still didn't understand, he'd said yes when she popped the question.

A friendly waitress handed them menus and took their drink order.

"Says here they're famous for their coffee," he said. "Does caffeine keep you awake?"

"Do chickens cross the road?" She laughed. "But sometimes, it's a good thing. I'm way behind on lesson plans, and if I can get them done by the end of June, it'll seem like an extra week fell out of the sky."

Nate opened his menu. "Lesson plans? But school doesn't start for months."

"I'm a huge Mark Twain fan." She opened her menu, too. "A whole lot of his quotes just *fit*, you know? Like this one, for example— 'It usually takes me two or three days to prepare for an impromptu speech.'"

"That fits, does it?" Nate asked, grinning. "Coulda fooled me."

If she noticed that the musical sound of her laughter drew the attention of nearby diners, Eden gave no sign of it.

"It fits—at least I think it does—because I hate waiting until the last minute to do things. I've learned the hard way that life has a way of sneaking up and—" Eden placed one hand over the other, imitating an alligator's mouth "—*chomp*, right when you least expect it." She lifted a shoulder in a dainty shrug. "So I figure if I'm a little ahead of the game, I can laugh when life bites."

Someday, maybe she'd tell him which lessons she had learned the hard way.

Eden stared at her menu. "This tuna wrap looks good," she said. "And so does the tomato basil soup. Think I'll order both." She closed the menu. "I'd order fries, too, but I didn't see them on the menu."

He should be home, checking the hay fields and making sure the cows hadn't wandered too far from safety. Instead, he was having lunch with a gorgeous gal who wasn't worried that hard work might chip a fingernail, who liked being out in the fresh air—even when it was this breezy—and actually enjoyed food.

"What's on your menu that isn't on mine?"

He met her eyes. "Huh?"

"Well, you're grinning like the Cheshire cat…"

"I, ah, I just think it's funny that the tuna wrap sounds good to me, too. Great minds think alike, and all that."

"Every time my grandfather heard that, he followed up with 'and fools seldom differ.'" She grinned. "I can't decide which category we fit into."

The couple at the next table had shifted their chairs to make it easier to kiss. Long, noisy kisses, and Nate and Eden weren't the only patrons who'd noticed.

"If that's bothering you," Nate whispered,

leaning closer to Eden, "I can have a word with the manager."

"What makes you think it's bothering me?"

Because it's bothering me, he thought. And envy was the only plausible explanation.

"So what's up with you and Brett?"

"What do you mean...what's up? I'm his tenant, and he's the greedy, thinks-only-of-himself landlord."

"Ah..."

"Why?"

"No reason." Why not just ask her, straight-out, if she'd dated the guy?

"Can I ask you a personal question?"

Eden sipped her coffee. "Mmm, this is delicious. No wonder this place is so well-known for their cappuccino." Then she looked him square in the eye. "You can ask me anything, but I can't promise to answer."

"How much is Michaels asking for Latimer House?"

She quoted Brett's price and deadline. "Truth is, even if he gave me a year, it's way out of my range. Well, I could afford it if I was willing to sell Pinewood. But I won't do that."

"So the only thing stopping you and the boys from relocating is putting the place back into livable shape before Michaels's deadline." He didn't like keeping her on the hook, but if Eden wanted to take him up on his offer, she'd have to say so. He wouldn't risk having her think that he saw her as a helpless, needy female.

"Can I ask you another question?"

"Wait. Don't tell me. You're a part-time reporter for the *Denver Post*."

Nate chuckled. "You wouldn't say that if you'd seen the kind of grades I got in English class."

"I'm sure you did fine." She tilted her head slightly. "But you were going to ask me something?"

"Yeah, I was going to ask what *you* were going to ask me last night."

Eyes wide, her mouth formed a small O. "How—how did you know?"

"I don't like to broadcast it because it sounds conceited," he said, tapping his temple, "but I'm a genius."

"Not just any old genius. A humble genius."

"I'm not a mind reader, though."

Eden rolled her napkin into a thin tube. "It's a character flaw, I think, the way I wait for the perfect moment to talk about certain…things. Because as we all know, there's no such thing as a perfect moment."

"Thinking before speaking is hardly a flaw."

She took a big gulp of air, let it out slowly. "Well, I was going to ask if—"

The woman at the next table tumbled from her chair, taking the tablecloth and everything on it with her to the pavement. She lay in an untidy heap amid spilled soup, espresso, sandwich fixings, and broken glass. If not for a quick-thinking waiter who blocked her boyfriend's descent, the man would have landed on top of her.

In a blink, Eden was beside her, gently blotting the woman's face and hands with a napkin. "Lucky for you, I don't see any cuts or scrapes."

"Lucky for me?" she shrieked. "Are you blind or just plain stupid? Can't you see I'm covered in blood?"

Despite the girl's near hysteria, Eden remained calm and quiet. "It isn't blood, sweetie." She showed her the condiment-covered plate that had held her burger. "See? Your dress is messy, but you're perfectly fine."

The waiter and boyfriend managed to get the woman to her feet, leaving Eden on her knees in the murky puddle of soup, coffee and food. Nate waited, thinking surely one of the three would thank her for trying to help. When they didn't, he held out a hand. Eden hesitated, no doubt concerned that the mess on her fingers and palms might transfer to his.

"Don't give it another thought," he assured her. "I'm overdue for my monthly shower, anyway."

That inspired laughter, and she put her hand

into his as the waiter returned with a damp towel. "Here you go, ma'am. Sorry you had to get involved in that."

"Thanks," she said, wiping her fingertips. "I'm just glad she's all right."

"The owner said your meals are on us, and that he's happy to cover the cost of your dry cleaning. I'll just check on your order."

"I don't think dry cleaning will be necessary," she said, returning to her seat. "But be sure to thank him for lunch."

Nate relieved her of the towel and crouched beside her chair, and in the fraction of a second it took to wipe a smudge of cappuccino foam from her cheek, he noticed a small scar on the bridge of her nose. He blamed the freckles scattered across her cheeks for sending his heart into overdrive.

"Poor thing," she said, breaking eye contact to look toward the couple, now arguing near the exit. "I guess now we know what inspired the song 'Love Hurts.'"

"You're one of a kind, Eden Quinn," he said, chuckling as he sat across from her.

"So I'm told."

Three or four members of the waitstaff appeared, some to deliver their food, some to clean up the kissing couple's mess. It didn't surprise him in the least when Eden tried to help.

But why did she seem so eager to get involved in other people's messes, from her career choice to the one created by the amorous duo? Did the troubles of others distract her from her own?

Something told him the sale of Latimer House was but the tip of the iceberg. He could finance the repairs at Pinewood, but did he have what it took to help with her emotional baggage?

He'd always done his best thinking on horseback, and it seemed to him it might just take a long hard ride to figure out what to make of the Eden-inspired emotions swirling in his gut.

CHAPTER SEVEN

SIDE BY SIDE, they returned to the parking lot. Standing between their vehicles, Eden said, "We should do this again. I enjoyed it."

"I agree."

Maybe next time, she'd remember to ask him about the loan.

His cell phone rang, and after a quick glance at its screen, Nate slid it back into his pocket. "So what do you think? Will you and the boys spend July Fourth at the ranch?"

"I'm not sure yet."

He looked like a pickup truck ad, leaning against his driver's door, one pointy-toed boot crossed over the other. So good, in fact, that Eden wondered if he'd struck the pose just to impress her. If so, he'd succeeded.

"We don't have a parade, but I think we can make it memorable for the kids."

To hear him tell it, folks might assume his family gathered for a low-key backyard barbecue, but Eden knew better. She'd read all about the Marshalls' Fourth parties in the *Denver*

Post. Three generations of Marshalls, the article had said, along with friends and neighbors, chowing down a spit-roasted pig while a Grammy-winning country band played in the background. They hired clowns and set up games for the kids, and after dark, put on a magnificent fireworks display. A man cut from a different cloth might boast—and he'd have every right to—but Nate wasn't like any man she'd ever met.

"I think y'all should come the day before, stay until the day after."

"Oh, you do, do you?"

Guilt flashed in his gorgeous blue eyes. Nate uncrossed his ankles and stood up straight. "Sorry. Didn't mean to overstep." He held up his hands. "Just want you to know you're more than welcome."

"Please," she teased, "put your hands down. People will think I'm an undercover cop and you're my perp."

Laughing, Nate folded both arms over his chest. "So have you heard from that Templeton guy?"

"No, and I'm not happy about it, either."

"Think he'll make good on his promise to deliver appliances and whatnot?"

"I hope so."

"I'll take that to mean he hasn't provided you with the names of contractors, either."

"No."

"Well, I still know some reliable people. The guys who built my barn and house, actually. If you're interested, I can call, see when they're available for a walk-through."

Ask him, she told herself. *Ask him right* now!

"Oh, I'm plenty interested…if they're willing to work for free…"

Eden whipped off her baseball cap and covered her face with it. "I can't believe I actually said that out loud." She put the hat back onto her head. "It'd be real easy to blame you for my bad behavior, you know."

"Me!" Nate looked every bit as surprised as he sounded. "What did I do?"

"You're too easy to talk to."

"Ah, I see. Maybe I should hang around with Michaels, see if I can pick up a few bad habits, rough myself up a little."

"You do that, and it's over between us."

It's over between us? As her own words echoed in her ears, Nate took half a step back. She wouldn't blame him if he climbed into his truck and sped away so fast that he left black streaks on the parking lot. The silence lasted all of a blink, but Eden had a feeling she'd relive the embarrassing instant over and over again. And Nate might not soon forget it, either.

"Did I tell you there will be fireworks on the Fourth?"

Eden pretended she hadn't read the article. "No."

"And a band?"

"No kidding?"

"It's usually a headliner." He regained the half step backward he'd taken. "Do the kids like country music?"

"I'm trying to broaden their horizons by making sure they listen to *all* genres."

Was she speaking in a monotone, or did it just sound that way because somewhere between leaving the DCS building and now, her brain had turned to pudding? Eden would have hugged him for letting her off so easily, but the way things were going, she'd probably tromp on his toe or bang her hard head on his chin.

"The other night after supper, a couple of your boys asked me when they could come back to the ranch."

Yes, Eden had heard them. Heard the diplomatic way Nate had explained that although he'd love to have them, the decision was entirely hers.

"They'd have to stay at my house this time," he continued, "since the ranch hands will be in the bunkhouse. It'll be a little tight—I only have four bedrooms—but we'll manage."

"I'm sure they'd love that." And they would, too…if she got over her embarrassment in time to take him up on his offer. "I wouldn't want to intrude or impose, though. Won't you need the extra space for out-of-town relatives?"

"The only one staying at my place is Sam, and he won't mind bunking down on a cot in my room. He's a firefighter in Nashville. He can easily keep the boys entertained with on-the-job stories. He's got hundreds of 'em."

"Nashville is almost as far from the Double M as Baltimore…"

"He had dreams of cutting a record," Nate explained. "That's what got him down there. To bring in a few bucks while he waited for his big break, he slung hash at a diner, and to fill his off-duty hours, joined a volunteer company. Turned out *that* was his calling, and when the city recruited him, he said yes."

He glanced at his watch. "I've kept you standing here nearly as long as it took us to have lunch. Better let you hit the road, and do the same myself."

"Lunch was lovely. Thanks, Nate."

He was half in, half out of his truck when he added, "My offer still stands, you know. Just let me know how much you need and I'll cut you a check. No questions, no strings."

At the corner, as he waited his turn to merge with traffic, he stuck his arm out the window and waved.

Eden waved back and decided she wouldn't mind a few strings. Wouldn't mind them at all.

NATE WASN'T PARTICULARLY comfortable speaking in front of crowds—not even when the majority of the gawkers shared his last name—but thanks to his seasons with the team, he'd learned to fake it for the few minutes it took to answer reporters' questions. He knew exactly what he wanted to say, and when The Bandoliers finished their song, Nate climbed the stairs, crossed the stage and stepped up to the microphone.

"Y'all know Travis Miller, don't you?" he began, pointing into the audience. A few hoots and hollers and a smattering of applause indicated that the boy had made a good impression on kinfolk and ranch hands during his day and a half at the Double M. "Well, I'm here to tell you that Travis is leaving for Fort Collins in a few short weeks, where he'll be a veterinary student at Colorado State." This time, the applause was longer, louder and punctuated by a shrill whistle or two. "Full scholarship," Nate added. "And although the hour-long drive means he could come home every weekend, this young fella has signed on as a vet assistant near the university to help defray costs. So my advice is, do your backslapping and handshaking now, because for the next eight years, you're only going to see this kid on holidays."

As he left the stage, Brett Michaels clapped him on the shoulder. "Next time I attend a town meeting," he said, smirking, "I'll let 'em know you're available for a council position. Who knew a cowboy could give a speech that didn't involve livestock?"

Nate ignored the implied insult. He had more important things to discuss with the guy than what cowboys could and couldn't do.

"Walk with me," he said, heading away from the bandstand and out of the barn. He'd been thinking about this for days, and decided that his idea would help Eden and the boys without making her feel obliged to him. The only glitch, as he saw it, was trusting Michaels to keep his mouth shut.

"We step any deeper into the shadows, people might think we're cooking up a real estate deal," Michaels joked. "Don't know how I feel about folks thinking I associate with ranchers."

Nate ignored the gibe yet again. "How 'bout extending that deadline you gave Eden?"

The question made Michaels stand up taller

and painted a smug expression on his face. "And how 'bout you mind your own business?"

"I know exactly what that old place is worth." Nate recited the day's fair market value. "I find it hard to believe anyone in his right mind offered twice that, especially in these hard times, but it seems to me the guy can wait a month or two longer, give Eden more time to fix up her grandparents' place before you kick her and the kids to the curb."

"I'm the first to admit that what happens to those delinquents is of no concern to me, but I'm not completely heartless. If she needs more time, *she* can ask for it."

"And you'll give it to her?"

"What's it to you, Marshall? You sweet on the gal?"

Nate ground his jaw. "For her sake, I'm hoping you'll keep this discussion between us."

"Ah, so you do have feelings for her, and you're worried she'll kick *you* to the curb if she finds out you've been meddling in her business."

Nate searched for a way to deny it without telling a full-blown lie.

"What are you two whispering about over here?" Cora wanted to know.

Her sudden appearance startled both men, and Nate wondered how long she'd been there… and how much she'd heard.

"You know better than to wander around in the dark, Ma. If you turn your ankle on a clump of grass, you'll be months, recuperating."

Cora aimed a strained glance at her son. "Your concern is touching." Her expression softened as she squeezed Nate's forearm. "That was some speech you made on behalf of Travis. I had no idea you were such a smooth talker."

"I have a feeling there's a whole lot you don't know about this guy," Brett said.

"Melissa Peters was looking for you." Cora pointed toward the bandstand. "She told me you promised her a waltz."

"Yes, yes I did," her son said, winking. "Mmm-mmm-mmm, that girl sure does fill out a pair of jeans, doesn't she?" He elbowed Nate. "Remind you of anybody? Nice talking with you, Marshall. And don't worry, mum's the word."

Nate could only stare as Michaels swaggered away.

Cora placed her hands on her hips and shook her head. After a moment, she met Nate's eyes. "You're making a big mistake, son. He's my boy and I love him, but I don't trust him this far." She held her palms an inch apart.

He no longer had to wonder how much she'd overheard. "That boy of yours might fool us both and keep his word." He grinned. "I won't have to worry about you, will I?"

She exhaled a weary sigh. "See that blade of grass over there?"

Nate followed the invisible line between her fingertip and the green blades growing around a fence post.

"Pick it for me, will you?"

He looked at her uncertainly, but she kept pointing, so he went over and picked a random blade from the soil.

"Take a good long look at it."

Again, he did as she asked. Had she succumbed to Alzheimer's disease?

"What do you see?"

Nate shrugged and stated the obvious. "Grass."

"And what's going to happen to it, now that you've picked it?"

"Well, I guess it'll die."

"And it would die sooner or later, even if you'd left it right where it grew."

She wasn't making much sense. He took Cora's elbow. "Why don't we find you a place to sit and some lemonade? Maybe I can scare up a slice of pie or a piece of cake."

She allowed him to lead her closer to the crowded dance floor. "Too loud?" he asked, dusting off the seat of a chair.

"I'm fine," she said, slumping into it. "Wish I could say the same for you." She pointed at the blade of grass, still pressed between his thumb and forefinger. "Mark my words. He'll turn on you faster than that will turn brown."

Eden joined them, a red plastic cup of lemonade in each hand. "What are you two whispering about over here?" Handing one to Nate, she put the other on the table beside Cora.

He held up the cup, as if toasting the older woman. "Seems to be the question of the day, doesn't it?"

Now Cora was pointing at the dance floor. "They're playing your song."

Nate met Eden's eyes and read the concern on her pretty face. He held out one hand, and she slipped hers into it. "Didn't know we had a song, did you?"

He led her away from Cora, until they were out of earshot.

"What was all that about?" she asked.

They stopped at the edge of the parquet tiles. "Nothing really. Michaels was worried she'd break a leg in a gopher hole, wandering around in the grass, so I put her someplace safe."

"That was sweet of you."

The lively song ended and the band slid into a soft, slow ballad as he drew her onto the floor.

"Think the kids are having a good time?" he asked, pulling her close.

"Definitely. Better than they had over Memorial Day, and that's saying something."

He couldn't take his eyes off her long enough to find a couple of boys to verify her statement.

"You look amazing. You should wear your hair down more often."

If the lights hadn't dimmed, he'd probably see a blush coloring her cheeks.

"You clean up well, too."

She'd better quit gazing up at him through those long, dark lashes, or he'd have no choice but to kiss her right there in front of the band and her boys and the whole Marshall clan.

But he still didn't know enough about her or her past. And until he did, he'd bide his time. Nate didn't want to hurt Eden, but he sure as shootin' didn't want to be hurt, either. Holding her closer still, Nate shut his eyes and buried his face in her silky, sweet-smelling curls.

"I've always loved this song," she said, pressing an ear against his chest.

"Me, too. I memorized it back in high school, thinking it would help me coax a kiss from Katie Marley at the end of a date."

"Ha. Really? And did it work?"

"Might have…if she'd said yes when I asked her out."

Eden laughed and snuggled closer. "So let's hear it, Romeo," she teased.

"You want me to sing?"

"Why not?"

"Oh, you're a brave one, I'll give you that."

"Quit stalling. The song will be over before you know it."

Nate sighed, then started in soft and low. "I feel the wind sigh, the eagle soaring by…"

"Don't stop. You have a beautiful voice."

"Patches doesn't mind it, but I've never sung it to a real-live *girl*."

"Be quiet, unless you're going to sing."

He harmonized with the lead singer, who signaled Nate to join him at the mic. They'd danced close enough to the stage that Nate could reach out and grab the microphone stand from where they were. Instead, he shook his head and sent a signal of his own: There was no place he'd rather be than right here, in Eden's arms.

CHAPTER EIGHT

EDEN WAS FOLDING bath towels when the doorbell rang.

"Wow," Brett said when she opened the door. "This place looks better every time I see it." He stepped into the foyer and pointed over his shoulder at the flowers growing along the walk. "Where did you find the money for seeds?"

"I didn't buy them. I saved them from last year's blossoms."

"I should have known. But how do you find time to plant and prune and weed, with everything else you do around here?"

"Kirk and the boys help," she said, closing the door behind him. "A lot. And as you know, we have plenty of volunteers, too."

Hands in his pockets, he glanced around and nodded appreciatively. "Yes, the place looks good, real good."

Good enough to sell, right now? she wondered, heart thundering. "It's too hot to bake, so there aren't any cookies, but I have lemonade and iced tea in the fridge."

"Surprise me," he said, and followed her down the long hallway. "What do you call those flowers in the hanging baskets out there?"

"Petunias," she said, dropping ice into a glass.

"They're really purple, aren't they? Do they have a name for the shade?"

"Violacea, I think." Chitchat wasn't Brett's style, and the fact that he'd chosen to partake in small talk today unnerved her.

He slid onto a bench nearest her laundry pile. "That was some party at the Marshalls' last week, eh?"

"Yes. I think everyone had a lovely time."

He smirked. "Seemed like *you* did, all pressed up against that cowboy on the dance floor. Made me wish they had one of those betting wheels, so I could make a few dollars guessing when he'd plant one on you."

"You would have lost." She could have added that Melissa looked more like a decal on his shirt than a dance partner, but the happy memory of being in Nate's arms took the steam right out of it.

"New curtains?"

Eden added a folded towel to the tidy stack on the table. "Yes and no. They used to be pillowcases, but when the hems frayed, I hung them in here."

"Frugal, talented and gorgeous. What man could ask for more?"

If she didn't know him so well, Eden might say he was flirting with her.

"Have you eaten? I could make you a sandwich." Eden hated her tendency to cook and bake when she was worried. Hopefully, he'd say no.

"No, thanks." He held up his glass. "This'll do."

Eden breathed a sigh of relief. "An ice-cream cone, maybe?"

"What flavor?"

"Neapolitan."

"Okay, sure. Why not?"

Will you hush! What in the world is wrong *with you!*

"It's awfully quiet around here. Where are the boys?"

"They're out back, tossing a football around with Kirk."

"Ah, Kirk Simons, former Stanford quarterback. Hard to believe he settled—"

This wasn't like him. Not like him at all. Why had he stopped himself from delivering the insult? A chill snaked up her spine, despite the mid-July heat.

"Any word from Templeton?" he tried.

"No." She stopped folding. "Why do you ask?"

Brett shrugged. "Paying him to do nothing is part of the reason you're having problems making ends meet. Seems to me if he'd done his job, the tenants wouldn't have ruined Pinewood, and you could sell it. Think what a great cushion that much cash would make in your bank account. Peace of mind. All that good stuff."

"I wouldn't need a cushion," she said, snapping a fresh towel, "if you weren't bound and determined to sell Latimer House out from under me."

If he noticed her brusque tone, Brett chose not to mention it.

"I was sorry to hear Judson turned down your loan request."

How did he know about that? She'd told only three people about that meeting—four, counting Judson, and she found it hard to believe any of them would tell Brett about it.

"Have you seen Stuart lately?" she asked him.

"Not in person. Why?"

Unless he was lying, that left only Nate. She hadn't thought anything of it when the two of them had walked off to chat on the Fourth. But now—

"You know what I wish sometimes?"

Eden had no interest in Brett's wishes. Or his hopes and dreams, for that matter, but rather than spew a third gruff retort, she added another folded towel to the pile.

"I wish you'd give up this counseling stuff and come to work for me. With your management skills, you'd whip my whole office into shape inside of a week. Your people skills are unrivaled, and the amazing progress you've made with Travis Miller, former breaking and entering expert, is proof. Who would have thought he'd earn a full scholarship to Colorado State? I hope he knows it's because of you that he graduated with honors."

"First of all, Travis earned those honors himself. And secondly, *all* of the boys had issues when they came here." Breaking and entering, truancy, car theft, solicitation, shoplifting, armed robbery—the list of their combined offenses would fill the chalkboard in the back hall. "But they've all worked hard to overcome those difficulties, and for the most part, they've been successful."

She hoped the same would be true for Thomas someday, too. Eden plucked another towel from the heap and gave it a good flap.

"From now on, I'd really appreciate it if you didn't refer to them as 'kids like that,' okay?"

He tossed what was left of his cone into the trash can and rinsed his hands. "I'm sorry, Eden. I hope you know I meant no disrespect."

She knew nothing of the kind. But fear that he might put a rush on the sale of Latimer House kept her from admitting it.

"You're right," he said, sitting across from

her again. "They've come a long, long way, due largely to their own work. But there's no denying how big a role *you* played in their successes."

Eden could kick herself for offering him that ice-cream cone. Why didn't he just hurry up and leave, or at the very least tell her why he'd stopped by today. This verbal Ping-Pong match had already grown tiresome.

"I hated my stepfather when he first moved in with us," Brett mused.

Where was this going?

"But if it wasn't for his firm hand, I probably would have ended up just like your kids. You're doing everything you can, but you can't be a male role model." He grinned. "I mean, just look at you."

She imagined herself stuffing a towel into his mouth and smiled slightly.

"My mom is always after me to volunteer for something. So what if I stepped into that position, here? I could dole out a little fatherly advice—or discipline—when it's called for."

Put the man who'd once kicked a trash can all the way down the driveway because the lid wasn't on tight enough in charge of impressionable, vulnerable teenagers? Yeah, right!

"I appreciate the offer, but they have Kirk and Stuart, and occasionally, Shamus." *And Nate.*

"Yeah, but Stuart isn't here enough, and Kirk

is here too much." Brett walked around to her side of the table. "This whole house sale thing has been eating at my conscience."

Funny, I wasn't aware you had *a conscience.*

"Let me know how much time you need to get Pinewood into shape. I'll shave a few bucks off the asking price of the house and ask for a little more time. That'll appease the buyer and take some pressure off you."

What had Cora said or done to bring this about?

"What would you say if I hired someone to help with the housework and yard chores?"

I'd say, "Who are you and what have you done with Brett?"

"I'm guessing with Travis leaving for college, the state will send a new kid to take his place," he continued. "You'll need time to help him adjust, in addition to your usual duties."

In all the years she'd known him, Eden had never witnessed Brett do anything without first considering how it might benefit him.

"Wonderful as it all sounds, I can't afford the added rent you'll have to charge every month to defray the cost of hiring people to help."

Brett began to pace the kitchen. "Do you really think that little of me? You think I'd make an offer like that just to take advantage of you?"

There were a dozen things she could say to

defuse his claims, but she literally couldn't afford to rile him.

Brett stopped pacing. "Look, Eden. I'm aware I haven't been the best landlord, and that I've sometimes been unfair, stingy and difficult to deal with."

Sometimes?

"I'd like to see if Mom is right about this giving-of-yourself stuff. She says it makes people feel good about themselves. I don't know where else to start."

At a loss for words, Eden only shrugged.

Brett took a step closer and, hands on her shoulders, licked his lips. "Okay. I can take a hint."

She looked up into his face, and for a second there, he seemed almost sincere.

"You don't trust me. I get that. And I have no one but myself to blame."

Then, in less than a blink, there it was again—the mocking, almost antagonistic glint she'd come to recognize as his only genuine character trait. Eden had no idea what he hoped to gain from his offer, and she didn't want to find out.

"It's a generous offer," she said, "but I'm so stuck in my ways and persnickety, I'd make a housekeeper or yard crew so miserable, they'd quit the first day."

"Yeah, I guess." He took a step back. "I'll see myself to the door."

Eden followed him to the foyer, where Brett paused on the threshold.

"Let me know how much time you need to bring your grandparents' place up to code, so I can give my buyer some kind of time frame."

"Okay."

She leaned onto the porch, looking for his car. But Brett pocketed both hands and walked, head down, across the lawn. Had he wrecked the vehicle? she wondered.

The towels would have to wait. She needed to do something physical, something that would help her work out her agitation. That way, if the boys asked about her flushed cheeks, she could blame the exertion. In the laundry room, she filled her garden bucket with tools and carried them outside. After the boys turned in, she'd call Nate. It was time to get them out of this place, and the sooner the better. It meant setting aside her pride and working out a deal that wouldn't insult Nate or leave her feeling beholden to him.

Like it or not—and she did not—she needed to trust that he was every good thing he seemed to be.

Because if she found a Brett Michaels hiding under his caring, gentlemanly facade, it would break her heart.

NATE DECIDED IT was high time to repeat his offer. He didn't like thinking that embarrassment or fear had left Eden twisting in the wind. The way he saw it, the loan was a good thing for everyone concerned. Cora's warning had fused itself to his brain, and he couldn't stop worrying that at any moment, Michaels might boot Eden and the boys to the curb.

He deliberately arrived midway between lunch and suppertime so that Eden wouldn't feel obliged to feed him. Again. Memories of how she'd felt in his arms out there on the dance floor had been cause for much speculation at the Double M. Hard as it was to admit, they'd been right: He *had* started falling for her.

Why not give in to it? If ghosts from her past rose up to haunt her, maybe he could help.

The decision felt good. So good that on the way to Latimer House, he stopped at a corner flower mart, grabbed a pretty bouquet and hoped the boys had been right when they'd said daisies were her favorite.

Parking out front, as usual, he made his way up the walk, where flower beds, hanging baskets and plants that spilled artfully from heavy urns on each side of the front door showed further proof of her constant care. The door's brass hinges and knob gleamed, and he wondered if the woman ever slept.

The money-stuffed envelope in his shirt pocket crinkled as he transferred the flowers to his left hand. Instead of the first notes of the Westminster chimes, Nate heard a dull *thunk*. Probably nothing more than a loose wire, easily fixed with a screwdriver.

Nate followed the flagstone path that led to the back of the house and, rounding the corner, he saw Kirk and the boys at the far end of the yard. Red-faced and sweating, they were so focused on drills that they didn't see him. It seemed providential, since now he and Eden could discuss his investment in Pinewood without interruption.

The interior door to the mudroom was ajar, no doubt to encourage cross ventilation. If that cheapskate Michaels would fork over a few bucks to have the antiquated air-conditioning system repaired, everyone at Latimer House would rest easier.

He hid the flowers behind his back and prepared to knock. Quiet voices coming from the kitchen stopped him. One belonged to Eden, he knew that much. But the other...

Brett Michaels? Why hadn't he seen the guy's sleek sports car out front?

Nate peered inside, and saw them, wingtips to sneakers and locked in deep conversation.

The jealousy swirling in his gut made no

sense. It had been easy to believe her when she'd said Michaels was her landlord and nothing more. The guy made her life miserable, after all, threatening the boys' security.

Nate sat on the top step, the bouquet dangling blossoms-down between his knees, free hand clapped to the back of his neck. He'd never even kissed her, so why did it bother him, seeing her toe to toe with Michaels?

Behind him, he heard footsteps, retreating down the hall. When Eden and Michaels reached the door, would she kiss him goodbye?

The daisy petals trembled, and he clasped the stems so tightly that a few drops of water seeped from the wrapper and landed on the toe of his left boot.

Out in the yard, the boys were running plays now, but the boxwood hedge planted around the yard hid him from view. A good thing, since he probably looked as if he'd been mowed down by one of their maneuvers.

He could count on one hand the number of times he'd cried since reaching manhood, and have fingers left over. Thomas strolled up and sat down beside him. "I hate football."

"It's a rough sport."

"Yeah, but that isn't why I hate it. I don't like being hit. Or hitting people."

He'd overheard a couple of the boys say that

Thomas's mother had died in prison, and that his father had put him in numerous dangerous situations. It was hard enough wrapping his mind around the fact that a parent could desert his own child, but learning that the boy might also have been physically abused only heightened Nate's contempt of the man.

"Guess you're real glad, then, that everyone here likes and respects you."

Thomas's eyes widened. "They do?"

"'Course they do. You probably can't see it because you live with them. We tend to overlook things we see every day. But I noticed."

Thomas glanced into the yard, where his housemates laughed and hollered as they mimicked Kirk's moves. "Well, maybe." On his feet, he said, "I need to get my chores done."

"See you later, then."

Thomas paused just inside the screen door. "I notice things, too."

Nate turned to get a better look at the kid.

"If you're sad because you think Eden doesn't like you, well, you're wrong."

With that, he disappeared inside.

Nate had no idea what Thomas had seen to inspire such a comment, but he knew he'd do everything in his power to protect these kids. The money in his pocket would help her turn

Pinewood into a home that no one could ever sell out from under them.

As he got to his feet, the back door opened with a *whoosh*, and out stepped Eden, wearing jean shorts and a sleeveless white shirt.

"Hey there!" he said as she plowed right into him.

If he hadn't gathered her close, she might have fallen down the back steps. Eden met his eyes, a grateful smile turning up the corners of her mouth. Had she looked at Michaels this way a few minutes ago? If you want something bad enough, his grandpa had advised back when donning a major-league uniform had seemed impossible, you'll fight for it. Nate had taken the advice, working harder than he had in his life. Hours in the gym, sacrificing soft drinks and pizza, paid off, because he made the team. Was it crazy to want to fight that way...for Eden?

"Wow," she said, pointing at the garden tools that had tumbled to the flagstone walk. "It's a good thing you were out here, or that's where I'd be." Using a fingertip, she turned his head gently. "Look what my big hard head did to your chin. How will you explain that to your family?"

"Same way you'll explain the goose egg on your forehead."

Eden stepped back and adjusted the hem of

her blouse. "It'll be better before I'm married."
She bent to grab the handle of her bucket.

"My grandmother used to say that," he said,
passing her the clippers and shears that had
landed on the stairs.

Eden picked up the flowers he'd brought,
spent a moment tidying the stems and petals.
"Another casualty of my klutziness," she said,
holding out the spray. "Sorry."

"Those are for you."

Nate hoped she wouldn't ask why he'd bought
them. "Because the boys said they're your favorite" or "I saw them and thought of you" sounded
even more idiotic than the jealousy he'd felt seeing her with Michaels.

"But now that I compare them to these—"
he swept his arm to encompass the colorful,
healthy plants lining the back walk "—I'm the
one who's sorry."

"You'd think something this pretty would have
a powerful fragrance, wouldn't you?" She stuck
her nose into the bouquet. "I've never had any luck
growing daisies, so thank you. They're beautiful."

He went back to retrieving tools, and she said,
"I'll get those later. Can you come inside for a
minute? I'd like to get these into water and show
you something."

Once inside, she poured him a glass of lemonade. "Check out the boys' bulletin board," she said, grabbing a vase from under the sink. "A and B-plus essays, all written about you and the Double M."

Nate stepped up and read the titles. "How to Saddle a Horse." "A Clean Bunkhouse Is a Happy Bunkhouse." "Fail-safe Way to Feed a Sugar Cube to Horses."

He turned to Eden. "All this from what they picked up Memorial Day and the Fourth?"

"Amazing, isn't it, especially when half the time, it sometimes seems like they're not even listening."

"And what's this one, a thank-you note?"

"Travis wrote it, and Silas typed it up," Eden said, arranging the flowers in a yellow vase. "I suggested mailing it, but they wanted you to pick it up here."

Nate plucked the thumbtack from the cork, grabbed the paper and read aloud:

Dear Nate,
We know that most people think that be-cause we got a rough start in life, we'll never amount to much. It's people like you and your family who let us know that the only real limitations in life are those we put on ourselves.

Thanks for teaching us so many life les-sons, and for showing us a good time, too.

We're real lucky to have met you, and real proud to call you our friend.

And it was signed by the boys—and Eden and Kirk.

"Man," Nate said, waving the note, "it's a good thing I'm not the sensitive type, 'cause a thing like this could put a tear in a man's eye."

Eden headed into the mudroom. "Would you mind very much setting the table while I pick up those tools?" In the doorway, she added, "Unless you can't stay..."

He shouldn't. There had been another cougar attack on a neighbor's ranch, and he needed to check the herds. And yet he heard himself say, "I can."

Moments later, when she returned to the kitchen, Nate said, "So what was Michaels doing here earlier? Moving up your move-out date?"

"Not exactly." Frowning, she sighed. "I don't understand how a guy like that came from a woman like Cora. The only thing they have in common is their last name."

"I think I have the solution to his threats."

"Threats," she echoed. "I wouldn't have put it quite that way, but I guess that's exactly what they are."

Nate held out the envelope.

"What's that?"

"My donation to Latimer House. Or Pinewood. So you can get out from under that idiot's thumb, once and for all."

Eden stared at the bills, then met his eyes. "Nate, that's far more than we need. I can't ask you to—"

"Seems to me we've been down this road already. You didn't ask. I offered. It isn't a loan, remember, it's a contribution."

The cheerful sound of the boys grew louder, telling him the football game had ended and they were heading inside to clean up for supper.

"We'll wrap this up later," he said, sliding the envelope back into his pocket as one by one, the teens bulldozed into the room, laughing and high-fiving on the way to the fridge.

Kirk sidled up and whispered to Nate, "Need a word with you, if you have time after supper."

He didn't. But he said, "Let me make a phone call, make sure Carl has things under control." Rising, Nate put his cell phone to his ear and stepped onto the back porch.

"Hey, boss, what's up?"

"Just checking in. What's the latest?"

"Told the hands what you said, and sent four of 'em out in the Jeeps, armed with binoculars and rifles. They have radios, too, so if they see something, I'll be the first to know."

"I'll be back before dark," he said. "Call me if anything happens."

Both men knew what that meant: if one of the hands saw the cougar, he would shoot to kill.

"You got it, boss," Carl said, and hung up.

Nate didn't like the way things were unfolding. That cat should have moved on by now. The fact that it hadn't told him it saw the Double M as a reliable food source, that it was probably a female with kittens to feed. It seemed a crime against nature to kill her, but she hadn't left him any options. If it came down to protecting the cat or defending every living being that called the Double M home...

The sound of clattering plates and flatware drew his attention inside. Nate pocketed the phone and headed back into the kitchen, where Eden was setting the table.

He stepped up to the sink to wash his hands. "Where is everybody?"

"Taking showers, doing chores, completing their reading assignments."

"Good. I want to pick up where we left off." He sat at the table, and patted the empty space to his right.

She gave him a look that said, "I have a dozen things to do," but sat beside him.

He slid the fat envelope from his shirt pocket, laid it on the table, and covered it with his hand.

"Nate, I—"

"Humor me, will ya? Now, promise me that you won't say anything until I'm finished. I have a one-track mind, and interruptions tend to derail me."

"Okay," Eden said, biting her lip.

"First of all, let me repeat—this is *not* a loan. It's a straight-up donation. In a way, it's an investment *and* insurance, because once you bring Pinewood back to its former glory, it'll mean no one can ever threaten the boys' stability again."

He slid the envelope directly in front of her.

"I don't know what to say."

He lifted her chin. "Say you'll find a safe place to keep it until you need it for a contractor, new appliances and other repairs."

"A safe place?" She sighed. "Is there such a thing these days?"

"Would you feel more comfortable if I held on to it? Say the word and name the amount you need, and I'll be right over to deliver it." He grinned. "Probably at mealtime."

Eden focused on something beyond his left shoulder. Was she considering her options, or wondering just how easy—or difficult—it might be to wait for him to dole out the money?

"The contractor you recommended...do you think he'll meet with me later this week?"

"I'll give him a call, have him get in touch

with you so you can set up a time that works for both of you." Nate slid the envelope back into his pocket. "Okay if I give him your cell number?"

"Of course."

Nate couldn't pinpoint the change in her expression. Anger? Fear? Shame?

"Thank you doesn't begin to cover what I feel."

"No thanks necessary. I like those kids." *And I like* you. "I'm glad I can help out a little."

"A little?" Eden laughed. "I took a writing class a few years ago," she said, "and the instructor stressed two things, over and over."

"Oh?"

"One, don't undervalue your contributions." She leaned in close, real close.

"And what's number two?"

"Show," she whispered, "don't tell."

Eden pressed her lips to his, a lingering, heart-pounding kiss that left him breathless, wanting more.

When it ended, he looked into those striking storm-gray eyes and found a word to describe the subtle shift in her mood, and it hurt like a roundhouse punch to the gut: obligated.

CHAPTER NINE

SAVED BY THE BELL, Nate thought when his cell phone pinged, ending the kiss.

Carl's text gave him just the excuse he needed to leave, right away.

"Much as I'd like to, I can't stay for supper."

Travis walked into the room. "Something to do with that cougar, I'll bet," he said.

"'Fraid so."

As the rest of the kids filed into the kitchen, Nate held out the thank-you note. "I'm gonna frame this. Thanks, guys. You're the best."

"No, *you're* the best," traveled up and down the table like a curious echo.

From the doorway, Nate said, "This meeting of the Mutual Admiration Society is hereby dismissed." To this point, he'd avoided eye contact with Eden. She'd sent mixed messages, and evidently, he wasn't savvy enough to read them. The kiss told him she was grateful for his offer, that she had feelings for him that had nothing to do with money. Nate couldn't decide if the peculiar look on her face meant she resented him for making the offer…or resented herself for needing help.

He risked a glance to say, "Thanks for the invite, though." All the way down the walk, he pictured the boys' curious expressions. They were probably already pummeling her with questions about his hasty departure. He was about to insert the key into the ignition when Kirk rapped on the driver's door.

"I won't keep you, but I need your advice about something."

"Okay, but advice isn't exactly my strong suit."

"For starters, let me say that I appreciate everything you've done for the boys. If you're helping them because you're interested in Eden, well, that's none of my business. But those kids have had it up to here," he said, drawing an imaginary line across his throat, "with people who've let them down."

In other words, *if you and Eden are having problems, don't make them the boys' problems, too.*

"I thought you said you needed advice."

Kirk swallowed, and Nate summoned his patience as the younger man worked himself up to whatever he was about to say. "Well, Brett Michaels has been sniffing around here a lot lately. He's getting sneaky. Parking on the next block and walking over so nobody will see his car. He's up to no good. Why else would he go to all that trouble?"

Good question. And now he understood why he hadn't seen Michaels's car out front earlier.

"Every time he's here, he drops hints."

"What kind of hints?"

"He never actually comes right out and says anything, but the implications are clear: If Eden doesn't come up with the money to buy Latimer House, soon, we're all out on our ears. Eden won't talk about it much, but I've known her long enough to see it's weighing on her."

"How?"

"She's quiet. Way too quiet. Doesn't eat much. And the boys told me they've heard her pacing in the middle of the night."

Moving to Pinewood would solve all of that. Would she actually call him when she needed money to make repairs? Or had she just agreed to his suggestion to put the subject to rest?

"Can I trust you with some confidential information?" Nate asked.

"Depends. Who'd I have to hide it from?"

"Everybody. Including Eden."

Kirk frowned slightly. "I can't give you my word on that. Not until I hear this confidential information."

"I appreciate your honesty." It told Nate the guy could be trusted. He patted his pocket. "I offered this money to Eden today—not a loan, but a straightforward donation—so she can get Pinewood inspector-proof."

"So we can move over there."

"Exactly."

Kirk narrowed his eyes. "Aw, man. She turned you down?"

"Not exactly." Nate licked his lips, remembering that kiss. He frowned, too, recalling how beaten-down she'd looked afterward. "I'm just concerned that after she thinks about it for a while, she'll turn me down."

"No, she'll take the money and get Pinewood fixed up. She'd do anything for those kids."

Including swallowing her pride…

"None of this would be necessary if the Hansons weren't such losers. And if Brett Michaels wasn't such a greedy, narcissistic pig. Wouldn't you love a chance to get into that twisted mind of his?"

"No, thanks." He turned the key and fired up the truck. "I dislike him enough already."

Kirk stepped back as Nate shifted into Reverse. "Good luck capturing that cougar."

Capturing? Nate understood that hearing how they'd solve the cat problem could upset someone who hadn't been raised a rancher, so he simply said, "Thanks. Catch you later."

He glanced into the rearview mirror, saw

Eden on the porch, waving. Summoning Kirk to supper, or saying goodbye to *him*?

"MAN, EDEN," STUART SAID, "I need to drop by more often." He helped himself to another oven-fried chicken thigh. "This is better than Gran's."

"Have you had her homemade fish sticks?" DeShawn asked.

Stuart was too busy separating meat from bone to look up. "Can't say as I have. But if it's half as good as this, I'll bet it would turn a fish-hater into a connoisseur."

"Nate was s'posed to eat with us, but he had to get back to the ranch," Devon said. "To kill a cougar."

Carlos looked surprised, and a little afraid. "Kill it? Really?"

"He's a rancher," Travis began. "Protecting your livestock can sometimes be ugly business."

He'd become a young man, right before her eyes, Eden admitted to herself, reflecting on his mature statement and the thoughtful way he'd delivered it.

The boy shook his head. "Wish there was something we could do to help."

"Like what?" DeShawn asked. "Strap on a gun belt, draw a bead on that cat and say, 'If you know what's good for you, you'll git on outta town'?"

"You watch too many old movies," Thomas said.

DeShawn harrumphed. "Better than those cartoons *you* watch."

"Boys," Eden said, "your fries are getting cold. Who wants to help me crank the handle on the ice-cream maker after we clean up this mess?"

"I will," Thomas said, "if it's chocolate!"

"I'll do it no matter what flavor it is," Devon said. "Homemade ice cream is the best!"

Stuart chimed in with "How about we take turns?"

All eyes turned to him.

He feigned defensiveness. "Hey. I'm a cop. Negotiation is part of the job." With a devilish smile, he added, "Besides, grown-ups enjoy cranking that handle as much as kids do."

"Hey, Eden," DeShawn said, "think Nate has ever made ice cream?"

"Born and raised on a ranch, I'm guessing at least one of his grandmothers had a great recipe. So yes, I imagine he has."

"Grandmothers are like that," DeShawn observed. "Wish I'd had a chance to get to know mine."

The others agreed by way of a quiet murmur that traveled up the table and down again.

"Hey, Kirk," Thomas said, "what were you and Nate whispering about out there in the driveway?"

Eden had wondered the same thing, and waited for her assistant's reply.

"Oh, nothing much. I told him to be careful rounding up that cat." He scraped crumbs from his plate into the disposal.

"Coulda fooled me."

Kirk didn't ask what Thomas meant, and neither did anyone else. Eden had a feeling she knew the answer. Her assistant moved like a cat himself, padding through the house on white-socked feet, surprising everyone with sudden appearances. Had he overheard Nate's offer?

Stuart put his plate into the sink. "Where do you keep the ice-cream maker?"

"In the pantry, middle of the bottom shelf."

"And it'll be right there, too," Travis observed. "Was she always like this, Stu?"

"Yeah, 'fraid so."

Eden rolled her eyes at her brother. Stuart—and just about everyone else—had been calling her a clean freak since before she lost her first tooth.

"In my opinion, it's a positive trait," Travis said. "One that all of us benefit from."

"How do you figure that?" Carlos asked.

"Because we always know exactly where our stuff is."

Jokes went up and down the table, covering the gamut from teacher's pet to apple polisher, but Travis seemed unfazed as Eden assembled the ingredients for ice cream. Once she'd filled the bucket and added ice, the boys took turns cranking.

"They make electric ice-cream makers, y'know," Carlos said.

DeShawn grunted as he powered the handle. "Yeah, but what fun would that be?"

They talked less and turned more, and soon, the cream, sugar and flavorings began to thicken.

"Think Nate's having this much luck catching that cat?" Thomas asked.

"If he cares about his livestock, he won't catch it, he'll kill it," Stuart said.

The boys fell silent.

DeShawn frowned. "Never saw Nate as a killer."

"He isn't," Stuart said. "He's a realist. That cougar is eating his livestock. Might as well be taking food right out of the Marshalls' mouths. Plus, a lot of little kids live at the Double M. All it'd take is for their parents to get distracted for a second, and the cat might decide to make a meal out of a toddler."

Eden thought of Nate, alone out there in a wide-open pasture. No doubt he'd have a rifle at the ready. He might even be shouting distance from his foreman and ranch hands. Still… She almost preferred picturing him on a date with some pretty socialite. At least he'd be safe.

Eyes closed, Eden remembered their kiss. She had initiated it, intending it only as a quick thank-you peck. But when Nate's arms automatically slid around her, one big hand pressed to the back of her head as the other cupped her chin, she gave in to the moment. He'd held her close, so close she'd felt and heard the steady *thump-thump* of his big, caring heart.

"What's the matter, big sister, got a headache?"

Eyes wide-open now, she felt the telltale warmth of a blush creep into her cheeks. "No, Stuart, I'm fine."

"Got a crush on the cowboy, eh?"

"When you're wrong, little brother, you're wrong." It was far more than a crush.

Eden licked her lips and glanced at the ice-cream maker.

Cody groaned. "Isn't that stuff thick enough yet?"

Stuart lifted the lid and withdrew the dasher. "What do you say, guys?" He held it high enough for all of them to see. "Is this stuff thick enough, or is it thick enough!"

It pleased Eden to see them happy and content, well-adjusted and interacting like brothers. The only thing missing, she decided, was a father figure. Not Kirk, their teacher or Stuart, the like-an-uncle visitor, but someone who'd give them advice and guidance in caring doses, as needed. Someone who'd guide them into manhood with his own good example.

"You sure you're okay?" Stuart asked. "Looks like you've seen a ghost."

Laughing, Eden said, "You know I don't believe in stuff like that."

Fortunately, the boys had turned their attention to Stuart, who'd started plopping equal portions of ice cream into ramekins.

Her reply had been truthful. She'd never really believed in beings from the spirit world.

But Eden had a feeling that kiss would haunt her for a long, long time.

IN THE WEEK since the afternoon of the kiss, Nate had called Eden twice…on the same day. Once to give her the contractor's phone number, once to correct it when he found out his guy had changed his number.

She'd wasted no time scheduling a walk-through. Any day now, she'd find out how much work and expense it would take to restore Pinewood to the warm, cozy home it had been for her and Stuart.

Now, with the boys in bed and Kirk gone for the day, it almost seemed she had Latimer

House to herself. Eden had always loved the big old-fashioned kitchen, with its white metal cabinets and black-and-white-tiled floor. Kirk and his dad had built the long trestle table and matching benches to seat twenty, and Cora had raised the funds to replace the old fridge with an up-to-date model.

She guessed that the boys would choose the family room as their favorite, with its well-worn, L-shaped leather couch and wide-screen TV, donated by Duke shortly before his death.

She sat on the recliner end of the sofa and put up the footrest. It wasn't often she had a chance to relax—her own fault, admittedly. Yes, she could have hired someone to help with the dusting, vacuuming and laundry, but the money saved by doing the chores herself meant she could splurge now and then, providing the boys with better cuts of meat or brand-name sneakers.

The big, drafty place had been a haven for every scared, bedraggled kid who had arrived lugging a backpack that held all his worldly possessions. They considered it home now, and she hoped they'd feel just as safe and comfortable at Pinewood…and that it wouldn't take long to move them there. They didn't know it yet, but she was considering taking them to the initial meeting with Nate's contractor, so they could ask questions and make suggestions. She'd be able to tell a lot about the honesty, integrity and patience of the man, just by watching him interact with a dozen inquisitive and rambunctious teenagers.

Eden aimed the remote at the TV and scrolled until she found the old movie channel. A classic Western would begin in just a few minutes.

It wouldn't be fair to ask Nate to join them for the contractor meetings, not with all his other duties and responsibilities, but what was the harm in calling to ask if he'd solved the cougar problem?

She dialed his cell number and counted the rings. One…would he answer from inside his rustic log house? Two…from the well-equipped barn? Three…or was he scouring the property in search of the killer cat?

Eden hit the end button without leaving a message. If he was out looking for the cougar, he'd probably set his phone to vibrate or turned it off altogether. Disappointed, she settled in to watch the Western. It was the story of a rough-and-tumble cavalryman and the estranged wife who refuses to let him—or any man—control her. Despite the danger around them and hard words between them, they gave in to a moment when a soldier sang "I'll Take You Home Again, Kathleen." When their kiss ended, the actor's expression reminded Eden of the way Nate had looked at her last week—hopeful, loving, tender... He had feelings for her. How else could she explain the way he'd trembled slightly when she pressed her lips to his?

"Fool," she muttered. "Shouldn't have started something that can't go anywhere."

But...why couldn't it? She had feelings for Nate, too.

Because with all of your other commitments, you can't commit to Nate, that's why.

Eden turned off the TV and tossed the remote to the other end of the couch. Maybe a cup of tea would soothe her.

Eden popped her favorite mug in the microwave.

Taking care of others was in Nate's DNA. Watching him interact with his family, with her boys, was proof of that. So when he learned about her financial dilemma, of course he'd offered to chip in. And if she hoped to continue helping the kids, Eden needed to accept the offer. If it turned out his motives were less than pure, well, she'd deal with that later.

Better watch it, Miss Scarlett O'Hara; not everything is better tomorrow.

The microwave beeped, and as she dropped a teabag into her mug, the phone rang.

"Hey there."

Her heart fluttered in response to the sound of his voice. Eden smiled to herself. She needed a better word than *fond* to describe her feelings for him.

"I saw that you called. Is everything all right?"

"Everything's fine." She tucked the phone into the crook of her neck and spooned sugar into the tea. "I was watching a Western and started thinking about you out there on the Double M, looking for that cougar. Did you find it?"

"No, 'fraid not. But we found tracks and other signs that give us a pretty good idea where she's holed up."

"Are you sure it's a she?"

"Pretty sure, yeah. For one thing, she's hanging out where the Double M butts up against the Rocking K property, taking a cow here, a horse there, from both of us. Usually, cougars kill once a week, if that, then feed off the carcass a few days and rest up while scoping out another meal. The fact that this one is killing so often tells us she has kittens to feed."

She could hear the strain in his voice. And who wouldn't be tense, knowing that his major income source was shrinking with every kill. "Could it be more than one cat?"

"It's possible, but not likely. They're solitary animals."

"I wish I knew more about them. About ranching," she admitted.

"Why?"

"So I could think of something supportive, something reassuring, to say."

His quiet chuckle filtered into her ear. "It's plenty reassuring, just knowing the subject doesn't bore you to sleep."

"Bore me! You're kidding, right?"

There was a long pause before he said, "Let's just say not every woman is as obliging as you."

His mother and aunts had been ranchers most of their lives, and so had his sister, Hank. So he must have been referring to the fiancée named in the *Sports Illustrated* article. She was curious about the woman—about the relationship.

"I take it your fiancée wasn't as understanding as the Marshall women?"

Another long pause made her think she'd overstepped her bounds.

"Let's just say she was cut from a different cloth."

"Still, it must have been hard, losing her that way."

"Yeah, but I expect you know something about loss."

A hint that he was curious about the details of her parents' murders? Maybe another time…

"I was young when I lost them. Kids adjust and adapt quickly. It isn't so easy for adults."

"Miranda was a casualty of my can't-say-no habit. I knew things weren't working between us, but I didn't know how to admit it without hurting her. I should have been up-front with her. She would have kicked me to the curb, and we wouldn't have been together that night."

"I hope that doesn't mean you blame your-*self* for—"

"Yeah. I do. But…"

He punctuated his pause with a heavy sigh.

"But enough about me. Why did you call?"

"To make a confession. And to thank you."

"Oh?"

"It isn't fair to put you in the position of dol-ing out money. You're not my dad, and I'm too old for an allowance."

He chuckled, giving her the courage to finish with, "So if it's still okay with you, I'll take your donation, all at once." *And someday, somehow, I'll repay every dollar.*

"I'm disappointed."

Eden's heart thumped a little harder. Had she misjudged him? Was generosity nothing but camouflage to hide his control freak tendencies?

"If I'm not delivering dollars in dribs and drabs, what excuse will I have to come to supper?"

Relief surged through her, prompting a nervous giggle. "You're family, Nate. So you're welcome, anytime."

"I, ah, thanks."

"So about this cougar," Eden said, changing the subject. "If you're forced to kill her, what will happen to her babies?"

"Ever hear of 'survival of the fittest'?" Sad acceptance tinged his voice.

In other words, he didn't expect they'd last long without their mother to feed and teach them to live and thrive in the wild. Nate's tone also told her he took no pleasure from that fact, and it gave her a whole new reason to admire him. She had a better understanding what he was up against, every day of his life, and didn't envy what he might have to do next.

"I'd sure hate to be in your saddle, cowboy."

Nate laughed, and yet again, Eden's heart fluttered.

"You sure do have a way with words. And speaking of words, here's one for you—Thanksgiving."

"What about it?"

"My mom gave me strict instructions to invite you and the boys to join us this year."

Eden glanced at the calendar. "She sure does like to plan ahead, doesn't she!"

"Yeah, that's because the Marshall women are always looking for excuses to decorate the party barn. The more the merrier, and all that. But if you tell any of them I said that, I'll deny it."

"I've always enjoyed planning and cooking big feasts, but—"

"I get it. And I told her you might have other plans. She'll be disappointed. We'll *all* be disappointed—"

"You didn't let me finish. I was going to say it might be nice not to have all the work and worry in the middle of a big construction project."

"Ah, so you called my contractor?"

"I did. I'm meeting him at Pinewood next week. A formality, really, since I can already tell he'll work magic over there."

"When's the walk-through?"

"Wednesday, between eleven and three."

"Want me to meet you over there?"

"Thanks so much, Nate, but I can't ask you to carve four hours out of your day to babysit me. Besides—"

"I hate to sound redundant, but you didn't ask, I offered."

She laughed quietly. "And I've said *this* before—you didn't let me finish. The boys are going with me. I think it'll be good for them to see the place while it's still a mess, let them have some say in how we'll clean it up."

"That's a great idea." After a long pause, he added, "How would you feel about bringing them out to the ranch tomorrow, just for the day? Last time I was there, they said they'd like to go riding. Might want to swim a little, too. And I could show 'em how to recognize predator signs, maybe even get in a little target practice."

"Target practice? You mean with *guns*?"

"That's kinda what I had in mind, yeah. If they're going to spend time out here, they should learn proper firearms safety, in case we ever encounter something during a trail ride."

"Oh, I don't know, Nate. I'm afraid if the Division of Community Relations got word that I'd allowed them to handle weapons, they'd take away my license so fast I'd need stitches to close up the paper cuts. They'd take the boys away, too, put them into foster homes and halfway houses all across the state. *Then* what would become of them?"

Another lengthy silence. "Man. I hadn't given any of that a thought. Growing up out here, rifles are tools of the trade. Knowing how to shoot is as vital as knowing how to ride. But you're right. I won't even mention it to them."

Relieved, Eden blew a stream of air through her teeth. "Thanks for understanding."

"If you guys can make it tomorrow, give me a call first thing, so I can have the horses ready."

"I have a feeling we'll be there, probably around lunchtime."

"Sleep well, Eden," he said, and hung up.

Carrying her tea into the family room, Eden flipped through the channels, stopping when the you-need-kissing-by-someone-who-knows-how scene from an old classic lit up the screen. Instantly, the memory of that sweet moment with Nate came to mind. She'd liked standing in the circle of his arms. Liked the way his gentle lips had responded to hers. She could almost hear his smooth voice uttering the same words as the movie star.

Oh, she was falling for him, all right. Would she feel this way if she *wasn't*?

CHAPTER TEN

EDEN WOKE LONG before her alarm rang, and after a few minutes of tossing and turning, she flipped the covers back and got up, working the kinks out of her neck and shoulders.

While Kirk and the boys took advantage of the pool, Eden had let Hank talk her into a long ride across the Double M's acres. If she'd known her backside would protest this much, she might have said no when Nate's sister asked how she felt about taking a seldom-used trail back to the barn.

But there wasn't time to pamper her achy muscles. This afternoon, she and Travis would make the hour-long drive north to Fort Collins. It had taken a little finagling, but Eden had secured him a semiprivate dorm room with its own bathroom, and by tonight, he'd be pretty much settled in Piñon Hall. Just last week, she'd taken him shopping, so he could spend his graduation gift cards on clothes, a backpack, linens and a hamper, a desk lamp and alarm clock. Thanks to Nate, Travis could contribute a TV and DVD player to the shared space, and Kirk had provided a microwave. Cora donated the small fridge and coffeepot from Duke's office, and the rest of the Latimer House boys pitched in with headphones, an assortment of cords and accessories for Eden's old computer and printer. He'd be pleasantly surprised, she thought, to discover that she'd been stockpiling toiletries, hygiene products and a box filled with his favorite nonperishable snacks. She'd bought him an inexpensive cell phone, and right before saying goodbye, Eden would make him promise to call her at least every other day.

Soon after sunrise, she dressed in sweatpants and a T-shirt and headed outside to weed the walk. She figured she had two hours before the boys woke. By then, she'd have the front yard looking shipshape.

On her hands and knees, Eden weeded between the flagstones leading to the old park bench Kirk had salvaged and refinished, then snipped spent blooms from the red-and-white impatiens that grew alongside the path.

When the deep rumble of a motorcycle grew closer, she looked up to see what inconsiderate dolt would ride a noisy vehicle in the neighborhood so early in the morning.

The rider, dressed entirely in black leather,

turned into the driveway, and she recognized him instantly.

"G'mornin'," he said, removing his helmet and aviator sunglasses. The silver chains draped from his square-toed boots clanked as he walked toward her. The man was Thomas's father. The initial supervised meetings between father and son had taken place downtown, and the social worker in charge made it clear that Eden's presence was not encouraged.

"Name's Thomas Burke," he said, extending a hand. "I understand you've been taking care of my boy."

Most of her boys had no idea where their parents were. The few who did rarely heard from them. A good thing, in Eden's opinion, because seeing the mom or dad who'd neglected or abandoned them could lead to major setbacks. Thomas had been with her almost as long as Travis, and despite his issues, he'd made amazing progress…until *this* one showed up.

The man adjusted his black-and-white do-rag. "So is Tommy here?"

She didn't know what reason he'd have to lie about his relationship to Thomas, but Eden wasn't taking chances. Not after learning the hard lesson taught by the father of a former resident in her care. After flashing a legitimate death certificate, Will Keegan took his son home, and within weeks of leaving, young Malik died during a gang initiation. If the department had investigated the father's background, it never would have released Malik into his care.

"There's no one here named Tommy."

It seemed as though he'd suddenly taken on a great burden. Head down and shoulders slumped, he groaned quietly. And when he reached into his studded jacket, Eden flinched and gripped the handle of the garden tool tighter.

Burke produced a zipper bag filled with photos and handed it to her. "Will you give this to him? I told him about them last time we met, and he seemed interested, so…"

Eden motioned toward the bench behind her, and joined him when he sat. Something told her she had nothing to fear from this pierced-and-tattooed man. Whether or not *Thomas* had anything to fear remained to be seen.

She went through the photos, and Burke explained when and where each had been taken: Thomas in a striped hospital nursery cap, moments after birth. Thomas with his arms akimbo, learning to walk. Thomas grinning and showing off his first baby tooth. Burke appeared in many of the photos, and in some, so did a pretty, sad-eyed young woman.

"Thomas's mother?" Eden asked.

"Yeah, that's Nicole. I guess you already know what happened to her."

Unfortunately, she did. Thomas's mother had been sentenced to life without parole for the murder of her drug dealer, who'd turned her into his one-woman mule. She'd continued distributing drugs while incarcerated, and when a deal went wrong, she paid with her life. According to Thomas's file, Burke served time, too, for the use and distribution of drugs and for neglecting his son.

The Latimer House boys had a chance to take different roads than their parents had. Thomas was on the right track so far...as long as his father didn't divert him.

"Guess you're wondering where I've been since getting out of jail."

She was holding Thomas's baptismal certificate, proof that at some point in his early years, one or both of his parents wanted their son to live a normal, happy life. Yes, Eden wondered where Burke had been, but the better question was, what went wrong in the first place?

Burke began telling her how Nicole met a man more than twice her age, who left his wife of twenty years to run off with her. And Burke—hurt, humiliated, angry and overwhelmed by the day-to-day pressures of raising a toddler all on his own—found solace at the bottom of a bottle. Next thing he knew, Thomas was in foster care and he was in the county jail. Upon his release, he swore to clean up his act. Unfortunately, he continued, little changed, except that he swapped whiskey for beer and pills, which were cheaper and didn't make him so mean. His third DUI arrest would have put him away for years, so he jumped bail and ran off to Alaska, where he signed on as a big-equipment operator with a gold mining crew. While recovering from a near-fatal on-the-job accident, he read an article about recidivism, which included a sidebar about the large percentage of children who ended up like their parents—or worse.

"It made me realize what a mess I'd made of my life…and Tommy's. So I came home, turned myself in, and when I got out that time, I got clean and stayed that way." He looked Eden in the eyes. "Earned my two-year chip a few months back. Got a job and a decent place for me an' Tommy, I mean Thomas, to live. I figure there's a lot to make up for and not a lot of time to do it. But I aim to try."

For his sake and Thomas's, Eden wanted to believe him. But she'd been fooled before by the seemingly sincere promises of parents and guardians.

She started to hand him the photos.

"No, I told you, Thomas asked to see them.

Maybe they'll bring back some good memories and he won't be so opposed to visits with me."

"You were honest with me, Mr. Burke, so I feel it's only fair to tell you the truth. It isn't likely the state will deny your request to visit with Thomas, but there are no guarantees where full-time custody is concerned. If you're serious, you'll have to do this by the book." She paused and gave him a hard stare. "I'd hate to see Thomas lose all the ground he's gained, looking at these pictures and dreaming of something that might never happen, or that it might be taken out from under him if it does."

Eden thought it odd that Burke hadn't asked one question about Thomas. Didn't he want to know the details of his son's life at Latimer House? If he was healthy and fit? If he got good grades and stayed out of trouble?

"I'm curious," she said, "about how you found Thomas. It was my understanding that you made no attempt to stay in touch, all those years you were...away."

Standing, Burke said, "Man makes a lot of useful friends on the inside." He handed her a slip of paper. "That's my contact information at home and at work. Will you call me if Thomas wants to see me?" It was his turn to pause. "Or even...even if he doesn't?"

What could she say, except, "All right."

He held out his hand and, getting to her feet, Eden put hers into it, hoping she hadn't just struck a deal with the devil.

EDEN AND SHAMUS were sipping iced tea and engaged in a lively conversation when Nate pulled into the driveway. And since she'd sworn him to secrecy about their deal, Nate didn't mention that he'd stopped by to deliver the cash—every penny she'd need to remodel Pinewood. After exchanging pleasantries, Eden stepped inside to get him a glass while Nate slid a rocking chair closer to theirs.

"So did you get Travis all set up in his dorm room?" he asked when she returned.

"As set up as I could get him." A feeble smile lifted the corners of her mouth. "He had pretty strong ideas about where and how to stow his things."

Nate reached across the space that separated them and patted her hand. "That's a good thing." And when her brow quirked, he added, "It's proof you taught him to think for himself."

"I suppose."

And Nate supposed it was only normal that she seemed a little subdued. Having lived under the same roof with the kid for years, helping him cope with disappointment and celebrate success, she wouldn't be Eden if she didn't miss him.

But something more was going on here, as evidenced by the mood shift between her and Shamus.

"Didn't mean to interrupt you guys," Nate said.

"You didn't interrupt anything." Shamus clucked his tongue. "I just wish you'd shown up half an hour ago. Maybe that bonehead Brett Michaels would have driven right on by if he'd seen your truck."

Nate glanced at Eden, who sighed quietly.

"What did he want this time?" His mind was reeling.

"Well, he wasn't too pleased to see *me* here, let me tell you," Shamus said, "'cause he knows I'm not impressed with his peacock strut." Shamus growled before adding, "I know he owns the place, but for cryin' out loud, if a man can't smell his own BO, he can't get upset when nobody wants to rub elbows with him."

Eden had told Nate about the older man's tendency to mix metaphors. He had to admit, it could be pretty funny...if a person could untangle the message. Nate wasn't the least bit amused, though, that Michaels still felt entitled to come and go as he pleased. One day soon, Eden could tell the guy he could do whatever he wanted with this old rattletrap, because she was leaving it for good.

"I take it he's stopping by more than usual?"

"Don't ask *her*," Shamus spouted. "She's too nice to give you the down and dirty." Leaning an elbow on his knee, he said, "Back in Korea, we had ways of dealing with guys like Michaels."

Nate wasn't about to ask what those ways might be, not in front of Eden, anyway. He liked Shamus, and appreciated that the old guy looked out for her.

"I called to tell him the dryer finally died," Eden said, "and he brought a friend by who fiddled with the innards in hopes of nursing it along for a few more loads. But the fix didn't hold, so I had to call him again."

"And the bum won't give her a straight answer about replacing it," Shamus said.

"You'll need a dryer at Pinewood. Why not buy one now, and move it over there once the renovations are done?"

"I thought of that," she said tentatively, "but I was hoping to leave this place—and everything in it—and just start fresh."

The older man drained the last of his iced tea and put the tumbler down with a thump. "Well, I'd better get back. Tomatoes are fallin' off the vines, I tell you, off the vines!" He gave Nate's shoulder a fatherly squeeze, and leaned in close to whisper, "Something more than that confounded dryer is eating her, but darned if

I can figure out what. See if you can get any-thing outta her."

After hugging Eden, he was on his way.

"He must think my hearing is defective," she said when he drove off.

"Well? Is he wrong? Or is something eating you?"

Eden looked around, then held out her hand. Nate was only too happy to take it and let her lead him to the bench beneath the big maple.

"I had a visitor this morning," she began. "Thomas's father."

He remembered the boys saying that for days after the supervised visits, the kid was tough to handle.

She gave him a breathy rundown of Burke's unscheduled visit. "I have no idea where he stored all those photos during his years in prison," she said. "I don't know, maybe he broke into another relative's house and stole them."

"If Thomas has other relatives, why didn't any of them step up when the Burkes went to jail?"

"I'm sure you've noticed that Thomas has... issues. I'm sure they did, too."

"Well, if it goes as far as court, I'll stand front and center, tell the judge and everyone present what a positive influence you've been in the kid's life. I wouldn't worry about it, though. Chances are good the guy won't keep his word."

She didn't look convinced the authorities would see things that way.

"You've given all these kids a firm foundation, Eden. They can build good, productive lives on what you've done for them."

"But Thomas is so young, emotionally. Life is constantly testing all of us, and kids deserve to know they have a safe place to land when they fall."

"Don't you mean *if* they fail? You're not giving yourself enough credit. Not giving *Thomas* enough credit, either. You can't be certain that he'll forget everything you taught him the very first time he's faced with choosing to do right or wrong."

"But…the most critical decisions he's made in all the years he's lived here were whether or not to change his socks and underwear every morning. He's been completely insulated from anything life-changing!"

Nate had never seen her angry, but he had a feeling it was something he could do without.

"Then I guess we need to make a good case for keeping Thomas here *if* the state decides he's better off with his father. If we buy enough time, his old man will show his true colors, and they'll have no choice but to let the kid stay."

"We…"

"I had no idea you could speak French." He smiled and added, "Yes, *we*."

She'd proven how tough and capable she was, but no one—not even Eden—could handle a guy like Thomas Burke all on her own. She buried her face in the crook of his neck. Her tears dampened his collar, and she held on tight. Her way of saying yes, she'd accept his help, finally?

He hoped so. *Man,* he hoped so!

Eden sat back, and when she closed her eyes, a tear crept down her cheek. He caught it with his thumb, and as he studied her lovely face, he realized there was no going back: He loved this woman.

"Sorry about that," she said, knuckling her eyes. "And thanks."

He might have asked "Thanks for what?" if she hadn't kissed him again.

CHAPTER ELEVEN

WHILE NATE HELPED prepare lunch, the first sparks of an idea flared in his head. The boys devoured sandwiches, chips and sliced apples, and he did his best to participate in their animated conversation. It wasn't easy with the concept growing, taking shape, convincing him of its workability. And it wasn't easy waiting for the boys to finish so he could run the idea past Eden.

"I know a few people," he explained when at last they were alone. "People who could look into Burke's background. If they look closely enough, they're bound to find something. It doesn't have to be much...just enough to convince the department to write him up as an unfit parent."

"But what if these people find something that isn't even relevant anymore, and it turns out that Thomas's dad really *has* changed?"

"That's why the supervised visits are a good idea for the time being. If the guy has turned over a new leaf, he'll do whatever it takes to prove himself, not just to the state, but to Thomas. And if he hasn't?" Nate shrugged. "We'll have bought the boy some time to see for himself that he has a safe place to land."

"I'm not sure I like having my own words used against me."

"Against you? I'm one hundred percent *for* you!"

She looked exquisite, standing at the sink as afternoon sun poured through the window, giving her hair a coppery glow.

"You've never been here to see what a visit with his dad does to him," she said. "He's never been what I'd call a quiet, easygoing boy, but the changes are startling."

"How so?"

"The others steer clear of him because, tiny as he is, they've learned he can inflict some serious harm when he's angry."

"Can't you explain that to the social worker who arranged the visits?"

"Mrs. Josephs would only see it as proof that she's right…group homes do more harm than good…and Thomas belongs in a more hospital-like facility."

"What if Thomas told her that he isn't ready to spend time with his dad?"

"She'd think I wasn't doing my job."

"That's ridiculous."

"Maybe, but she's under a lot of pressure. Every staff member over there is doing the work of three people. And they're exasperated by having to stretch limited funds without adding to sixty-hour workweeks."

"Sixty? What are they whining about? You work eighty."

She exhaled a frustrated sigh. "Nate, I appreciate your confidence in me, and what you're trying to do here, too. But you just don't get it. How could you? The red tape I have to deal with is like a boa constrictor. If you aren't careful, it'll choke the life right out of you."

"Here's what I don't get—if Thomas is that volatile after a meeting with his dad, it isn't safe for any of you to be around him. So why fight so hard to keep him here?"

"Because he needs me, needs *us*. And, as the saying goes, he's all bark, no bite…for the most part."

"For the most part? That isn't very reassuring."

Eden all but slammed the dishwasher door. "You can't have it both ways, Nate. Either you believe I know what I'm doing—that I know these kids and what's best for them—or you don't."

"I'm not trying to second-guess you. But you have to admit, this whole Thomas and his dad thing might put you guys in danger."

"I don't have to admit any such thing."

"It could."

"It *won't*."

"You hope."

Eyes blazing, Eden jabbed a forefinger into his chest. "Let's set a few things straight. I appreciate—no, I *need* the money you offered, because as you so astutely pointed out, it's the only way we'll ever get out of here and into a place where we'll never have to worry about being displaced." She jabbed him again. "But if you think your big fat donation gives you carte blanche to tell me how to do my job, *think again*."

He'd been right that he could do without seeing Eden angry.

He didn't have her background in psychology, but it didn't take a genius to figure out what was going on here. Eden was angry with Burke and Michaels and her boss. She didn't trust any of them to listen without making her—and the boys—pay a high price.

But she trusts you, Nate acknowledged. Grinning to himself, he rubbed the spot she'd poked. *But it wouldn't hurt if she trusted you a little* less...

"Sorry," he said. "You're right. I have no business telling you how to do your job. If you need a sounding board, I'm your guy. If you want to vent, feel free. But from now on, unless you ask for my opinion, I'll butt out." He held up his right hand. "Word of honor."

"I'm sorry, too."

"What? Why are *you* sorry?"

"Because misplaced hostility is an exercise in futility." She picked up the dish towel and gave the faucet a final polish. "I shouldn't have taken my exasperation out on you."

Nate waited, sensing she had more to say.

"Truce?"

He swallowed. Hard. Because when she looked up at him that way, he wanted to kiss her, not forgive her! *Don't do it, Marshall. Don't even* think *about doing it!*

"What's going on that requires a truce?"

Eden gasped and pressed a hand to her chest. "Good grief, Carlos, I'm going to have to put a bell around your neck!"

"Why?"

"So I can hear you coming. You move like a cat."

"But…aren't you always telling us to walk slowly and quietly?"

"Well, yes, but—"

He looked at Nate. "Women. Will I ever understand 'em?"

Nate was suddenly stuck in the proverbial "There is no right answer" scenario.

"Sure. I guess. Probably sometime between now and…"

"…when you're married," he and Eden said together.

The phrase broke the tension, and their laughter sent Carlos from the room, shaking his head and muttering, "Grown-ups. I'll never understand them, either."

DURING THEIR FIRST trip to the ranch, the boys had whined incessantly about the long ride, worried they might get fleas from the horses or get cow dung on their favorite sneakers. What could they learn from some hick cowboy…how to spit tobacco into a bucket or pick their teeth with a blade of grass?

One of these days, Eden would have to share that story with Nate. Right now, a glance in the rearview mirror was all it took to prove the guys didn't feel that way anymore. They were all smiling eagerly, pointing out landmarks that were now familiar to them.

They made no secret of the fact that they'd rather be at the Double M than just about anywhere else. And was it any wonder, with dozens of activities to keep them occupied and so many people willing to give them their time. Seeing the positive changes in the boys made it next to impossible for Eden to say no when the Marshalls extended yet another invitation. Now that school was back in session and the visit would once again keep them away from the classroom for several days, Eden justified the trips by blending ranch activities with daily studies.

As part of their math class, for example, she helped the boys measure the girth and length of horses and cows, and taught them how to calculate the animals' weight. For science, Kirk asked them to research the life cycles of livestock, as well as seed germination and the weather's impact on growing seasons. Essays comparing their experiences at the Double M to details from classic novels made for perfect English assignments. They still grumbled about the assignments, but Eden overlooked it by focusing on their joy at being in the outdoors.

There were life lessons, too. Carl, Nate and his cousin Zach took the boys on overnight treks in the mountains, teaching them wilderness survival and first aid skills. Back at the ranch, Mrs. Marshall showed the boys how to make her famous lasagna and meatballs, and his aunts shared biscuit and pie-making tips.

The positive changes in them were obvious and—Eden hoped—permanent. Every boy's self-confidence had risen far higher than she'd ever thought possible. They were no longer standoffish, shy or overtly aggressive when out in public. Interactions with the men of the Double M had taught them the importance of respect and trust…and that both must be earned. These simple yet profound principles would take them far in life. And she owed all of it to Nate. Her only regret was that she hadn't found him sooner. For the boys' sake, of course.

She'd stopped for gas, and as she stood at the back of the van to scan her credit card, Eden listened in on the boys' conversation.

"What's wrong with her?" Ben muttered to Carlos.

"Shh," Wade warned. "She'll hear you."

"No, she won't," Cody countered. "She's busy at the pump."

"You sure?"

Thankfully, they hadn't figured out that even when she appeared busy with other things, there wasn't much that missed her notice. Eden had learned early in the job that sometimes, being privy to conversations they thought she couldn't hear could give her the opportunity to forestall or prevent trouble.

"I'm positive. Watch and learn." Cody leaned forward. "Hey, Eden…"

She kept her back to them and hid a grin.

"See?" Cody sat back. "So, you were saying?"

"What's wrong with her is we're getting closer," David observed.

DeShawn looked back from his second-row bench seat. "Why would being closer to the Double M get her all weirded out? She *likes* it there."

Weirded out? So, despite her efforts to keep her emotions in check, they'd noticed a mood shift?

Eden got back into the van. "Everybody buckled up?"

Following a series of metallic *clicks,* she put the vehicle into gear and continued west.

From the rear of the van, DeShawn said, "Only thing wrong with those two goofballs is that they're too stubborn to admit they're in love with each other." He punctuated the observation with a grunt.

"Which two goofballs?" Devon wanted to know.

"*You're* a goofball," DeShawn said. "Nate and Eden, who else?"

Devon chuckled. "I think they *did* admit it. More than once." He exhaled a deliberately loud and wistful sigh.

Ben piped up with "What's he talkin' about?"

"Yeah, smart guy," Chuckie teased, "tell us what you know."

A moment of good-natured shoulder slapping

and shoving passed before Devon explained. "I saw 'em kissing. Twice. And it was the real deal." Eyes closed and lips puckered, he wrapped his arms around himself, inspiring another round of boisterous laughter.

Eden quickly looked away from the rearview as silence descended. Would they take Devon's comment seriously? *Keep laughing, boys. Keep laughing!*

"Aw, ma-a-an," Carlos said. "I'll probably have bad dreams for a week, picturing that."

"I don't know about the rest of you," Devon said, "but I think it's cool. People their age shouldn't live alone. What if one of 'em fell down and broke a hip or something? When that happened to my grandmother—"

More rowdy laughter. Eden bit her lower lip to avoid the temptation to join them.

"Dude!" DeShawn said. "You talk like they're, like, *old* or something. They could be our parents. Age-wise, anyway."

"I dunno," Chuckie countered. "Nate goes off by himself a lot, whispering into his cell phone and looking around to see who's listening."

"That's easy," DeShawn said. "*You're* listenin'. You're always listenin'! And anyway, ain't no law against private phone calls."

"'Specially on your own property."

Wade agreed with Silas. "He was just doing ranch business, I'll bet."

"Okay. Maybe," Chuckie allowed. "But if all he wants is privacy to discuss ranch business, why does he drive off in his truck after half those calls? And stay gone for hours? Got an answer for that, DeShawn?"

Silence fell upon the van again, as Eden wondered why she hadn't noticed any of that. Not that it mattered. Yes, they'd kissed, but that didn't mean Nate wasn't seeing someone else. The possibility bothered her more than she cared to admit. He had so much to offer a woman. Strength of character. Compassion. Generosity. With a common-sense approach to life that infected everyone around him. He was sensitive, too, in an almost pushy way, often identifying what she or the boys needed, then meeting those needs whether she wanted him to or not.

If there *was* another woman in his life, wouldn't someone at the Double M have mentioned her?

He laughed at her jokes, even when they weren't funny. Found ways, despite his hectic schedule, to spend time at Latimer House, and took advantage of every opportunity to be alone with her. And those kisses…

Be a grown-up, she scolded herself. *Quit*

stalling and let him know you're interested in something more than friendship.

But what if he got the idea that her actions were prompted by the financial contribution?

And what if after she repaid him, she realized it was true?

Worse still, what if the realization caused hard feelings between them and Nate pulled back from the boys...boys already scarred by abandonment.

Far better to err on the side of caution, as her grandfather was fond of saying.

The Double M's massive wrought iron gate came into view, and the sight of it made her heart beat a little faster.

"So you really think, you know, what you said before?" Ben asked.

Devon elbowed him. "Shh! You want her to hear?"

A second, perhaps two ticked by before he added, "And yeah, I really do."

Wrong or right, Eden had to admit that Devon might be right.

CHAPTER TWELVE

"HEY, NATE," CARLOS shouted from the diving board. "Watch this!"

Carlos's belly flop soaked everyone, Nate included, and provoked brotherly taunts and threats that sent the kid scurrying for cover. Though it did his heart good to see the boys enjoying themselves, Nate found it tough to take his eyes off Eden.

She had been sitting poolside when her phone pinged, and now she was hurrying to the pool house, bare feet splashing through the shallow puddles left behind by the boys.

For one thing, she looked fantastic in the body-skimming white top that covered her bathing suit.

For another, she seemed worried or scared as she paced behind the sliding glass doors.

Sam padded up on big bare feet and flopped onto the lawn chair beside Nate's, and he was glad his cousin had decided to spend his week-long vacation at the ranch. Sam held out a frosty can of soda.

"Don't say I never gave you anything," he said, handing it to Nate. "And don't chug it, or you'll get an ice-cream headache." He pressed a forefinger between his blond eyebrows. "Ask me how I know."

Nate popped the top and took a swig. "Thanks," he said. "That hits the spot."

Sam gave a quick nod toward the pool house. "What's all that about?"

Nate shrugged. "Who knows? Could be the contractor who's rehabbing her house." He shot a quick look at Thomas, who was about to do a backflip from the board. "Or that one's ex-con dad, who wants back in the kid's life. Or her landlord, Brett Michaels."

"*That* jerk? Man. I haven't thought about him in years." He paused. "Remember the time he stuffed shrimp between the coils of the science lab's heaters?"

Nate groaned. "If I think about it too hard, that stink still burns my nose."

"I'm still traumatized. Can't eat shrimp to this day."

The cousins shared a quiet chuckle.

"Wonder when things went sideways?" Sam mused. "I mean, how does a guy go from harmless pranks to being...*Brett*?"

"Don't know, don't care, long as he steers clear of me." *And Eden. And those boys.*

"Oh, you've got it bad, don't ya, cuz. Real bad."

He'd stolen a glance at Eden. Again. And Sam had caught him. Nate swiped condensation from the side of the soda can. "I think you've been sitting in the sun too long. You're babbling."

"Me think thou does protest too much."

Nate laughed. "Should have read the actual play instead of the CliffsNotes. Maybe then you'd know how to properly quote that line."

Sam rolled his eyes. "Whatever."

Over in the pool, Ben was on the diving board, trying to decide whether or not to try a backflip.

"Just do it!" Cody bellowed.

DeShawn agreed. "You'll never know if you can or not if you just stand there!"

"From the mouths of babes," Sam said, nodding toward Eden.

"There you go, babbling again."

Sam sat sideways in the chair and looked Nate in the eye. "Just do it. It's good advice when you're trying something for the first time." He glanced toward the patio doors, where Eden was now frowning at her phone.

"Woman like that doesn't come along every day, y'know."

In other words, tell her how you feel before she gets away.

She emerged and headed toward them, and

Nate thought he could watch her slight, womanly sway until he was old and gray. Then he felt Sam's eyes on him and realized he was grinning like a buffoon. If she wasn't within earshot, he'd have a few choice words for his cousin.

"Get everything settled?" Sam asked as she sat on the other side of Nate.

"More or less."

"Things looked pretty grim from out here," Nate said. "Anything I can do?"

She sent him a smile so sweet, he wondered why his teeth didn't ache.

"Nothing I can't handle," Eden said. "Aren't you going to introduce me to your cousin?"

Sam stood and reached across Nate. "This guy has the manners of a caveman. Name's Sam."

"Oh, right. You're the firefighter cousin. The youngest one, right?" she said, shaking his hand. "So how was the drive from Nashville?"

"Used my frequent-flier miles this time. Gives me an extra couple days with my favorite cousin here."

She pointed at the redheaded boy in the pool. "That's Nick Smith. For the past year or so, he's been talking about becoming a firefighter."

"Well, he's sure big enough to handle the ladders and hoses," Sam observed. "I'll catch up with him later, recommend a couple of the books I read before making the commitment."

She smiled at Sam. Not the same beautiful smile she'd aimed at Nate a moment earlier, but a nice one, nonetheless. She got to her feet, handing Nate her phone.

"I'm going to take a few laps," she said. "Would you time me?"

The cousins watched her cross to the far end of the pool and dive into the water.

"Is there anything she *can't* do?"

Sam's question reminded Nate of the way she'd kissed him. "If there is, I haven't seen it yet."

Nate leaned back and took in the scene, Eden gliding serenely through the water, the boys laughing and horsing around.

"So what are you waiting for?" Sam said after a few moments, startling him.

Nate didn't get it, and said so.

"You're in love with her, so—"

Eden splashed to the surface and folded her arms on the edge of the pool. "So, how'd I do?"

Nate had totally forgotten he was supposed to be timing her. He fumbled with the phone, then repeated the numbers on the stopwatch.

Grinning, Eden gave herself a thumbs-up and swam back to the ladder. She grabbed a towel and wrapped it around herself as Thomas ran up to ask her a question. She gave him her full attention. Nate believed that was her secret. Eden didn't believe in doing anything halfway. Someday, she'd be a great mom. And the guy lucky enough to call her his wife—"Well?" Sam asked. "What are you waiting for?"

"To be honest, cousin, I don't know."

But it was high time he figured it out. Because Sam was right...a woman like that didn't come along every day.

THOUGH THE TEMPERATURE sometimes rose into the seventies and eighties during the daytime, the Double M could be downright chilly at night. Today was no exception. When Sam suggested firing up the brick oven, Nate thought it made perfect sense. The boys were enthusiastic, too.

"That thing throws off enough heat to warm your whole house," Eden said.

Nate agreed. "We've cranked her up to five hundred and fifty degrees a time or two, but only when Sam's around."

Eden laughed. "It's like a work of art, Nate. There isn't a brick or stone out of place. How long did it take to build?"

Too long, Nate thought, *and not long enough*.

"About a month, start to finish," he said. "The week my surgeon gave the go-ahead for me to fly back to Colorado, I went to work for the ranch, ordering supplies, paying bills, balancing the books. Drove me nuts, sitting at a desk all day. And then one morning, while sorting the mail, I found an ad for an oven like this." He shrugged. "I'd always been pretty good with my hands, knew my way around a few power tools, so I thought, why not build one of my own?

"The family thought it was too soon for all that manual labor, so I promised to take my time.

"As it turned out, the exercise was good for me." *And the hard work kept my mind off the accident.*

"If it was a little bigger," she said, "a person could live in it."

"Well, it's sturdy enough to live in, I guess."

She looked into his face, then took his hands in hers, turned them this way and that, tracing every line and contour with the tip of her finger. "It didn't leave you with any scars," she said, releasing him. And meeting his eyes again, Eden added, "So why don't you like it?"

No one, not even his mom, knew his true feelings about the oven. But Eden had picked up on it straight away.

"I like it fine," he began. "It's just...seeing it wakes old ghosts."

The boys were in the house, some making

pizza dough with Zach and Summer while the rest cut up toppings with Hank and Sam. Nate didn't know how it had happened, exactly, but somehow, his last-minute pizza party had turned into a full-fledged family gathering. Not his first choice, but he had to admit, at least no one would notice when he took Eden aside.

This was as good a time as any to tell her the whole story. She had a right to know the truth. If nothing else, he'd have a better idea how to answer next time Sam asked what he was waiting for.

CHAPTER THIRTEEN

AFTER DARK, THE BOYS placed the chairs around the fire. Huddled under blankets and holding tight to mugs of hot chocolate, they leaned back and pointed out the constellations visible on this bright August night.

"There's Aquila," Wade said. "The eagle that carried messages to humans on earth."

Chuckie pointed out Bootes, the bear driver. "Took me forever to find the spear and hunting dogs, until Eden told me to look for the handle of the Big Dipper."

"Job's star," Cody added, nodding.

"My favorite is Auriga."

"Why's that?" Nate asked.

Ben looked over at him. "Because it has two cool stories. One about a crippled guy who invented a four-horse chariot to get around—"

"The PC police are comin'," Carlos said. "I hear the sirens!"

"There wasn't any such thing as political correctness when the myths were written," Ben huffed.

"Boys? I'd like to hear the other story, wouldn't you?" It seemed all it took to quell the minor disagreement was the sound of Eden's voice.

No surprise, there. Smiling as the kids tossed balled-up paper napkins and blew white paper straw coverings at one another, Nate gazed around the circle, the boys' faces seeming younger in the amber-orange glow. He closed his eyes and listened to their banter, trying to determine who'd cracked the latest joke and who had laughed at it. They felt at home here at the Double M, and he wouldn't have it any other way. This was what life could be like if he and Eden got together and headed up this odd menagerie—

"So there was this shepherd," Ben continued, distracting Nate from his reverie. "And one of his pregnant goats went missing. So he looked and looked and finally found her stuck on some cliff..." He paused for dramatic effect. "With her two babies! So the shepherd hangs her over his shoulders and makes his way back down to the pasture with one of her kids under each arm." Ben frowned. "Don't know how that has anything to do with a chariot, but hey, I aced that quiz, so there y'go."

"Some people," Nate inserted, "think the kids represent the two daughters of the king of Crete, who brought food to the baby Jesus in Bethlehem."

"I'm impressed," Eden said.

"Me, too," Thomas agreed. "*That* part of the story made me all starry-eyed." He leaned left and gave DeShawn a poke on the shoulder. "Get it? Starry-eyed…"

Laughing, DeShawn shook a nonthreatening fist. "Yeah, I get it, pip-squeak. And if you poke me with that bony finger again, *you'll* be starry-eyed."

"Listen to us," Silas said, "doing science homework and *liking* it."

Eden feigned shock. "Silas, does that mean you don't *always* enjoy science class?"

"I, ah, well…" He turned toward Nate. "Hey, what's the story of the ranch? Bet it's got all kinds of cool history."

"Nice save, kid," he said, winking. And linking his fingers behind his head, Nate told them that in the 1880s, his great-great-grandfather Malcolm Marshall and his twin, Martin, bought and tamed the original acres. "While other men spent their energy digging and panning for gold, he and his brother turned barren land into planting fields. While Martin was off rounding up mustangs, Malcolm tended the oats, rye and pasture grass."

"The stuff to feed horses," Carlos said.

"Yup. And to feed themselves, too. They put together a big sturdy cabin." He pointed at the barnlike structure that now housed the tractor, baler, tiller and harvester. "But when the brothers married, they built another house." Again, Nate pointed, this time at what had become the bunkhouse.

"You don't mean...those are the original buildings?" Eden asked.

"Back then," he said, smiling, "they built things to last."

At last count, he told them, a couple dozen outbuildings and thirteen homes, each belonging to his cousins, aunts and uncles, and parents, stood on Marshall land.

"I'll bet Double M stands for Martin and Malcolm!"

"You got it, Thomas," Nate said.

Nodding, Silas stroked his chin. If he wasn't careful, Nate thought, he'd rub that sparse beard of his clean off.

"I have a weird question for you," the boy began. "Everybody here at the ranch told us that was Sweet Mountain." He pointed at a nearby peak. "But I searched for it on the internet, like, a dozen times, and there *is* no Sweet Mountain."

"That's because it exists only in the hearts and history of the Marshall clan. See, Mount Evans wasn't always called Mount Evans. In the late 1880s, it was known as Mount Rosalie... which just so happened to be Martin's wife's name. We still have Rosalie's diary, and there's a passage where Rosalie claimed to start every day facing 'her' mountain. When the sunrise hit the snow-capped peak, she'd say, 'My mountain is winking at me!' Martin refused to call her anything but Sweet, so she renamed it. Sweet died giving birth to her first child, who grew up thinking his mama must have been one special woman to have a mountain named after her. Before long, all the Marshalls referred to it that way. These days, when I look up at Sweet Mountain at first light and the mountain winks at me, I understand what Rosalie meant."

When he stopped talking, Nate heard nothing, save the pop and hiss of the firewood in the belly of the oven. Had the tale bored them all to sleep? He glanced around the circle, and was startled to see everyone's eyes zeroed in on him.

"You tell a real good story, Nate."

"Thanks, Thomas. I can't take any credit, though. I only repeated the story I've heard a hundred times or more."

"Can I ask you a question?" Thomas glanced around. "Could there be a cougar out here, watching us?"

Every kid in the circle looked over his shoulder. Twice.

"Nah. They're afraid of people. And fire. And people sitting *around* a fire."

Eden hid a smile behind one hand.

"Yeah, well, last time we were here, I thought I heard one growl."

"It was probably wind in the trees. Or a gate that wasn't fastened tight…plenty of the hinges could use a shot of oil. Cougars only caterwaul in the movies. In real life, the only time you hear one is when something spooks them, or if they feel threatened."

"Seen any cats lately?" Greg wanted to know.

"No, and we're hoping it means she got tired of horse meat and decided to go up into the mountains for some elk or mule deer."

Cody yawned, and David stretched.

"I'm goin' to bed," Wade said. "You should go, too," he told Thomas, "before you scare yourself to death."

Without being told, the boys put the lounge chairs back where they'd found them, and draping their blankets over their shoulders, shuffled into Nate's house.

He was glad Eden hadn't gone with them, because there were things he needed to tell her… and things she needed to hear.

"THEY'RE GOOD KIDS," Nate said. "No telling where they might have ended up if you hadn't been there for them."

"We provided safe haven, but they decided to make it work."

"I don't buy it, and if you asked them—or anybody else—neither would they."

"But I didn't do it alone. I have help. A lot of it. Kirk for one, on his next-to-nothing salary, Cora, your family…" She spread her arms wide. "Every memory and experience the Double M has given them is all thanks to you. You taught them things I couldn't have."

Nate cleared his throat. "I, ah, wondered… have you heard from Travis lately?"

How like him, Eden thought, to take the spotlight off himself by giving her something else to focus on. "He texts me at least once a day, usually to ask where I put something in his dorm room." Eden opened her phone and showed Nate Travis's responses to her pictures of tonight's pizza party. You're mean! said one, followed by, No fair! and a smiley face.

"Travis is a good example. He *chose* the right direction," she said. "He *decided* not to let anything get him off track. That's his accomplishment, not mine."

"Yeah, but—"

"Look at it this way—if he'd taken a different route, started using drugs or robbing stores or something, would you expect me to take the blame?"

"Okay, I see your point."

"You have to love a man," she said as he crossed to the stone oven, "who isn't afraid to admit when he's wrong."

He added logs to the fire. "Well, you don't have to, but it sure would be nice."

What did *that* mean?

"That's the last of it," he said, dusting his hands together. He glanced at the dwindling woodpile. "Looks like I need to schedule a day to split firewood." Settling into the lounge chair again, he crossed his ankles. "So about that phone call earlier...what got you so riled up?"

It didn't seem fair that his talent for reading faces far outweighed hers.

"It was Thomas's dad. He's tired of being judged for his past bad behavior."

Nate harrumphed. "What's he gonna do, storm City Hall with a picket sign?"

"Sort of. He went to the mayor's office and refused to leave the room until the man agreed to hear him out. And he brought along a friend who works for the *Denver Post*, who threatened to write a piece connecting ex-con recidivism with disinterest on the part of politicians. Naturally, the mayor agreed to look into the matter. Although I can't imagine it going further than that. Custody, visitation...it's a matter for the courts."

"So the mayor spewed some politician-speak for 'fat chance,' to get rid of Burke," Nate said, frowning. "I'll say this for the guy...he's shrewd. But that doesn't mean he's father material."

"My thoughts, exactly. He doesn't know it, but I have a few friends in high places, too. After I got off the phone with him, I made a few calls. They can't ignore his request—legally—but they can shelve it until I can figure out how to explain the whole mess to Thomas. Which I have to do soon."

"You'll do the right thing," he said. "You always do."

Well, he had promised not to offer his opinion unless she asked for it. "Not always."

Nate faced her. "You'll need a really good story if you expect me to believe that."

Eden shivered at the memory of that awful morning...

"Oh, come on," he said. "It can't be *that* bad."

Could she tell him?

He grabbed her hand. "Ever play Truth or Dare?"

She wondered if he'd been on the debate team in high school or college because he sure knew how to change the subject.

"I played once," she answered, "and promised myself, never again."

He leaned forward. "Humor me?"

"Fine, but whatever happened to ladies first?"

"Is that supposed to scare me?" He laughed. "Bring it on, Eden. Bring. It. *On*."

She matched his challenging stare, blink for blink. "Have you ever been married?"

"What a marshmallow," he teased. "Thanks to that goofy article, you know that I was engaged—*once*." Wiggling his eyebrows and wringing his hands, he smirked. "My turn."

Her heart rate accelerated a blip or two.

"When we were discussing Thomas's dad, and you said you didn't always do the right thing—what did you mean by that?"

Suddenly thirsty, Eden took a sip of her lemonade. "Let me see if I remember the rules correctly. Either I answer your question, or I have to accept your dare?"

"That's the idea."

"I choose Dare."

Nate was a good man. A loving son and sibling. A loyal friend to his cousins. And generous to a fault. What did she have to fear from any dare he might issue?

A wicked grin crept across his face. "All right, I *dare* you to tell the whole, unvarnished truth about the time you didn't do the right thing."

Shoulders slumped, Eden hung her head. "Well," she began, stalling with another sip of lemonade, "it was early September. A Tuesday morning. Bright. Sunny. It was my six-month anniversary on the job, but I had nothing to celebrate. I'd been haggling with my supervisors, trying to convince them the boys would be better off if I hired an assistant, so I could homeschool them to spare them all the smug attitudes and nasty looks and snide remarks they were getting at school, from students and teachers alike."

"I didn't realize you had a degree in education."

"For your information, Mr. Suspicious, I double-majored. Not that it mattered, because they said no."

"Why?"

She rubbed her thumb across her fingertips, the universal sign for money. "I didn't fight them because…well, why rock the boat? I was new, one of the first and only female group home administrators, and I didn't want to risk being demoted. So on this beautiful September Tuesday, after I'd fed the boys their breakfast, I said all the expected things when they listed their fears—about undeserved detention, locker room brawls, teachers who turned a blind eye to it all—and I put them on the school bus."

"Look," Nate said, pointing skyward, "a shooting star. Make a wish."

"Okay—I wish you'd stop changing the subject."

"You know what they say…speak the wish aloud and it won't come true."

"Something tells me that even if I believed in wishes, *that* one wouldn't come true."

"Ha. Very funny. But you were saying. So on that beautiful September day…"

"Malik was a high-functioning autistic kid. Chubby. Afraid of bugs and strangers, and he hated noise. It broke my heart to see him crying when those doors hissed shut. 'It'll be okay,' I told him. 'Just give it a couple days.'" She let out a long, shaky breath. "The bus rolled away from the curb, and I never saw him again."

Nate took her hand again. "I never should have forced you to tell that story."

"You didn't ask. I volunteered, remember?" She sat up straighter. "Besides, you can't take back a dare. Rules are rules, right?"

His sympathetic smile almost broke the last strand of her control.

Almost.

"His father had been out of jail for a few weeks, and the department approved regular visits. He picked Malik up from school that day, and he never came back to Latimer House."

"Oh, Eden. I'm sorry. What happened?"

"The officer assigned to the missing child case told me that Malik's father was a major player with a Denver gang."

"And the cop thought that's where the kid ended up?"

Nodding, she bit back tears. "So there you have it. Self-centeredness, pride, survival instinct—whatever you want to call it—I put my needs and fears of being demoted or losing my job ahead of the kids' well-being. If I hadn't given up so easily, if I'd fought for them, instead of—"

"What happened to Malik is on his father, not you."

"There you go, giving credit where it isn't due. Again."

"You want to know what I think?"

She'd just confessed her ugliest truth, and dreaded the answer.

"You're beating yourself up over something you couldn't control. Even if you'd been able to take the boys out of public school sooner, that's no guarantee Malik's dad wouldn't have found another way to take him."

She hadn't allowed herself to cry, not once, since Malik disappeared. But when Nate's arms went around her, she more than made up for lost time.

CHAPTER FOURTEEN

NATE HADN'T MEANT to upset her, but when Eden insisted on shouldering the blame for Malik being swallowed up by his father's gang, well, words exploded out of him.

"Why are you so determined to be a martyr!" he demanded, letting go of her hand. "Not smart, kiddo. Not smart at all."

Eden branded him with a flinty glare, and he prepared himself for the tongue-lashing that would follow. He could take it…if it helped him figure out why she ran hot and cold with him.

"I know what I'm talking about," he continued. "My family spent hours—*years*—trying to convince me the accident wasn't my fault."

She turned away from him. "Apples and oranges."

That stung, but he wouldn't admit it. He'd used the same tactics, facing his parents, his cousins and Hank. They hadn't given up on him, and he wouldn't give up on Eden.

"You had a tough childhood," he said. "It

makes you mistrustful. Just tell me one thing, and I'll back off."

She met his eyes. "What?"

"Don't you trust me by now?"

"I'm a guest in your house, or I'd…" She bit her lower lip.

"You'd what?"

"I'd say you don't know me nearly as well as you think you do."

Oh, she was a force to be reckoned with, all right. But Nate's patience was growing thin and he was growing tired of being her scapegoat.

"Okay. You're right. You're an enigma. So help me understand you." He leaned into the space between them. "I *want* to understand you, Eden."

"Why?"

An easy question. Too bad he didn't have an easy answer.

"Look, I want to help you. But how can I do that when you put up roadblocks at every turn?"

She licked her lips, and he thought, *what a weird time to remember those kisses.* Then she blinked, and he noticed that her thick eyelashes were still damp and spiky from the tears she'd shed just moments ago.

"I think I'll turn in," Eden said.

Halfway between the fire and the house, she turned to face him.

"Good night, Nate. I'll see you in the morning." And without another word, she went into the house.

Hot and cold. *Should have kept your distance. Should have stuck to the rules*: Do Unto Others and Just Say No.

By morning, she'd pulled herself together so well that, all through breakfast, he thought maybe he'd dreamed the argument.

She disappeared as he helped the boys load their duffel bags into the van and said his goodbyes. They made their way to the corral to watch the new horses, and she was still nowhere to be seen.

Just as well, because Nate was in no mood to pick up where they'd left off last night. He went around back and popped his truck's hood. Changing the oil was a messy job, but it beat saying an awkward goodbye to Eden.

It was quiet down here under the truck, just his own thoughts and the quiet splat of oil draining into the pan. He heard footsteps. One of the kids, he hoped. But one glance at those snow-white sneakers and he knew luck wasn't on his side this morning.

She got down on both knees. "There you are."

Nate slid out and got to his feet.

"Hey," he said, wiping his greasy hands on a rag.

"We're leaving in just a minute, and I wanted to say bye. And thank you."

Thank you? Nate drove a hand through his hair. The woman was going to drive him crazy.

"For being a man of your word," she added. "I know you meant it when you said 'no strings attached,' and what happened last night doesn't change that. So…" Eden shrugged. "So thanks."

What was he supposed to say? A halfhearted *You're welcome* or a phony *Don't give it another thought*?

"I talked with your mom about Thanksgiving. She wants us to get here a day early, so the kids can goof off and I can help in the kitchen."

Great. More opportunities for her to vent her frustrations in his direction. But, "Still a long way off," is what he said.

"Gives me time to get the boys settled and find my grandmother's pecan pie recipe. Your mom says it's one of your dad's favorite desserts."

She did you a favor, he thought, squinting into the sunlight. If she hadn't flown off the handle, he might never have gotten back on track.

"So the contractor starts on Wednesday…"

Ah, that explains the 'no strings' reminder.

"Give me five minutes," he said, tossing the rag to the ground, "to grab that envelope."

She looked hurt and surprised when he turned

on his heel and left her standing there, alone.
Guilt squeezed at his conscience, and it riled
him. He hadn't done anything wrong—unless
offering her a helping hand was wrong—so why
did he feel like such a heel?

The boys were in the van when he returned,
and Eden stood beside it.

"I didn't want the boys to know," she said
when he held out the envelope.

"Why? There's no shame in admitting you
need help. No shame in accepting it when it's
offered, either."

Nodding, she tucked the money into her purse.

"The boys would love it if you'd stop by Pinewood on Wednesday."

But would you, *Eden?*

He liked those kids, so Nate said, "Sure. I'll
bring fried chicken."

She smiled, but only a little. "Sounds good."

Nate leaned on the gate, watching as she
climbed into the van and fired up the clunking
engine. The boys waved, and he waved back.

Then she drove away...

...and he let her.

A DOZEN TIMES a day, Nate checked his phone,
hoping to see her number in the missed calls
list. It was just as disappointing to discover that

she hadn't left a message on his home answering machine, either.

He'd spent another restless night tossing and turning, then pacing the quiet house in the hope of figuring out why, despite her mood swings and stubbornness, he missed her like crazy.

Unfortunately, every room held reminders of her. The way she'd refilled, then repositioned the canisters to make more space on the kitchen counter. In the now-spotless fridge, condiments, jellies and dairy products were grouped together. She'd karate-chopped each throw pillow on the family room sofa because "that's what the designers are doing these days." And alphabetized the fan-shaped array of outdoors and sports magazines on the coffee table.

He liked being surrounded by her womanly touches. Was he crazy to feel this way?

It only took an hour or so of aimless wandering before he surrendered and got into the shower, and as the steamy spray hit his face, Nate admitted he didn't like the distance between them.

"So what are you gonna do about it?" he muttered.

He lathered his face, and peering into the mirror, decided he couldn't just stop by or pick up the phone.

Unless…

She still hadn't given him a precise arrival time for the Thanksgiving weekend. Yes, it was still a long way off, but he couldn't think of a more reasonable way to break the ice than to ask.

Distracted, Nate nicked himself with the razor. Muttering to himself, he plugged the small leak with a patch of toilet tissue and returned to the kitchen for coffee and a bowl of cereal. He'd no sooner stuffed his mouth with corn flakes than he heard footsteps on the back porch. He knew by the silhouette—and baseball cap atop a mass of curls—who'd come calling.

"Make a wrong turn on I-70?" he asked, opening the door.

In place of an answer, she stood on tiptoe and peered over his shoulder. "Do I smell fresh coffee?"

Nate returned to the table. "Help yourself. You know where things are." He hadn't gotten a good look at her face, and her stance told him nothing about her mood. *Guess you'll just have to wait to find out why she's here.*

Eden pulled out the chair nearest the head of the table and pointed at his bowl. "Got any more of that?"

"Sure."

While she rummaged for a bowl, a spoon, cereal and milk, Nate wished she'd just get to the point. Why did she seem to delight in his misery? Then again, he thought, remembering what she'd said the night of the pizza party, maybe it was good that she'd decided to draw things out. At least this way, he had a few minutes to steel himself, in case she'd come to finish him off.

"You were right about your contractor. He's great."

"I've always said he's worth double what he charges."

"You should stop by Pinewood, see how much progress Max has made."

If he could get her words out of his head, he might not feel uncomfortable in his own house. *I need the money, but I don't need* you. "You're probably wondering why I'm here, alone, so early on a Saturday."

Nate didn't trust himself to meet her eyes. "The thought crossed my mind," he said, lifting his mug.

"I was going to call, but decided it would be cowardly, considering..." She took a deep breath. "We didn't exactly part on good terms."

When Nate met her eyes, he half hoped to see bitterness or anger, anything that would make it easier to ignore the fact that he'd fallen boots over Stetson for her. What he saw instead—no emotion at all—hurt almost as much as what she'd said that night.

"So? Why *are* you here?"

Was it his tone or the words themselves that made her flinch?

Nate didn't like the person he was turning into, and he knew that this...this *thing* between him and Eden was behind it. His surly mood had put him in the position of having to apologize a dozen times over the past few days, to his family, to Carl and the rest of the ranch hands, even to Patches.

Eden wrapped both hands around her mug. She'd barely touched her cereal, but for a second there, she looked like his old Eden, sweet, sensitive, caring. Nate clamped his teeth together. *She's not* your *Eden, so get your head on straight.*

She rose slowly, carried her mug and bowl to the sink, and stood with her back to him for what seemed like a full minute. Nothing was stopping him from walking over there, taking her in his arms and telling her how sorry he was that he'd stuck his nose where it didn't belong. Now he wished he hadn't offered her that money. He should have given it to Cora; the woman would have understood, and he could have trusted her to get it to Eden. But he couldn't help wondering if she would have found some other excuse to keep him at arm's length.

"I think maybe the sages are right," he said, choosing his words carefully.

She took a few steps closer. "About?"

"Money is the root of—"

"Please." Eden held up both hands. "Don't say it."

Was he imagining things, or were there tears shimmering in her gray eyes?

"You need to know," she began, struggling to keep that full lower lip from quivering, "I was wrong to fly off the handle at you. It isn't your fault that I shirked my responsibilities at Pinewood, allowed the Hansons to destroy the place. If I'd taken the time—and mustered the nerve—to do my *job*, the boys and I could have moved right in. And you wouldn't have felt cowboy-bound to rescue me."

Nate watched her, standing as tall as her five-foot-two frame would allow, doing her best to sweeten a sour situation with a halfhearted smile.

"Well, I should go," she said, opening the back door. "I just wanted to apologize in person—and in private. Besides, you probably have a million things to do today."

"Give me a heads-up next time you bring the boys to Pinewood. I'd like to see what Max has done with the place. I'll bring pizza or burgers."

"Will do."

She fired up the van's rumbling, pinging motor. *Take a good long look*, he thought, waving as she drove off. *This is what saying yes cost you.*

"Travis? Hey, yourself, kiddo. How are things going in Fort Collins?"

The boy gave him a quick rundown, which included tutoring a cheerleader who thought he had beautiful brown eyes.

"Look, Nate, real reason I'm calling is, I just talked to the guys. They're all worked up over this move to Pinewood, and I thought maybe if you went over there…"

Eden probably hadn't even made it back to Latimer House yet, so their brief, awkward meeting was still raw in his mind. "I, ah, I'm not sure when I can get away."

"Yeah, I heard about the fight."

"Fight? What fight?"

"Between you and Eden." Travis sounded uncertain about how to continue. After a moment, he said, "I don't know any of the details. They only said that you two haven't talked in more than a week."

Until this morning. "It wasn't a fight. More like a misunderstanding. But it'll work itself out. Sometimes it's best to let the dust settle."

"And sometimes, it just gets redistributed."

Very astute for an eighteen-year-old. "You worry about school, and let me worry about dusting."

Travis told Nate about his ethics class, the only one that had been a struggle so far. "The professor is like…like this burned-out hippy. He says the course is designed to help us develop our own theories and opinions, but he wigs out any time we don't agree with him. Either his brain is completely fried, or he grew up in a bubble, because the guy has no clue! If I didn't need an A in his class, I'd tell him that life is rarely just black or white, right or wrong. Even I know it's mostly gray, and I don't have a PhD."

"Right on, man!"

Travis laughed, and Nate added, "I know you didn't ask for my advice, but here it is, for what it's worth: you've already figured out what you need to do. Keep giving the guy what he wants and everybody will be happier."

"Really."

A statement, he noticed, not a question.

"Gotta go. Thanks, Nate. Tell everybody I'll see 'em soon." And he hung up before Nate could reciprocate, or confirm that he'd deliver the message.

TWO DAYS AFTER Eden's visit, Nate headed for Latimer House.

"Man," he said, "this place is a mess."

The boys stopped packing and gave him an enthusiastic welcome.

"Where you been, dude?" Devon asked.

"Takes planning, hard work and long days to get a ranch ready for the winter."

"Did you get that cougar yet?"

He turned to Ben. "Haven't seen any signs of her lately, kiddo, so we're hoping she moved on."

"Maybe a bear ate her. Or another cougar."

Both possibilities had crossed Nate's mind, too. He nodded toward the boxes, stacked in the foyer. "The big day is getting closer, huh?"

"Yeah. This Saturday. Woo-hoo."

Sarcasm at its best. Proof that Travis hadn't exaggerated: the boys weren't looking forward to the move.

"Where's Eden?"

Silas glanced up from the DVDs he was packing. "Getting groceries. You just missed her, but if you can hang around for an hour or so…"

"Sure." He rolled up his sleeves. "Long as I'm here, tell me how I can help."

"You can talk Eden out of this." DeShawn grunted, then thumped the heel of his hand against his forehead. "Oh. Right. You're not talking to each other. *Duh.*"

He sat on the right end of the couch, and it didn't take long for the sectional to fill up.

"So what's really bugging you, guys?"

They all started talking at once, spouting reasons to stay at Latimer House. Nate let them get it off their chests before weighing in. "This house is old, and hasn't been very well maintained by your landlord. You know better than I do that every day, something goes wrong. Eden does her best to hold things together, but she wants to get you out of here, into a place that's safe, where she won't have to worry about the ceiling caving in or one of you being electrocuted or something."

He read their silence to mean he'd at least begun to reach them. "I'm going to share a few things with you, things I'm sure Eden would clobber me for telling you."

If he didn't have their attention before, he sure had it now!

"Did you know that she uses her own money to pay a *lot* of the bills around here?"

Eyes widened, jaws dropped and brows rose, so he continued while he had their full attention.

"And did you know that every time Brett Michaels raises the rent, she sells something of her own to make the monthly payments? Or that while you're sleeping, she's up doing laundry, cleaning, making casseroles and freezing them so you'll have good, healthy food on nights when meetings with her bosses interfere with mealtime?"

"She has always done way more for us than our parents," Greg admitted.

Devon said, "Bet I know what Travis would say if he was here."

"'Sorry'?" Cody suggested.

Nate frowned. "Why would Travis need to apologize?"

"For leaving us," Thomas said. "He knew how to talk to her. And talk her out of stupid stuff like this move."

Nate was lost. "Now wait just a minute. I find it hard to believe Eden ever did anything stupid, especially where your best interests are concerned."

"Dentist appointments? Flu shots? Ten o'clock bedtime?" Thomas complained. "If those aren't stupid, what is?"

"Hey, c'mon now. All those things are for your own good, and you know it as well as I do."

Pouting, the boy shrugged.

Devon shook his head. "No, Travis wouldn't say he's sorry. He'd tell us to stop whining and crying like a bunch of spoiled brats and quit making trouble for Eden."

Carlos looked at Nate. "So we have to pretend we're okay with this move?"

"Just for the time being. It'll be a big change, there's no denying that. I remember when I first went to Baltimore and had to move from the ranch house into a downtown apartment. I hated it. But after a while, it grew on me."

"Gimme a break," Wade said. "You liked the big city better than the Double M?"

"I'd be lying if I said that. But I got used to the change. And after a while, I saw as many positives as negatives."

"What positives?"

"It didn't take an hour's drive to get into town, for one thing," he said with a shrug. "And I didn't have to spend every Saturday morning mucking stalls and picking dung from horses' hooves. Or freeze my fingers off in the middle of winter fixing fences." He showed them the raised red scar on the palm of his left hand. "Barbed wire is vicious." Grinning slightly, he continued. "My advice is to take things one day at a time. And try to keep in mind that if Eden had a choice, she'd never uproot you this way. Michaels wants to sell the place, and she can't afford to buy it." He shrugged again. "What choice does she have?"

"You could buy Latimer House," Thomas said.

"This place is a firetrap and a plumbing nightmare." He remembered only too well that money had destroyed what might have been a fulfilling relationship with Eden. "I don't believe in wasting money, and neither does Eden."

"I thought they were in a fight," Carlos whispered.

Devon said, "So'd I."

"Then why is he stickin' up for her all over the place?"

"We aren't fighting, we had a disagreement," Nate told them. "In a few years, I hope you'll understand the difference. Eden and I have a lot of respect for one another. This will blow over."

They didn't seem fully convinced, and frankly, Nate wasn't 100 percent certain about that last bit himself. But what he felt didn't matter. All he cared about was that they were listening, and it gave him hope that they'd come around eventually. Most of them, anyway. Thomas…he could never be sure what was going on in that kid's mind.

He'd no sooner completed the thought than Thomas said, "If I could talk Eden out of sharing the new address with my father, I'd be okay with moving. It isn't like any of us have a choice. Where we gonna go from here…foster homes? Juvie?" He snorted.

"I saw your dad once," Carlos said. "He doesn't look so bad."

Thomas whirled around and scowled at his housemate. "How would you know? And anyway, when did *you* see him?"

"He came by once. Sun was barely up, but I saw him and Eden from the upstairs window, sitting on the bench out front, looking at pictures or somethin'."

"I saw him, too," Wade said. "Dunno what kinda person he is, but he sure *looks* cool."

"What you mean?" DeShawn wanted to know.

"He's got long hair. Wears it in a ponytail under a do-rag. Has an earring, too, and tattoos. And his whole outfit was black leather."

"With *studs*," Carlos said. "And he rides a big black Harley." He rotated both fists forward, as if powering up an imaginary chopper.

"He isn't cool," Thomas snarled. "He's a loser, and after everything he did to me, I don't want anything to do with him."

"I know he did you wrong," DeShawn said, "but that was years ago. How do you know the man didn't change? People turn over new leaves every day. Eden says so all the time."

The baleful expression on Thomas's face told Nate it was time to put an end to the discussion. He got to his feet and clapped his hands once. "So, where should I start?"

"You're taller than us," Carlos said. "You could take down the curtains."

The others chimed in with things that still hadn't been done: boxing up pots and pans, wrapping the glassware and plates in paper, rolling up rugs, clearing out the linen closet.

For the moment, at least, it appeared as though they'd decided to take his advice.

All but Thomas, who slumped on the sofa, arms crossed and scowling.

"Think we should order a couple of pizzas?" Nate asked.

"Better wait," Wade said.

"He's right," Carlos agreed. "Eden might have bought something at the store."

"And she might not like finding out you showed up uninvited *and* decided what to fix for supper," Thomas said.

Message delivered and understood. Evidently, the kids knew more about the disagreement than they were letting on. Either that, or they were even smarter and more people-savvy than he gave them credit for.

Thomas in particular.

CHAPTER FIFTEEN

THE BOYS HAD been hauling boxes and bags since shortly after breakfast, and had earned every moment of R & R they were enjoying now.

Eden's grandmother would have loved to see her furniture come back into style, though she wouldn't be surprised that it was as functional today as it had been when she'd ordered it from the 1945 Sears catalog. "Cost an arm and a leg," Gramps always boasted, "but they stood behind our soldiers when they needed 'em most, so it's the only place I'll ever buy furniture from again." And as far as Eden knew, he'd stuck to his guns. Gram sometimes accused him of overthinking things, but even she couldn't deny that once he'd made up his mind, that was that.

Clearly, Eden hadn't inherited that trait. If she had, she wouldn't feel like a human Ping-Pong ball when it came to Nate Marshall.

A thump upstairs brought her back to the present. Dresser drawers opened and closet doors closed as the boys padded around on white-socked feet. She could hardly wait to see how they'd arranged their new rooms.

"Hey, where is everybody?"

Eden hurried into the foyer at the sound of the familiar voice. "Travis! What are you doing here?"

"Nate called yesterday," he said, "asked if I wanted to be here for the move." He hugged her. "How could I say no?"

She looked over his shoulder at Nate, who carried the boy's duffel bag.

"Laundry," Nate explained, setting it down inside.

"But what about finals?" she asked, relieving Travis of his backpack. "Shouldn't you be studying?"

"Don't worry, I've got this," he said with a wink—a wink exactly like Nate's.

What choice did she have but to take him at his word? Correction: What choice had Nate left her, bringing Travis here without discussing it with her first?

She took a step back and gave the boy a quick once-over. "Is it just me, or have you grown taller?"

Laughing, Travis rubbed his well-groomed goatee. "It's probably just my man-hair."

Tilting her head, she examined the beard. "Is it me," she repeated, "or is your hair longer, too?"

"Quit worrying, okay? I promise to cut it before I get married."

It was a phrase she'd often used to soothe the boys when skinned knees, sprains and splinters threatened their tight hold on masculine bravado. It touched her to know he'd adapted it for his new, independent life.

"Are you hungry? Did you have breakfast?"

"I'm fine." He patted his flat stomach. "In fact, I'm stuffed. Nate brought me a breakfast burrito."

Just what he needs, Eden thought, clenching her jaw. *Greasy, processed cheese and fake meat.*

"Are the guys upstairs?"

"They are, and you know how much they love surprises. They'll be thrilled to see you!" Eden led him to the stairway. "The top step squeaks," she whispered, "and so does the floorboard in front of the first bedroom."

Travis took the stairs two at a time, leaving Eden and Nate alone in the living room. She could tell by his hopeful expression that he expected her to thank him for driving all the way to the college to pick up Travis. But before she got the chance, Kirk came in from the kitchen, a stack of empty boxes in his arms.

"Hey, man," he said as he peered around his load and noticed Nate. "Glad you made it! Did you, ah…is…"

"Yes," Eden said, "Travis is here. He's upstairs saying hi to the boys." She faced Nate. "Guess you two hatched this wily little scheme for my benefit?"

A chorus of "It's Travis!" and excited laughter echoed above them.

"You make it sound like I was plotting a corporate takeover or something," Nate said. "I had no devious intentions. I just figured if nobody knew, nobody would be disappointed if Travis couldn't come." His voice dropped. "You, mostly."

Kirk, always the peacemaker, stepped up. "Don't mind her. She's been working like a mule, pulling all-nighters to get ready for the move. You can blame her short temper on exhaustion."

Or an aversion to being treated like a child.

Kirk's anxious expression distracted her. Eden could count on one hand the number of times she'd seen him looking anything but upbeat.

"So, Nate," he said, "what do you think of the place?"

"I think it's a great old house. And once the kids have a chance to settle in, I think they'll think so, too."

"Ya think?" Kirk teased. "But you're right. It's a whole lot safer than the old place, thanks to the renovations, and has a better layout...with one exception."

"And what's that?" Eden asked.

"Latimer House had all those great little rooms on the first floor, and they were perfect for classrooms. I don't know why we didn't consider it before, but here, there's just the family room. Figuring out how to make it work for science experiments and art projects might pose a challenge, but don't worry, I'll get 'er done!"

Nate had been listening intently, and she couldn't help but wonder how he planned to control *this* situation.

Kirk started for the hall. "Just two more boxes and I'll have the kitchen under control. Then if it's okay with you, I think I'll head out. I promised Janie we'd grab dinner and a movie tonight."

"Janie?"

"Oh. Guess I forgot to tell you I'm seeing somebody. Sort of." He grinned. "So far, so good."

"You've already given up half of your weekend, so don't worry about finishing up in there. I'll take care of it later." She hugged him. "Have a good time tonight. You deserve it!"

His mood was contagious, and he left Nate and Eden smiling in his wake.

"He made a good point," Nate said, "about the lack of classroom space."

"I've given it a lot of thought, but until I can afford an addition, we'll just have to make do."

"Mind if I have a look at the sunroom?"

He headed toward the back of the house before she gave the go-ahead, and like an obedient child—a *stupid* obedient child—she followed. She watched him pace off the width and length, and count windows and doorways.

"This area is huge," he said. "Plenty big enough to divide into four classrooms, way I figure it, two on either side of a hall."

Nate drew imaginary walls to help her envision what the space might look like. She pictured each room, equipped with desks and chairs, lab tables... "I hate to admit it, but it sounds good. Expensive, but good."

"Nah. Some two-by-fours and a few sheets of drywall, a little paint...job done in a day or two, for a couple hundred bucks."

"You really think so?"

"I know so."

"Why am I having trouble believing that?"

"Because you don't trust me anymore." He held up one hand. "There are good reasons for that, but you'll just have to trust me on this. And if Max can't do it, *I* will."

Eden pictured him, sleeves rolled up and a tool belt around his slim waist, hammering nails and taping drywall. She almost wished Max wouldn't have time to build those walls. First chance she got, she would unpack her old psychology textbooks. Maybe she'd find an explanation for the peculiar way she'd been behaving lately. Nate had called her behavior hot and cold, and she could hardly deny it. Until she figured it out, she'd thank her lucky stars for Nate's unwavering support…

…and hope he never developed a talent for reading minds.

WHEN PHIL NICKS called to report another kill on his property, Nate decided it was time for drastic action. Arranging a meeting had been far easier than expected, given his fellow ranchers' erratic winter prep schedules.

"Does this place ever change?" Phil joked, shaking Royce Marshall's hand.

Nate's father gave as good as he got. "Nope," he said, slapping his old friend on the back. "Riffraff has always been welcome here."

Every seat—on the U-shaped leather sectional, the matching recliners and counter stools, even the six chairs around the high-top game table in Nate's den—held a man in plaid and denim.

Zach's dad elbowed him. "We look like a blue jeans and Western shirts ad," he said, laughing.

"Boots and hats, too."

"And belt buckles," Pete Maxon added. "There's enough silver in this room to supply every dentist in Colorado."

Gus Jackson's hearty laughter filled the big den. "The only tooth docs who are still using silver are fogies, and I don't want an old codger poking around in my mouth with a drill!"

Nate made a circle of his thumb and forefinger, bit down on it and blew. The shrill two-note whistle instantly silenced the din of male voices.

Phil wiggled a fingertip in his ear. "Land sake, son! If you're lookin' to deafen the lot of us, you're on the right track!"

"Sorry," Nate said, grinning, "but as the saying goes, we're burnin' daylight."

Murmurs of agreement and nods of approval told Nate he had their permission to get the meeting under way.

"Hank here," he said, bringing their attention to his sister, "has volunteered to take notes, in case we need verification for—"

"Write down there on your li'l tablet how that brother of yours blew out my left eardrum," Phil interrupted, leaning over to Hank. "In case *I* need it for verification when I send him the bill for my hearing aid."

When the laughter waned, Nate finished his spiel. "Verification for the CWP agents. I thought we'd start by stating kill numbers. Here at the Double M, we lost two horses, two weeks apart. Would've lost a third, if not for Carl's eagle eyes. Saw the cat and fired a shot."

"And missed, doggone it," the foreman said.

One by one, the ranchers weighed in, and when they finished, Nate turned to Hank. "What's the tally, sis?"

"Six steers, five horses," she said, shaking her head. "And half a dozen near misses."

A moment of edgy silence followed her announcement, and then Amos Wagner got to his feet and tugged at the droopy ends of his white handlebar mustache. "Time to lay traps along the tree line," he said, hitching his faded jeans higher on his narrow hips.

"Aw, c'mon now, Amos. That ten-galloner of yours must be two sizes too small. If your brain was getting any blood, you'd know we can't do that."

"Why in tarnation *not*?"

"Because we're liable to catch our *own* animals, for one thing," Carl said.

"And it's against the law," Nate's dad added.

Notes of assent and dissent, shrugs and whispers floated around the room.

"What, then?" Amos demanded. "Get us some of those live animal traps and set 'em out, like a bunch of tree huggers?"

"Whoa, whoa, whoa." Nate raised a hand. "We'll never get anything settled if we talk over one another this way."

"The boy's right," Phil said. "This is worrisome, costly business, no question about it. But let's just settle down, hear each other out."

"We all know good 'n' well there's but one way to solve this."

All heads turned toward the gravelly baritone voice at the back of the room. It was Cam Mitchell, leaning against the doorjamb, calmly walking a toothpick from one corner of his mouth to the other.

His gaze scanned the room. "Y'all know me. *I* ain't no tree hugger." He removed the toothpick and used it as a pointer. "But I'll have no part in tearin' up a cougar—or any other critter, for that matter—in a steel trap. Trappin' it in some confounded cage won't work, either, 'cause sure as we're sittin' here, some pencil pusher down at CPW will decide the solution is to take it for a half-hour ride in his fancy SUV and rerelease it."

Grumbles of agreement circled the room.

"Now, by my count, we've got purt' near a hundred ranch hands between us. We'll write up a schedule and make assignments, so as to spread out the workload. Our boys will have instructions to hunker down and keep their eyes peeled. Anything looks like a cat?" Squinting one eye, he peered through an imaginary rifle scope and quietly said, "Pow."

"But that ain't legal, either, Cam. Not unless the cat is attacking."

"Well," he drawled, "don't know how y'all feel about it, but I say my land, my law." With that, he bit down on the toothpick again and fired off a two-fingered salute. "Happy huntin', neighbors." He left them to mull over what he'd said.

When Nate's double-wide front door clicked shut, Phil cleared his throat. "Hate to say it, boys, but Cam's right. My land, my rules." He walked toward the door, stopping to say, "Hope to see y'all at the fall hoedown."

One by one, the neighbors departed, leaving Nate, Hank and their dad alone.

"I have a bad, bad feeling about this," Hank admitted.

Every rancher who'd been there likely owned two or three long-range rifles, and equipped his men with the same.

And in the right hands, the powerful long guns could hit targets from three or four hundred yards away.

"Sounds to me like we'd better call a family meeting," his dad said.

And Nate knew why: to let Carl and the boys know they'd better keep their eyes peeled—especially when riding the Double M's boundaries—to protect *themselves*.

CHAPTER SIXTEEN

NATE SHRUGGED INTO his jacket and headed onto the porch.

Leaning into a slat-back rocker, he rested his boot heels on the railing and crossed both arms over his chest. Moonlight drew his eye to Mount Evans, where snow clung to the peak. "Evenin', Rosalie," he said.

A common nighthawk dipped and zigzagged across the sky, its plaintive *peent-peent* fading as it disappeared into the trees pines beyond the corral.

A splinter of light sneaked through the opening in the curtains behind him, and he could count every breath that clung to the chill September air. Shoulders hunched into the breeze, he blew into his cupped palms, and lured by the quiet purr of a single-engine plane, he looked up. Nate envied the pilot, for on a clear night like this, the man could likely see—

"There you are."

Startled, Nate nearly overturned the chair.

"For cryin' out loud, Zach, you just shaved ten years off my life."

"You're welcome," he said, taking the rocker beside Nate's.

"For scaring me out of my boots?"

"I hear the last ten years are the roughest, so…" He shrugged. "So you're welcome."

The cousins enjoyed a moment of companionable silence before Nate said, "So what's your take on tonight's meeting?"

"I think we might want to invest in body armor."

"Yeah, that's pretty much what Dad and I were saying earlier."

"The right night, the right weapon, the right ammo…" Zach shook his head. "A bad combination in the wrong man's hands."

"If it was Cam out there, I might not worry. But as somebody said tonight, there are a hundred or more hands working these ranches. Who knows which one will end up eyeball to the scope of a Winchester 270."

"Couple of the guys have grandkids on their payroll. Put one of *them* on the business end of a deer rifle," Zach said, "all by their green-as-snow-peas selves? In the pitch-dark? They'll fire at the first thing that moves—coyote, leaf, mosquito…"

"Man," Zach said.

Nate's mouth went dry just considering the grim possibilities.

"Let's look on the bright side. Maybe one of the grandkids is a sharpshooter, like Cam. Or maybe the cat will rub a bear the wrong way, and *it'll* solve our problems."

"Oh, that's a fine trade-off…a grizzly for a cougar."

"Good point." Zach got to his feet and stretched. "Well, cousin, it's getting late. I need to get home to my pretty pregnant wife."

Nate stood, too. "Remind me Summer's due date?"

"Christmas week, give or take a candy cane."

They crossed the porch side by side, and stopped at the top of the steps. "Did they tell you yet if it's a boy or a girl?"

Zach bounced down the steps. "Yup. But you know the old saying—"

"If I told you, I'd have to kill you," they said together.

"You going inside to call Eden?"

Nate pocketed both hands. "Nah, I'm beat. Think I'll call it a day."

Zach slid into his pickup. "Just be sure you're doing this for the right reasons," he said before slamming the driver's door.

Doing what? he wondered as the truck roared away. But Nate didn't really need an answer.

He'd bet his view of Sweet Mountain that Sam and Zach had talked about him recently.

Individually and as a team, they'd reminded him that Miranda had been an adventure junkie. She could just as easily have died rock climbing, they'd said, or skydiving, or any one of the dozen risky things on her bucket list.

What they didn't understand, and probably never would, was that blame couldn't be weighed and fault couldn't be meted out in portions. All that mattered now was that her parents lost a daughter, her siblings a sister, and Miranda the chance to cross even one more item off her list.

The only person who *did* get it was Eden, he thought, remembering the Malik story.

If THOMAS WITHDREW any further, Eden thought, he'd become one with the sofa cushions.

"It's just a visit, Thomas," she said. "Kirk and I will be right in the next room, and I promise, you aren't leaving with him."

At least, not today. She'd been down this road before. Parents who wanted to regain custody—and could demonstrate their fitness—were almost always reunited with their child. Even if she could spare Thomas this, Eden wouldn't do it. In-person visits provided the only measurable proof of a parent's interest in a child. If Mr.

Burke really had cleaned up his life, Thomas was better off in his care.

Leaning forward, she patted his knee. "You have a few minutes to change your clothes and comb your hair before your dad gets here…"

"No way. If I'm dirty and smelly, maybe he'll go away. Forever."

"All right then, that's your decision to make. But I think I'll put some drinks and snacks on a tray. That way, you'll have something to occupy your hands, in case you don't feel like talking."

He narrowed one eye. "Huh?"

The rules said she had to cooperate with Mr. Burke. Nowhere did it say she had to make it easy for him. In her opinion, the more difficult it was, the better. Any moms or dads who complied with months of court-ordered, regulated sessions to remain in their children's lives were more likely to survive the day-to-day stresses that came with parenthood once the arrangement became full-time.

"Well, it isn't polite to talk with your mouth full, right?"

That, at least, encouraged the hint of a smile, and she headed for the kitchen to prepare the tray. She'd already made sure the rest of the boys were busy in other parts of the house. The maternal side of her hoped Burke would change his mind or forget to show up, but the counselor in her understood how either scenario would remind Thomas of the many times his dad had neglected or abandoned him.

Thomas was understandably wary of the man. Part of Eden's job involved weekly counseling sessions with the boys. During his very first meeting with her, Thomas seemed eager to declare that it was his parents' fault that he'd been forced to live at Latimer House; he had nothing to do with the crimes they'd committed, so why did he have to serve time, too? It pained her to think he felt that way about Latimer House, but in his shoes, Eden might have seen it that way, too.

It was a question every boy asked upon arriving, and Eden told them the truth in ways she believed they could safely process. As time passed, sessions tended to center more on schoolwork, friends and their hopes for the future rather than family-related issues of the past.

Thomas was the exception.

The quiet roar of a Harley told her Mr. Burke had remembered the meeting. In fact, he'd arrived a full ten minutes early. Eden carried the tray into the living room as Mr. Burke rapped at the screen door.

"Would you like to invite your dad in?" she asked Thomas.

He tightened his crossed arms and said a firm, flat, "No."

"It's okay," Burke said, letting himself in.

It must have been the black leather that made him seem taller that day in the yard. He'd traded the do-rag for a leather band that held his ponytail in place and replaced his stainless gauge earrings with flesh-colored ones. The eagle, tiger and American flag tattoos were hidden under a long-sleeved white shirt, and he'd removed the chrome chains from his newly polished boots. And unless she was mistaken, he'd pressed a crease into his dark blue jeans.

His dark eyes went immediately to the coffee table, where three glasses of lemonade and three napkins flanked a saucer of cookies. Oatmeal raisin, Thomas's favorite. Eden fully intended to stay in the room until she was sure Thomas felt comfortable to be alone with him. Supervised visits meant she needed to stay within shouting distance, and Eden believed father and son would accomplish far more if she didn't hover.

"You're sticking around, right?" Burke asked.

"I'll be in the kitchen." She focused on his son. "Thomas, aren't you going to say hello?"

The boy grabbed a cookie and gave his dad a dull greeting.

"Please, have a seat, Mr. Burke, and help yourself."

Wisely, he chose the short end of the L-shaped sofa—directly across from his boy instead of beside him.

"It's good to see you again, Tommy."

"I told you a hundred times, they call me Thomas now."

"Oh. Right. Sorry." He looked at Eden and shrugged helplessly.

"Good things come to those who wait," she said. And to Thomas, "Why don't you tell your dad about your project for the county science fair."

"Why don't *you* tell him."

It would have been easy to feel sorry for the man. His every effort had been met with rejection. But looks could be deceiving.

"Do you have any questions for Thomas, Mr. Burke?"

"Please, call me Tom." He helped himself to a cookie and said to his boy, "Oatmeal raisin. You remembered."

"Eden baked 'em 'cause she knows they're *my* favorite." He leaned forward, balanced both elbows on his knees and clasped his hands in the space between. Exactly like Nate. "I didn't tell her they're your favorite, too."

Eden chose that moment to leave the room, but heard Burke say, "So what's the hypothesis of your science project?"

After Thomas summarized his work, Burke shared two stories from his own school days. At the end of the hour, Eden peeked around the corner, and saw that the boy had inched to the other end of the couch, handshake distance from his dad. "Not exactly a lovefest in there, is it?" Kirk whispered.

"Mr. Burke is trying. If he doesn't push too hard, too fast, Thomas might just meet him halfway."

Kirk headed for the sunroom-turned-classrooms. "I need to set up for Monday's lesson."

Earlier, she'd seen him carry in four huge chunks of modeling clay and a bag containing sculpting tools.

"We're making turtles," he said from the hall. "Who knows? Maybe we'll discover a prodigy."

"Is it okay with you if I send Thomas in when his dad leaves? Maybe while he's helping you, he'll share something that'll help us figure out how he feels about these meetings."

"Sure. That's a great idea."

On her way back to the living room, Eden wondered why she wanted Nate to share in this moment—what could be a major breakthrough for father and son.

"Guess my time's up, huh?" Burke said when she joined them.

She smiled. "Actually, it was up half an hour ago."

On his feet now, the man extended a hand. "Thanks, Miss Quinn, for suggesting we meet here. Things were a whole lot more pleasant than in that dingy old office downtown."

"Please, call me Eden."

He made a move as if to tousle his boy's hair. When Thomas pulled back, Burke tucked his fingertips into his jeans pocket.

"Maybe next time," she said.

"Saturday? Same time?"

"Sounds good. Thomas? Your dad is leaving."

Shrugging, he studied a hangnail. "Bye."

Eden walked Burke to the door. "These things take time."

"I know. And I know it's my own fault that he's behaving this way." He faced Thomas. "See you next week, buddy."

Thomas only rolled his eyes.

"I'll call if anything changes," Eden said.

Lowering their voices, they exchanged a few more words, and once he was gone, Eden sat beside Thomas. "That went better than expected, didn't it?"

"I wish he'd quit calling me Tommy and buddy. I've told him I hate it, but he doesn't care what *I* want."

"He's trying. That's all you can expect for the

time being. Maybe it wouldn't be so hard if you tried, just a little, too."

He was on his feet in an instant. "I don't want things to be easy. I hate him."

She knew better than to say something like, "You don't really mean that."

He cracked his knuckles. "Does everybody think I'm stupid? I read a bunch of stuff online. I can petition the court to make sure he can't regain custody. And if they say I have to live with him, well, I'll just have to resort to extreme measures."

Extreme measures? Scary words, made more terrifying by the malicious look on his face.

"Kirk is in the art room," she said. "Would you mind helping him set things up for Monday's art project? It's something to do with clay." She forced a smile. "And turtles."

"Clay turtles." He harrumphed. "Like that's gonna make everything better."

He left the room, but Eden couldn't help but notice that his fists were still balled up at his sides.

She'd have to keep him busier than usual these next few days to keep his mind off the next visit with his dad…and lessen any chance that his heated mood would flare into something more.

CHAPTER SEVENTEEN

NOTHING COULD HAVE surprised or hurt Thomas's feelings more than when Eden said that his dad could come back next week.

At first, he hadn't wanted to pack any of the cookies she'd baked. Wasn't it bad enough that his hair and eyes were the same color as his dad's? Did he have to share his favorite cookie with the loser, too? Now, as his stomach rumbled, he was glad he'd taken them.

Adults could be so arrogant. First of all, talking quietly within range of people with perfectly normal ears was just plain rude. When they started whispering out there on the porch, right beside the screen door, did they seriously think he couldn't hear what they were saying?

"How many more of these supervised visits before I can take him home with me?" his dad had asked.

He'd expected Eden to say, "*This* is his home," or "If you want to see him, you'll have to see him here, at *home*." When she said, "Let's just play it by ear," he almost wished he hadn't been paying attention.

They must have thought he couldn't think for himself, either, or wasn't smart enough to get on the computer and investigate some stuff before the visit. Stuff that would protect him in case his worst fears came true. Such as the fact that he was old enough to decide whether or not he wanted to live with his father. And the article that explained how adults could get in a lot of trouble if they took a runaway into their home.

The law paints a thin line, the reporter wrote, between kidnapping and helping a good kid escape a bad situation. An adult who did that could be charged for getting involved. Thomas was glad he'd taken the time to read that one because Nate shouldn't get into trouble on account of him.

When he got to the Double M, he'd take the reporter's advice and tell Nate to call the cops, explain how Eden Quinn, his official guardian, was planning to hand him over to his ex-con father, who'd left him at his girlfriends' houses and under pool tables and bar stools more times than he cared to remember. The cops would conduct a thorough investigation, find out he was telling the truth, and then *nobody* could make him go anywhere with his father. Well, unless he had nowhere else to go. But he had Pinewood and Eden, and in a pinch, Nate, too, so…

He should have worn a warmer jacket. Should have grabbed those gloves Eden stuffed into his stocking last Christmas. His teeth were chattering, but it was okay. He'd forget all about this temporary discomfort once he got to the Double M.

NATE ROLLED OVER and glanced at the alarm clock. A call at two a.m. could only mean one thing: Another cougar attack.

"Yeah?" he barked into the receiver.

When the ringing continued, he realized it was the doorbell, not the phone. *Must be really bad*, he decided, pulling on sweatpants, for his foreman to deliver the message in person.

He flipped on the porch light, wondering why Carl had come to the front instead of the back, as usual.

"What's up?" he asked, flinging open the door.

But it wasn't Carl on the porch.

"Thomas?"

Nate stepped outside for a glance at the driveway and was greeted by a cold blast of wind. "Where did Eden park the van?"

"She isn't here," the boy answered, shivering. "I came alone. Walked part of the way."

Frowning, Nate drew Thomas inside and tossed him a hooded sweatshirt from the hall tree. "Wait. You what?" And then it hit him. If the boy had walked *part* of the way…

"Don't tell me you hitchhiked!"

Thomas shrugged.

"Get into the kitchen," he grumbled, "so I can get some soup and hot chocolate into you."

He'd give the kid ten minutes to explain what he was doing here in the middle of the night, and then he'd call Eden.

"Chicken noodle or beef vegetable?" he asked, holding up two cans.

"Chicken."

Nate dumped the contents into a small saucepan, then filled a big mug with water and slid it into the microwave. While waiting for both to heat up, he leaned against the counter.

"So what gives, kiddo?"

"My father visited today," Thomas mumbled. "Eden is on his side." He shrugged again. "So I can't stay there anymore."

Eden had her flaws, but Nate would have bet the ranch that she hadn't taken anybody's side against one of her boys. He crossed his arms over his chest. "What makes you say that?"

The microwave dinged, and Nate emptied an envelope of cocoa mix into the mug.

"I heard them whispering about...stuff."

"Yeah?" He put the mug on the table and handed Thomas a spoon. The kid didn't take the opportunity to elaborate.

"Thomas, you risked your life—literally—

to wake me up at two in the morning, so that's not gonna cut it."

The soup began to simmer, and Nate gave it a quick stir as Thomas sipped his hot chocolate.

"You're the only person I can trust."

Nate ladled soup into a bowl and set in front of Thomas. "You don't think that's a little harsh? You've been with Eden for years. She has one conversation that you don't approve of, and suddenly she's untrustworthy?" He shook his head and sat across from the boy.

"I won't live with him. And nobody can make me."

Nate knew the kid looked up to him; if he used that, maybe he could find out what was really going on here.

"'I won't live with him, and nobody can make me'? Running away from home? Seriously? You're acting about six years old right now." As expected, the comment struck a nerve.

Thomas bristled. "Oh, yeah? Well what would you have done?"

"I would have asked Eden straight-out whose side she's on."

Thomas ate a spoonful of soup and shrugged one shoulder.

"What, you think she'd lie to you?"

"No, but…"

"But what? She's probably frantic right now, wondering where you are, if you're safe."

Thomas pushed noodles back and forth in the bowl. "She's asleep. I made sure before I left."

Nate sat back and let him take a few more bites of soup before saying, "You know I can't take you in, right?"

Nodding, Thomas pushed the bowl away.

"If you do, you'll have to call the cops, tell them that I left Pinewood and came to you for safe harbor. Otherwise, you'll get in trouble for harboring a runaway."

"Really?"

"I looked it up. So if you aren't going to let me stay, you should call 911."

"No need to involve the cops because I'm taking you home. Are you finished eating?"

Another nod, and then he downed the hot chocolate.

Nate needed to grab something to put on over his T-shirt. Some socks and shoes. But he didn't trust the kid to be here when he came back downstairs.

He stepped barefooted into his work boots and slipped into an old windbreaker hanging by the door.

For the first half hour of the drive, neither of them spoke. Nate tried to imagine how Eden would react when he knocked on her door.

"This is going to break her heart. But you already know that, don't you?"

He had no clue what response he expected from Thomas, but it sure wasn't tears that turned into quiet sobs. He let the boy cry for a few minutes, then reached across the console and squeezed his shoulder.

"She's gonna hate me now."

"No," Nate said, "and you know that, too."

"You're gonna say I'm acting like a six-year-old again, but..."

"But what?"

"But I want Eden to be my parent. It's just... How do I tell her I love her without sounding like a weirdo?"

A different kind of love, Nate realized, but he knew exactly how Thomas felt.

"Promise me you won't tell her I said that, okay?"

"Okay," he said, hoping he wouldn't have to go back on his word.

Because the last thing this kid needed right now was for another adult to disappoint him.

BEING AWAKENED BY the doorbell at six in the morning was just as unsettling as a middle-of-the-night phone call. Eden belted her robe and raced barefoot down the stairs, hoping it was just Shamus stopping by to share his morning paper. Even before throwing open the dead bolt, she recognized the broad-shouldered silhouette on the other side of the seeded glass pane. And then she saw Thomas, standing slightly behind Nate on the porch.

"What's going on?" she asked, closing the door on the frosty air that followed them inside.

Nate stood, one hand on the boy's shoulder, the other in his pocket. "Do you want to tell her, or should I?"

"Whatever."

Thomas had been crying, that much was evident. And Nate—hair askew and shadows under his eyes—looked as if he hadn't slept at all last night.

"He told me to call the cops so I wouldn't get charged with harboring a fugitive. I didn't, of course."

"The police! Okay, you guys are scaring me." She glanced up the stairs. "Let's go into the kitchen. No sense waking everyone else."

She started a pot of coffee, and then sat across from them. "Well?"

Nate scrubbed both hands over his face. "Well," he echoed, "as you can see, I had an unexpected visitor last night." He leaned both forearms on the table. "I'll let Thomas here tell you the rest of the story. And if he doesn't feel like talking right now, I'll fill you in later."

Eden pulled the robe tighter, as if that would shield her from the rest of the story. But the boy didn't seem overly eager to tell it.

Terrifying news reports about the awful things that happened to hitchhikers flashed in her mind. "How did you get all the way to the Double M?"

He rested his forearms on the table, too, and hid his face in the crook of one arm. "I, ah, walked," he said, voice muffled by his jacket sleeve.

It would have taken hours to walk all the way to the ranch. Hours, alone in the dark, on the side of heavily trafficked highways. She'd memorized every creak and squeak in this house, but hadn't heard a thing last night. Not the telltale groan of his bedroom door hinges, not the squeal of floorboards, not the pop of the top step. She'd unlocked the front door to let them in, meaning the bolt had been fully engaged. The boys didn't need keys, since either she or Kirk was always home. So how had he relocked the door and left the house without her knowing about it?

The coffeemaker hissed, startling her. She got up to fill three mugs and doled them out like playing cards, amazed that not a drop slopped over the rims. After delivering spoons, the sugar bowl and milk jug, she returned to her seat, hoping that once Thomas had consumed the adult beverage, he'd at least try to act like a grown-up.

It wasn't difficult to connect the dots: the previous afternoon, he'd confronted her about overhearing his dad ask when he could take Thomas home. He'd heard her reply, too, and hadn't been too pleased about either. He'd donned the My Life Stinks expression that she'd seen on all of the boys' faces at one time or another. It was part of his makeup to brood and pout, but never for more than a few hours. And based on his behavior at suppertime, she'd had no reason to suspect he hadn't gotten over the visit with his father.

"Have I ever lied to you, Thomas?"

He lifted a shoulder in a sulky shrug. "Not that I know of."

She ignored the sarcastic reply. "I have *not*, and you know it." Eden wrapped both hands around her mug, mostly to hide their trembling. But that worked for only a few seconds because the mug was hot. Hands clasped in her lap now, she said, "When all of this started with your father, what did I tell you?"

"That he wouldn't be able to take me home for a long time. If ever."

"Did you believe me?"

Nate, to his credit, had leaned back, giving her space to do her job, while sending the subtle message that if she needed backup, he was available. She'd thank him for that later. Unless she found out he'd encouraged her escapee in any way.

"Well? Did you believe me?"

"I remember what that shrink lady down at the department said: 'Children are always better off in the care of their parents.' And she's your *boss*, so..."

In other words, he'd convinced himself that his feelings didn't matter. Eden wished she could tell him that wasn't true. But he was young and hurting, suffering under the delusions born of his years of yearning for love—though he'd never admit it—from a man incapable of being anyone's father.

"How long have you and I been together, Thomas?"

Another shrug. "I dunno. Couple years?"

"You were two days shy of your eighth birthday, so it's been nearly seven years." She gave him a moment to absorb that. "And how many kids have come and gone during that time?"

Thomas sighed and took a sip of his coffee. "Lots."

"Thirteen," she answered for him. "And your place here has always, *always* been secure. Why would that change just because some long-haired dude on a Harley rode up the driveway one day?"

She saw Nate's eyebrows rise.

And Thomas, looking to *Nate* for an answer.

Eden didn't know which irked her more, that she'd slept right through Thomas's escape, or that he'd taken his problems to a man he'd met mere months ago. Responsibility for that rested squarely on her shoulders, though, because *she* had allowed the relationship to flourish, to the point where Thomas felt more comfortable turning to Nate than his state-appointed counselor.

Righting the situation—if it wasn't already too late—would require Nate's full cooperation. Asking for it wouldn't be easy, since he'd proved time and again how much he cared about the boys. Nothing like this had ever happened on her watch, but it would be unprofessional at best and dangerous at worst not to take steps to guarantee something like it would never happen again.

Nate helped himself to a second cup of coffee and refilled Eden's mug while he was at it.

Squeaking floorboards and the sound of bare feet hitting the ground overhead told them the boys were up. Any minute now, they'd rumble downstairs, laughing and jockeying for position at the fridge and toaster.

Thomas grabbed Eden's wrist. "Don't tell the guys what I did. *Please?*"

Eden met his dark, imploring eyes. She didn't have the heart to tell him that they probably already knew. Ben and Carlos spent half their time peeking out the windows when they were supposed to be sleeping.

"You have my word. I won't tell them."

"Don't look at me," Nate said, hands raised. "I'm an innocent bystander, here."

She avoided his eyes, because this wasn't the time to point out that he had contributed to the problem, however unwittingly. The minute they were alone, she intended to pick his brain for every detail about Thomas's reasons for running away.

Silas rounded the corner first. He took one look at Thomas and said, "How long have *you* been up?"

"Awhile."

"Where you been, dude?" DeShawn plucked at Thomas's jacket sleeve.

An uneasy silence hung over the table until Nate said, "He was outside with me."

Before they could ask why, Eden suggested pancakes with homemade sausage gravy. "Why don't you guys find something on TV?" she said. "I'll call you when it's ready."

Devon grinned. "You sure? You don't want us to help?"

"That's why I'm here," Nate said.

Eden breathed a sigh of relief when, to stave off wisecracks and comments, he added, "Saturday morning cartoons were my favorite."

They darted from the kitchen calling dibs on

the remote and the recliner, and when they were gone, Eden looked at Thomas. "You, too," she said with a flick of her fingertips, "or they'll get suspicious."

He carried his coffee mug to the sink and hung his jacket on a hook near the back door.

"Better find a way to fake 'happy,'" Nate advised, "or your goose is cooked."

There in the middle of the kitchen, Thomas hung his head. "Sorry, Eden. I didn't mean to worry you."

She drew him into a motherly hug. "It's already forgotten…" It was not, and he no doubt knew that, so she held him at arm's length and touched a fingertip to his nose. "…if you can convince me that nothing like this will ever happen again."

"It won't." He looked at Nate. "Sorry I dragged you into this, man."

"It's already forgotten," he echoed. "But next time something gets your goat, talk to her. She's a real good listener."

Thomas looked up at Eden. "I know."

Halfway to the door, he stopped, turning to Nate again. "Geese and goats, huh?" He shook his head, a wry grin lifting one corner of his mouth. "Old people say the weirdest things."

Nate's halfhearted smile told her that Thomas's sudden shift from dour to upbeat worried him, too.

CHAPTER EIGHTEEN

EDEN DROPPED A package of sausage into a black iron skillet. "I'm sort of glad we have a few minutes alone."

Sort of glad? He turned a chair around and straddled it, waiting for the hammer to drop.

"What time did Thomas get to your house?"

"Two, give or take a few minutes." She had enough on her mind without hearing Thomas had hitchhiked part of the way. "He was cold to the bone, so I sat him down, made him eat some soup."

"Unless my math is off, he was with you at least two and a half hours. It never crossed your mind to call me in all that time?"

And there it was again, that *I know best* look that could cut him to the quick and make his neck hairs bristle. "Of course I did, but why get the whole household in an uproar—in the dead of night—when I believed I could talk him into coming home before everyone woke up?"

Eden sprinkled a few tablespoons of flour on top of the sausage and stirred. Vigorously.

"Guess we're all real lucky you talked him into it then, aren't we?"

She behaved this way only when someone questioned her authority or abilities, and this time, Nate wasn't guilty of either.

"What did he talk about while he was with you?"

It was tempting to divulge every detail, especially with the relieved-then-angry look she'd greeted him with still so fresh in his mind. But he couldn't. Not without going back on his promise to Thomas.

"He's pretty steamed at his dad." That much, at least, was true. "And if even half of what he says about the guy is fact, the kid has every right to be."

A pinch of garlic powder and a shake of parsley went into the pan. "He was barely four when he entered the system. I doubt he remembers all that much about Thomas Burke's parenting style." She gave the gravy starter another stir. "That's why the rules were put into place... to protect kids from inaccurate memories that could hurt them down the road."

And if he'd followed *his* simple rules, none of this would be happening.

"If anyone at the department ever finds out that one of my boys snuck out in the middle of the night and walked *miles* to a stranger's house..." Eden exhaled an exasperated sigh.

A stranger? Nate blamed the stinging remark on fear. "You could lose your job," he finished for her.

She branded him with a defiant stare. "So while you were acting as Thomas's counselor, did you ask him why he felt it necessary to run away from home?"

"He thinks his dad is a master manipulator—my words, not his—and that you fell for the latest scheme. I'm preaching to the choir, here, telling you that he spent way more than his first four years with the guy. Either he's a skillful liar, or he suffered a great deal when he was in Burke's care."

Eden turned and looked at him—really looked at him—for the first time since opening the door. Maybe *he* was the one who needed counseling, because he couldn't take his eyes off her. She was gorgeous, backlit by a shard of sunlight slanting through the window.

Nate shook his head and cleared his throat. *Can't let yourself get sidetracked, Marshall. Just follow the rules...*

"Is that so?"

If she wanted examples, he'd give her examples, much as it pained him to repeat the boy's distressing stories.

"He said that a couple of times, Burke left him at girlfriends' houses for days—women he barely knew. Once, he spent hours in a closet because one of them had a big vicious dog. Hid under a pool table once, too, for fear of being trampled by the drunks in some dive. And another time—"

"It took me ages to get him to open up about all of that. I don't know whether to pin a medal on you or smack you."

"Smack me? For what?"

She handed him the whisk and added milk to the gravy. "Stir that, will you, while I make the pancake batter."

They stood in silence, Nate at the stove, Eden at the counter beside it.

After a while, she said, "You barely know Thomas, so why was he so confident that if he came to you, you'd help him?"

"Wait. Whoa. If you think I did or said anything to encourage it, you're—" A guy didn't just call a psychologist crazy. "Look, Thomas came to me. I brought him home. End of story. Or, at least, it oughta be. I don't know what's going on with you, Eden, but you need to ratchet it down a notch or two. I could have called the cops. I didn't. I could have called you, let you deal with the problem all on your own. I didn't. A little gratitude might be nice, even if you have to fake it."

If he sounded gruff to himself, Nate didn't want to think about what he sounded like to Eden. She buttered the griddle. Whipped the batter until it all but foamed. Okay, so maybe he'd been a little hard on her, but to this point, TLC sure hadn't worked.

He lowered the flame under the skillet, covered the gravy and tossed the whisk into the sink. The urge to hightail it out of there was so strong, Nate could almost smell the leather upholstery of his truck. But he had to stay, if only for Thomas's sake. The kid had been through a lot in twenty-four hours. Last thing he needed was to return to the kitchen and find Nate gone.

So he set the table. Made a fresh pot of coffee. Filled stubby glasses with juice and milk. Set out the syrup—even though Eden looked at him cockeyed—because his family had been topping sausage gravy with the stuff for generations.

If he bent over backward any farther, his spine would snap like a twig. For some reason, Zach and Summer came to mind: married, awaiting the birth of their first kid, their relationship thriving. Nate found it hard to believe they resolved disputes—and surely they had them, because what couple didn't?—with stony silence. But then, they'd overcome a lot, separately and together. Unity like that took time and effort. Mutual respect. And love.

Eden poured the gravy into two big bowls and placed them at opposite ends of the table. Stacked pancakes on two plates and put them beside the bowls.

"I'll get the boys in here, before things get cold," he said.

She nodded, and he would have sworn her lower lip trembled slightly as he left the room. A part of him wanted to go back in there, take her in his arms and tell her everything would be fine. But Nate steeled himself. Losing Miranda had nearly broken him. If he took it to the next level with Eden and things didn't work out?

Just follow the rules, he reminded himself, rounding the corner into the hall. Just two simple rules.

"WHAT DO YOU MEAN, you don't have a fax machine?"

Paul Otto snickered into the phone. "How old *are* you, Marshall?"

Times like this, Nate wondered how he'd lasted four years in the same dorm room with the guy. "I'll come pick up the report. It'll be faster than jawin' with you all morning."

"I can email them."

"No, you can't. My printer's on the fritz."

"All right, simmer down. The copy machine has a fax feature. I think."

Nate heard papers rustling and Otto muttering.

"There are only four pages here," he said. "Give me a few minutes to find the instruction manual and I'll send 'em right over."

"Thanks, Paul. I owe you one."

"You bet your Stetson you do." And laughing, his former roommate hung up.

Ever since hanging his private detective shingle, Otto liked to boast that he really could find the proverbial needle in a haystack, and Nate believed it. He'd traced his mom's long-lost brother from Chicago to Eureka, from California to Canada—by way of Houston, Miami, New York and Nashville. If Nate had any regrets about funding *this* search, it was that he hadn't put Otto on the trail sooner.

Something Thomas had mumbled during the ride back to Pinewood had set off warning bells in Nate's head. "I won't live with him. I don't care what I have to do." After getting home from delivering him into Eden's welcoming arms, Nate searched the internet for every scenario the boy had described, and found examples of each in news stories from all over the United States. He'd substituted his name in place of the other kids', and artfully passed himself off as the victim.

In his immature, fearful mind, his father's past deeds—desertion, neglect, landing in federal prison, then disappearing for years after that—predicted the man's future behavior. By inserting himself into those stories, Thomas hoped to damage his father's newly established credibility and ensure himself a permanent home at Pinewood. If his accusations were even partially true, Nate couldn't turn his back on the kid. Any minute now, he'd have black-and-white proof that would validate father...or son. Either way, Thomas stood to benefit, and that eased Nate's conscience.

While he waited for the fax to appear, Nate stretched out in his big office chair, boot heels on the windowsill and fingers laced behind his head, watching the Double M cows graze contentedly along the tree line. A perfect example of why setting cougar traps out there was a dumb and dangerous idea. It had been weeks since anyone reported a kill, but that didn't mean the threat had passed.

The sudden *bzzt-bzzt-bzzt* of the fax startled him and nearly sent him toppling. Feet on the floor, he rolled his chair closer to the machine, watching as the pages surged from the printer. When the machine quieted, Nate settled in to study the report.

Thomas William Burke Sr., it said, graduated from Colorado State with a major in education and a minor in psychology. Every infraction on his criminal record had a direct link to drug or alcohol abuse, and when sentenced for a third DUI, his name appeared on the state's Most Wanted list. To his credit, Burke had come back, served his time and hadn't stepped out of line since. And Nate believed he knew who had inspired his turnaround.

It gave him an idea, but for it to work, he'd have to talk with Burke, directly. He'd seen the man's contact information tacked to the bulletin board in the Pinewood kitchen, along with recipes, coupons and an oil change discount card. Nate called Otto back.

"What's the problem, old man? Did I forget to dot an i or cross a t?"

"The report was so perfect, it gave me another idea. What's your schedule look like for the next few days?"

"Got dates with some long, slender ladies. Other than that, I'm wide-open."

"Are you still telling that tired old joke?" Nate grinned, remembering how Otto had assigned girls' names to his fishing rods and golf clubs. "You need some new material, pal."

"What I need to get is some new *friends*."

He heard Otto's desk chair squeal and pictured him literally sitting on the edge of his seat.

"Now, why don't you tell me about this idea

of yours, and I'll tell you whether or not I'm willing to bail on my ladies this weekend."

WHEN KIRK HEARD what Nate planned to do with the information he'd gathered about Burke, the young teacher had volunteered to snag the man's phone number from the bulletin board.

Dealing with Burke had been anything but easy. Fortunately, Thomas's dad had agreed to meet him, but Nate wasn't at all sure he'd show. Not that he blamed the guy. If a total stranger had started a telephone conversation with, "You don't know me, but I have a proposition for you," he might not show up, either. Especially if he had a rap sheet like Burke's.

Now, with The Alley's menu open in front of him, Nate scanned the parking lot and hoped for the best. He'd just ordered his second cup of coffee when the Harley wheeled into a space not far from Nate's truck. Curiosity, it seemed, didn't always kill the cat. Sometimes it merely lured him.

"Can't stay long," Burke said, sitting across from Nate. "Trying to keep my nose clean and don't want to be late for work."

Nate extended a hand. "Thanks for coming."

He'd seen the guy's birth date in Otto's report. Without it, Nate would have guessed he was much older. Clearly, his lifestyle had taken its toll.

"I'll be honest," Burke said. "If you hadn't said this meeting could benefit Thomas, I wouldn't be here."

"It'll benefit you, too." Along with Eden and the rest of the Pinewood boys, and in a round-about way, Nate, as well. "How far between here and your job?"

"Not far. I'm on the new hotel complex near the airport. My AA sponsor recommended me, and when the foreman heard I can run heavy equipment *and* weld, he hired me on the spot."

His biggest challenge after returning from Alaska, Burke told Nate, had been finding an affordable apartment and transportation. "Rode the light-rail system for a while, thinking to save up for a car, a nicer place, but man." He shook his head. "Let's just say I'm not cut out for mass transit."

He'd spent two years in The Last Frontier, so Nate wasn't surprised.

Burke glanced at his watch. "So about this idea of yours…"

"I've always believed in laying my cards on the table, so I'll say right up front that I hired somebody to look into your past."

"I figured. That boy of mine doesn't talk to me much, but when he does, you're usually part of the conversation." Burke chuckled. "I was prepared not to like you. All that hero-worship talk poked the green-eyed monster, big-time. And reminded me why Tommy isn't exactly fond of me." He cleared his throat. "Thomas, I mean. Sheesh. There's another habit I need to break."

Nate had a feeling he'd succeed, based on habits he'd already broken.

"My guy is one of the best private investigators in the business, and he's looking into the how-to of getting your teacher's certificate reinstated. His dad is a politician. Lots of contacts." He held up a hand in response to Burke's scowl. "Hear me out. These are ideas, nothing more, and if you decide you don't like them, we'll pretend this conversation never happened."

"I loved teaching, but I'm guessing the state will frown on putting a former addict at the front of a classroom."

"You were never convicted of any crimes against children, so I'm guessing the opposite. You could keep your day job, at least for the time being, and maybe volunteer at Pinewood. Eden and Kirk could use some help."

Nate saw sparks of optimism in Burke's dark eyes. "Don't get your hopes too high just yet, though."

"Don't worry. I'm used to disappointment.

Something tells me dealing with the state will be a walk in a park compared to getting Eden's approval."

That surprised Nate because Eden made it seem as though she approved of the father-son meetings.

"I met a guy in Alaska who liked to brag that he shot his wife and her boyfriend. Some folks said it was all talk, called him Santa 'cause of his belly laugh." Burke paused. "Eden has a big robust laugh, and she's mighty protective of those boys…"

Nate frowned slightly. "She can be downright fierce where they're concerned, but no way she'd kill to defend the kids."

Burke shrugged. "Mind if I ask you a question?"

"You can ask…"

"What's with you two?"

Nate answered with a ragged sigh. The contradictions were more confusing than a Rubik's Cube. Thoughtful gestures and angry outbursts. Warm hugs and cold glares. Sweet kisses and "I don't need you."

Nate licked his lips. "To tell the truth, I don't have a clue."

"Maybe you ought to put your guy on it."

That inspired a chuckle. "Touché."

He hadn't expected to like the guy, but it was

hard not to. Burke seemed intelligent and rational. He'd overcome a lot through patience and persistence. "We need to keep this between us," Nate said.

"I agree."

The men shook on it, and after Nate paid the bill, they walked out together.

"Soon as I hear anything, I'll call you," Nate said as Burke snapped his helmet's chin strap.

"Extra time with Thomas and a way to earn back his respect? Yeah, I'm looking forward to hearing from you."

Nate stopped at Café Brazil on his way home and picked up a gift card to thank Kirk for risking Eden's wrath by supplying Burke's number. The guy had earned a free meal with his Janie, and then some.

Driving back to the Double M, a sense of unease overshadowed his relief that Burke seemed enthused by his idea. Nate told himself that only a fool *wouldn't* feel edgy, given the guy's record. That, and the fact that he'd bypassed Eden to ensure the meetings with Thomas Burke. He hoped history wouldn't repeat itself; if Burke went off-beam again, everyone would pay a price...

...but none more than Thomas.

CHAPTER NINETEEN

When he saw the Pinewood number on the caller ID screen, Nate almost didn't answer. But on the off chance that Eden had finally put the whole Thomas the Runaway business behind her, he picked up.

"Nate!"

He recognized Devon's voice instantly.

"Hey, what's up, buddy?"

"Chili. Like, buckets of the stuff."

Normally, he didn't appreciate any aspect of speakerphone, but hearing the other boys in the background, laughing and cracking jokes, made it tolerable.

"I used your recipe and it tastes great, but…" More laughter, and then, "Can we bring some over to your place? Maybe you could get your family together to help us eat it."

He'd doubled, even tripled the recipe a time or two. But Nate couldn't figure out how they'd ended up with *buckets*. It was Sunday, when the Marshalls gathered for a traditional, weekly home-cooked meal. The family would probably get a kick out of a spur-of-the-moment meal prepared by a horde of hardscrabble teenage boys.

"I'll see if I can round 'em up. But how will you get that much chili over here?"

"I found these giant jars down in the basement," Devon said. "Eden told me her grandmother inherited them from her mother, and that back in the old days, women used them for soup and stew when their men went hunting."

His own grandmother had used similar jars for rib-sticking meals to feed the hands when they moved cattle closer to home to sit out the winter.

"How many jars?"

"Seven."

"*Seven?* Where did you get enough meat?"

"Eden said she needed to use up the ground beef before it got freezer-burned."

"We had lotsa tomatoes and beans and spices," Nick said, "because she's a food hoarder. You need us to bring pots and pans, too?"

"I think we're okay with what's here."

"Guess what, Nate?"

"What, Carlos?"

"We got a new kid. To replace Travis. His name is Luke. Say hi to Nate, Luke."

"Hello, Nate. I've heard a lot about your ranch. I've never been particularly fond of horses, but that's probably because I've never met one before. So I'm looking forward to meeting one. And you, too, of course."

He hated to admit it, but while the boy rambled, his mind had wandered. Had the boys talked with Eden about this little plan of theirs?

"What time was Eden thinking of heading out?"

"Well, we're working on that."

Nate groaned quietly. "Gee, Ben. You mean you haven't run this past her yet?"

"Not exactly. We were thinking of telling her it's a surprise birthday party, so she can't say no."

"Whose birthday?"

Silence, and then, " Eden's birthday is the day after Thanksgiving."

Three weeks away. "Where is she now?"

"In the office, grading papers, I guess."

"Okay, here's the plan. You guys clean up the kitchen—"

"Already done," Devon said.

"Eden-style?"

"Well, no, but almost."

"When you're sure it'll pass her inspection, put the portable phone someplace where she'll be sure to hear it, and I'll call in about fifteen minutes." He'd need at least that long to figure out what to tell her. And plan his getaway in case the invitation didn't go over well.

After screwing up his courage, he dialed

Pinewood, and she answered with a breathy "Hello?"

"If I'm interrupting something, I can call back."

"No, I'm just a bit winded from running up and down the stairs with the laundry."

He came close to suggesting she let the boys do it, but fear of sounding tactless or intrusive stopped him. "Are you sitting down?" he said instead.

A moment of silence was followed by a short huff in his ear. *Oh, good gravy,* he thought, *don't let that be a sign she's still holding a grudge.*

"Where are the boys?"

"Out back, tossing the football around."

"If you go into the kitchen, you'll see that they've made chili…"

"I know. The whole house smells heavenly."

"…*lots* of chili."

He heard her boot heels clicking across the hardwood.

"Oh, my gosh! How many times did they double your recipe?"

"From the sound of things, enough times to feed all of you, and all of us. Twice." He considered the consequence of every word before saying, "They're planning a birthday surprise for you. They found two old canning kettles and jars in the basement. And did you a favor by using the canned goods and burger meat before it all expired. I'm supposed to take care of the cake and getting my family to show."

"They're something, aren't they?"

"Yeah, they are." He could hear the smile in her voice. "So what's this I hear about a new Pinewood resident?"

"Luke. He's adorable. And too smart for his own good."

In his opinion, they were all too smart for their own good.

"He isn't shy," Nate said. "I thought he'd talk my ear off when the guys introduced us."

"He's high-functioning autistic, so you'll notice a lot of stimming."

"Stimming. There's a term that's new to me."

"It's short for self-stimulation. We all do it to one degree or another—cracking our knuckles, tapping our toes, drumming our fingertips—but in kids on the spectrum, it's far more pronounced. They bob their heads or flap their hands, spin in circles, rock back and forth. Luke does it all to one degree or another, but handflapping seems to be his favorite stim."

"Well, from the way he talks, he sounds like a cool kid. I can't wait to meet him."

"So what time is this surprise supposed to take place?"

She sounded like the happy, upbeat woman

he'd met back in May. Hearing her talk this way made Nate want to say "Come over right now!" so he could enjoy it before something happened to flip the switch. Again.

"How's three o'clock?"

"That's doable. I'm looking forward to it."

"Me, too," he said, hoping he wouldn't be sorry later.

WHEN NATE BUILT the sixteen-by-six table for his dining room, every Marshall had razzed him. Tonight, even Hank gave it the thumbs-up.

"It's big enough for three or four more," she whispered with a mischievous wink and a nod toward Eden.

"That's about the craziest thing I've heard all day."

Hank feigned ignorance. "What do you mean, big brother?"

"Just take me at my word because it'd take a month to explain why that'll never happen."

"Tell you what. When I get back from Florida in a couple of weeks, I'll set aside a month. We'll sit down, just you and me."

"Florida?" their mother said. "Who's going to Florida?"

"I am, Mom. To Davie, for the Southeastern Circuit Finals at the Bergeron Rodeo Grounds. I told you about it, remember?"

"Yes, but you know how I try to block un-pleasantness from my mind." She laughed. "Will you be back in time for Thanksgiving?"

"Wouldn't miss it."

"Maybe you could teach us how to…what's it called again?" Wade said.

"Barrel racing."

Hank had performed in Steamboat Springs in August, and when Nate found out none of the kids had ever seen a real live rodeo, he bought tickets and treated Eden and the boys. Eden would have nixed the six-hour round trip if he hadn't suggested the boys could study the geom-etry of the barrel race figure eight. In the weeks since, it seemed the kids jumped on any ex-cuse to talk about roping, riding and Hank. No doubt they appreciated her horsemanship, but not nearly as much as her cowgirl good looks. Nate tried to imagine Eden in four-tone boots, a fringed jacket and a pearl button Western shirt. Tried to imagine her roping Thomas Burke into tagging along on the trip from Pinewood to the Double M. He studied Thomas's face, expect-ing to see anger, or at the very least, disdain. Instead, the kid seemed okay with the idea. So had *he* invited Burke? Or had Eden?

"Stop gawking," Hank warned out of the cor-ner of her mouth, "or you'll have to start that month of explaining right now."

Sure enough, half the people at the table had aimed watchful eyes his way.

A basket of corn bread sat in front of Eden's bowl, and Nate pretended not to see the other one within his reach. "Hey, Burke, how about passing that corn bread down here."

Nate's dad, seated to his left, looked confused. "We have our own basket already," he said, pointing. "And you already crumbled a slice into your chili."

"Oh. Right. So I did."

"You're not old enough to be senile," Zach teased. "I hear B vitamins help boost brainpower."

Nate was only too happy to be the butt of his cousin's joke, since it covered up the fact that he'd been staring at Eden.

"What do you call that thing," Cody asked Hank, "where a rider leans a horse almost on its side while she's going around the barrels?"

"I've never attended a rodeo," Luke said, "but I've watched documentaries and read books. That maneuver is called shouldering, and it's something riders work hard to avoid. Ideally, they attempt to keep the animal's shoulders and body straight up and down when they're making turns around the barrel."

Cody looked at Hank, who said, "He's right. Straight up is best, because the tilt could cause you to hit a barrel. And the judges deduct points for that."

"Has your horse ever been injured?" Luke wanted to know.

"Only once or twice, and not seriously. A rider tends to take very good care of the animal that's helping her earn fat purses."

"Hey, I have a question for you, Hank…"

Now all eyes were on DeShawn. "What's the deal with some horses getting all wigged out in the doorway at the rodeo?"

"The alleyway," she gently corrected. "It's called balking, and it's a bad habit some horses pick up. Mostly it isn't their fault. They could be reacting to the crowd, or some inconsiderate fool's litter rolling around on the ground. It could even be me, coming out so tensed up that the horse feels it in my leg muscles."

Chuckie, sitting directly across from Hank, flushed a bit when he said, "Did it take you l-long to l-learn all those tricks?"

"I'm still learning," she said. "If I ever get to the point where I think I know it all, I might as well hang up my saddle for good."

"Who taught you to ride?" Eden asked.

Hank glanced around the table at aunts, uncles, cousins, her parents and Nate. The Double M foreman had joined them, along with Jim and Bob, the only two hands who weren't out moving the cows up from the south fields. "I had a lot of good teachers," she said, smiling.

"Yeah, but it took some concerted effort," the foreman said, "and a lot of teamwork to break this li'l filly of her bad habits."

"You're fired, Carl," she said, winking. Getting to her feet, she smacked Nate's shoulder. "You're slacking, big brother. Don't we have one last job to do in the kitchen?"

"Oh, yeah, that's right." He stood, too. "I need two volunteers."

Hank gathered chili bowls and spoons, and Burke signaled Thomas, who followed. It didn't escape Nate's notice that he was frowning less than usual.

"You poke the candles into the cake," Nate told the boy. While lighting them, he focused on Burke. "Can you grab that stack of paper plates and make sure everybody gets one?"

Alone in the kitchen now, Nate gave credit to his family. They'd not only welcomed Eden's boys with open arms, overlooking the occasional crude remark and inappropriate gesture, and now, they'd accepted Thomas's father, no questions asked. Pride thumped in his chest. He'd do anything, anytime, for anyone at his table. His two rules did not apply to them.

He carried the cake into the dining room and slid it in front of Eden. He didn't know which glowed brighter, her dancing gray eyes or the flickering candle flames. She blushed prettily as the family sang a loud, off-key rendition of the birthday song, and when it ended, Hank handed her a knife.

"Time to earn your supper, girlfriend," she teased, plucking candles from the icing.

"Where'd you buy this, Nate?" his aunt asked. "It's delicious!"

"Didn't. Mom made it."

When the oohs ahhs died down, Eden said, "Thank you, Mrs. Marshall. I'm touched."

"Please. It's Maeve. Mrs. Marshall was my mother-in-law, may she rest in peace."

The warm family scene stirred something in Nate. Eden could be part of this, always—if he could just figure her out.

"You know what would top this day off perfectly?" Everyone turned to Hank. "A moonlight ride around the pond."

"Aw, man, that sounds awesome!" Ben said. He looked at Eden. "I know it's a school night and you wanted to hit the road by six, but if we promise not to goof off and get straight to bed, can we stay?"

Nate expected her to say no. Surprisingly, she said, "Sounds like fun!"

The boys cheered and the adults whistled.

"Do you know how to ride, Dad?"

It was the first time Nate had heard Thomas address Burke that way.

"I'm no rodeo cowboy, but I can sit in a saddle."

"Why don't you youngsters go have fun," his aunt said.

Nate's mom agreed. "Don't worry, this place will be shipshape long before you get back."

"I'll stay and help them," Zach said, pressing a kiss to Summer's forehead. "Just in case somebody around here decides it's time to add to the family this evening."

HANK LED THE WAY, and Nate brought up the rear. Luke, Burke and Thomas were directly in front of him.

"Are you having trouble staying balanced, Thomas?" Luke asked.

"Yeah, a little. But pipe down, will ya, or the guys will give me the business."

Luke glanced up the line. "Oh, I doubt that. As you can see, they're all far too busy concentrating on staying in the saddle themselves to pay any mind to you."

Nate chuckled as Thomas's shoulders slumped, a clear indication he didn't quite know what to make of the newest Pinewood resident.

"I read a book once that explained the physics

of balance, and I'm quite delighted to discover that the tactics actually work."

"Do you ever shut up?"

"Yes, of course…when I'm sleeping. Although I can't be certain that I don't talk in my sleep. Perhaps you can enlighten me some morning."

"Yeah. Sure. Okay. Whatever."

Luke seemed unaffected by Thomas's attitude. "It's important that when riders mount, they take the time to position themselves properly in the saddle before urging the animal forward. Take note of the way I'm sitting. Tall but relaxed, with no sway in my lower back. Both buttocks should meet the saddle with equal pressure. Imagine a line drawn from your ear to your elbow to your hip and ankle."

"You're my father," Thomas said to Burke. "Can't you save me from that?"

Burke laughed. "At least let him finish. I'm learning a lot!"

Luke continued. "Improper balance makes it difficult for some riders to follow their horses' motion. They use their legs, instead, to hold on. Or they grab the reins tightly. This can be dangerous, particularly when the rider attempts a turn."

"Luke, can I ask you a question?"

"Certainly, Thomas. Feel free to ask me anything."

"How long have you been talking like a college professor?"

"You know, I'm not sure. All my life, I imagine." He glanced over at his new friend. "Why do you ask?"

Burke cleared his throat loudly, and again Thomas's shoulders slumped.

"Just wondering, that's all."

"What's that noise?" Carlos asked.

"Just a cricket or somethin'," DeShawn said.

"Well, it's creepy."

"So are all those shadows in the woods." Nick cringed.

"And that creaky noise the trees make every time the wind blows." Ben did his best to emulate the sound, then gave an exaggerated shiver.

A nighthawk chirruped in the pines to their right. To the left, the throaty hoot of a great horned owl. The boys, typically talkative and inquisitive, grew quiet, and even Luke seemed content to scan the horizon, lulled by the steady thump of horses' hooves on the frosty loam. The only things missing, Nate thought, were guitars and the harmonizing voices of cowboys singing "Home on the Range."

"Hey, Nate," Ben called out. "I think my saddle cinch is loose. It feels like I'm sliding sideways."

He rode forward, slowing when Patches came up alongside the big gentle roan. It seemed fine

to him, but they'd been riding awhile, so he signaled the group to halt. They dismounted and
stood, holding tight to their horses' reins and
turning left and right in response to every buzz
and thud around them.

Eden joined them, watching as Nate snugged
up the cinch.

"Is everything all right?" she asked as he patted the roan's rump.

"Yeah, but they're looking a mite rough around
the edges," he began. "What say we turn back instead of riding the whole way around the pond?"

"I say that's a winning idea," Hank agreed. "I
need to get home and pack for Florida."

Suddenly, the calm was shattered by an ear-
piercing shriek. The terrified trumpeting of a
horse. A boy's screams and a man's shouts, all
in the space of a heartbeat.

Nate ran full-out toward the melee, and when
he reached the back of the line, what he saw
made the breath freeze in his throat: the cougar, trampled by Burke's horse, lay motionless
in a quickly spreading pool of blood.

Thomas pressed close to Nate's left side. Luke
did the same on his right.

"Is it…is it dead?"

"Yeah, Thomas, it is."

And from the look of things, so was his dad.

CHAPTER TWENTY

THE WAITING ROOM at Porter Adventist hummed with the low murmurs of what nurses had labeled That Marshall Bunch.

When the 911 operator heard "cougar attack," she'd radioed for a medevac copter. While waiting for it to arrive, Hank pointed out that the helicopter would spook the horses, and volunteered to lead the boys back to the barn. Eden stayed behind to be with Thomas, who refused to leave his father's side.

"He's breathing! I feel a pulse!" He repeated it so many times that at some point, it changed from a hopeful pronouncement to monotone acceptance.

After they wheeled Burke into the surgical suite, Thomas had leaned against the waiting room wall, chin up and back ramrod straight. In the three hours since, he'd slid to a seated position, hugging his knees, his face hidden in the crook of one elbow. And there beside him, with an arm across his shoulders, sat Luke.

Zach had met them at the ER, and now, he

and Nate walked out to the hall and slouched into two of six chairs lined up near the door.

"I don't get it," Zach said. "What would make the cat come out into the open that way, with so many horses and riders around?"

Nate drove a hand through his hair. It didn't make any sense to him, either. Unless…

"Her kittens must have been close to the trail. Burke and Thomas were the last two riders, and when I got back there, Burke's horse was snorting and stomping, partway into the woods."

"His horse stomped the cat?"

Nate nodded. "Only thing I could get out of Thomas was that Burke put himself between the cat and the boys."

"If he survives this, we need to buy him a saddle. Build him a house. Give him a car."

"And a job." Nate got up and peered through the window in the waiting room door. "Look at him, calm as can be. Hasn't shed a tear, either."

A nurse approached. "Mr. Marshall?"

"Yes?" the cousins said together.

She smiled up at them. "I just wanted to give you a heads-up that the police are on the way to interview Mr. Burke's son."

"You mean, they're in the lobby?"

She met Zach's eyes. "No, not yet. They were just dispatched, but they'll be here soon." She leaned closer and lowered her voice. "I know because my boyfriend is the dispatcher. I've seen how these accident interviews go. I'm sure the officers mean well, but they don't always take time for gentle diplomacy. So when I can, I like to give the families advance warning."

The cousins thanked her, and once she went about her business, Nate turned back to Zach. "The kid is doing his best to hide it, but he's already traumatized enough. If I can get some information out of him before the cops get here, maybe they won't need to talk with him at all."

Zach nodded toward Eden.

"You need me to run interference? Distract her while you take Thomas aside?"

"Nah." But he remembered all too well her reaction to his bumbling advice. This could go sideways, fast, and he knew it. He opened the door and hesitated in the opening. "But if she goes for my throat…"

Zach grinned. "Don't worry, I'll make sure Hank gets Patches."

As an afterthought, Nate walked up to the soda machine and bought two bottles of water. After handing one to Eden, he gave Luke two twenty-dollar bills. "Do me a favor, kiddo, and tell the guys they should go down to the cafeteria, grab a bite to eat. We'll meet you later."

Luke took the money and started rounding up his housemates.

Nate placed a hand on Eden's shoulder. "Maybe you should go with them. I'll stay with Thomas."

He thought she'd tell him to take a hike. To his surprise, she held up her cell phone. "Call me if there's any news?"

"You know I will."

Eden patted the hand resting on her shoulder, saying without words that she trusted him. He studied her face. Would she change her mind? He hoped not because he wouldn't hesitate to tell her that right now, this kid was priority one.

"Can I bring you anything?"

He held up his water bottle. "I'm good. But thanks."

She hugged Thomas and left them alone, and once she was gone, Nate sat on the floor next to him.

"Drink this," he said, giving Thomas the second bottle. "They won't let you in to see your dad if you pass out from dehydration."

Thomas unscrewed his bottle and nearly downed it in one gulp.

"Thanks," he said, scrambling to his feet. "I'm goin' crazy just sitting here, waiting. Can we go for a walk or something?"

Out in the hall, Nate pocketed his hands, and so did Thomas. They followed the shiny tiles to a dead end, where a bank of chairs overlooked the courtyard below. They sat, Thomas fiddling with a loose string on his jacket sleeve, Nate staring at the silent news broadcast on the TV hanging from the ceiling.

"He's gonna die, isn't he?"

"I don't know. But I can tell you this. Everyone in that waiting room is pulling for your dad."

"I'm glad the cougar finally got killed."

"How did that happen, anyway?"

Thomas gave one slow nod. "Well, it jumped out of the woods from way up high, like it had been in a tree. It came down real fast, making a weird, scary noise. It almost landed on my horse, but my dad yelled really loud. That's when everybody freaked."

The more he said, the faster he talked. Nate opened his mouth to stop him, but Thomas rushed forward.

"Then…then my horse reared up, and—and—and so did Dad's, and the cat did this kind of a crazy somersault in the air."

He was talking with his hands now, mimicking the cat's motions.

"Dad…he shoved me. And I fell, hard. The cat landed over by where Dad was standing. And then, and then I looked away. I heard the stomping and turned around. But by then—"

That must have been about the time Nate had

reached them, already talking to a 911 operator as he knelt beside Burke..

"Take care of him," Burke had rasped. "Tell him…sorry…and…I love him."

Nate handed Thomas his unopened bottle and relieved him of the empty one.

"Nate?"

He reached across the chair arms that separated them and gave Thomas's forearm a squeeze. "Yeah, kiddo?"

"What did he say to you?"

He'd thought Thomas was standing too far away to hear his dad speak. Apparently not. "He said he loves you."

Eyes closed, the boy said, "That's what I thought."

A fat, shiny tear dropped onto the back of Nate's hand.

"Figures," Thomas muttered. "Just when I get to where I almost like him, he leaves again."

"Have a little faith, kiddo. He's not gone yet."

"Yes. He is. I can feel it."

Drawing the boy close, Nate searched his mind for something to say, something deep and meaningful that might offer a morsel of comfort to this confused, heartbroken kid.

The sobs started slow and silent, then rose in volume and intensity.

"Mr. Marshall?"

He looked up, into the uncertain face of a uniformed officer.

"We'd like to have a word with—"

"Not. Now," he snarled.

"You're right." The cop put away his notebook. "This can wait."

Thomas sat up and rubbed his eyes with his knuckles. "It's okay, Nate," he said. "They just want to know what I saw." He gazed up at the cop. "Right?"

"You're sure you're up to this?" Nate asked.

"Might as well get it over with," he said dully. "Because when I go back in there, the doctor is gonna tell me that my dad is dead. And I probably won't be able to talk at all after that."

The officer met Nate's eyes. "Some kid," he said.

Nate would have agreed, heartily…if he thought he could get the words past the sob in his throat.

A WEEK AFTER Burke's funeral, the state assigned a new boy to Pinewood.

Connor Nelson, a month older than Thomas, spoke only in nods, grunts and one-word answers to specific questions. He'd been delivered, bruised and bloody, to the District 5 Police Precinct with a zipper bag safety-pinned to his jacket that held instructions for administering ADHD medications. Eden's reputation for reaching kids like Connor preceded her, so for now, Pinewood was his home.

Eden had taken Thomas aside and explained as much as she could about the boy's background. "He's terrified and probably doesn't understand anything that's happening to him. Can I count on you to look out for him, make sure he isn't exposed to too much noise or activity, at least until he has a chance to adjust?"

"Sure. Whatever."

She had a feeling it would be a good match. Connor was bright and resourceful, and although he communicated differently than Thomas, the boys had a lot in common. If they formed a bond, it would help Thomas continue to adjust to the loss of his father while helping Connor cope with his move to Pinewood.

That very evening, she found them alone in one of the classrooms, talking quietly.

"What happened to your face?"

Connor put a careful fingertip to the butterfly bandage covering his eyebrow. "My mother lost her temper," he said, running the tip of his tongue across his swollen, bruised lower lip. "But it wasn't entirely her fault."

Thomas tugged gently at the sling that helped support the fingers-to-elbow cast on Connor's left arm. "Still, she worked you over good, didn't she? Does it hurt much?"

The boy shook his head.

"So is your mom a drunk or a drug addict?"

"Depends on what she can get her hands on."

"Did the cops throw her in jail?"

"They will, when she's released from the hospital."

"Overdose, huh?"

"Not this time." He paused. "A neighbor complained about the noise. One thing led to another, and she fell down the stairs." He heaved a shaky sigh. "This time when she gets out, they're not gonna let me live with her."

Connor didn't know it yet, but Eden had learned that in addition to beating her son, officers had found drugs and paraphernalia in their home. She faced numerous criminal charges and the possibility of decades in prison. Eden didn't think she'd ever get used to hearing stories like Connor's.

Connor faced Thomas. "So I hear your dad died couple weeks ago?"

Thomas nodded, and recited a coolly impersonal version of what had happened.

"So he's a hero, then," Connor observed.

"*My* dad?" Thomas harrumphed. "Please."

Connor crossed the room and grabbed a battered copy of Webster's and read the definition. "Says here that a hero is a person admired for fine or noble qualities, '...as in putting one's life in jeopardy to save another, such as police officers, firefighters and soldiers.'"

He closed the book and returned to his seat beside Thomas. "I wrote a report about human DNA…got an A on it, too. It stands for deoxyribonucleic acid, the molecule that contains the genetic code of organisms."

Thomas slapped a palm to his forehead and whispered, "Oy. Not another Luke."

"Who's Luke?"

"Don't worry. You'll meet him soon enough. I'll give you a pair of my earplugs."

"Why?"

"Because he's like a walking Wikipedia. He never shuts up."

Connor put his fingertips together, raising and flattening them, like a spider doing push-ups on a mirror. "So anyway, like it or not, you're preprogrammed to be like your dad. You're gonna be a hero, too. Nothing you can do about it."

Thomas snorted. "Yeah, well, my dad was a drunk and a drug addict, and he served time in prison. Does that mean I'll do all that, too?"

Connor's brow furrowed as he considered the question. After a while, he said, "Guess that'll depend on the choices you make."

"How'd you get so smart?"

Connor sighed. "My IQ is 162. I'm not bragging. It's just a fact. I can't help being smart any more than you can help being a hero. Or, more accurately, becoming one someday."

Eden watched as Thomas slowly nodded, absorbing information that allowed him to love and respect his father despite his past.

Thomas slid an arm across Connor's shoulders. "Y'know, you're not so bad. Let's get out of this stuffy classroom."

"You should know that I don't like being touched.

"Bunk," Thomas said, giving him a sideways hug. "I'm not crazy about it, either. But since *smart* is in your DNA, you can figure out a way to deal with it. You know the old saying 'practice makes perfect'? Well, it's true. And you probably shouldn't put it off, because a lot of pushing and shoving goes on around here. It's the guys' way of saying they like you. Or they're mad at you. Or whatever."

They were walking toward the door. Eden didn't want to get caught eavesdropping, but she didn't want to miss a word of this, either.

"I appreciate the advice, Thomas. And just so you know? I was right about you."

"How's that?"

"Well, by alerting me to normal behavior here at Pinewood, you saved me from being razzed by the guys."

Thomas was nodding again. Then suddenly, he

laughed. For the first time since Burke appeared—and left—his life, he laughed as if he meant it.

"I hear ya, genius. But it's not heroism, like rescuing somebody or defending a village. That was just one friend helping another."

"Same thing, if you ask me."

"Not to blow your theory, but I have a confession. I wasn't always nice. It's something I learned from hanging around with an old friend."

"Does he live here? Because I think I'd like him, too."

"You'll meet him, but he doesn't live here. His name is Nate Marshall. He's a cowboy."

"Interesting. A cowboy hero…"

Eden ducked into the kitchen so they wouldn't catch her listening in. It felt good knowing that Thomas would be all right. That Connor would, too. And to think she'd almost decided against putting them together!

She was filling her Orioles mug with coffee when they entered the kitchen. It was the mug Nate always reached for when he was here.

"Hey, Eden," Thomas said.

"Hey, yourself. I hid some cookies in the microwave…"

"Awesome. Thanks." Thomas grabbed the plate and carried it to the table.

She pretended to focus solely on chopping vegetables for tonight's salad.

"Okay if I ask a personal question?" Connor asked.

Thomas poured two glasses of milk. "Depends..."

"Which tendency is your 'thing'?"

"I might tell you if I had a clue what you're talking about," he said, delivering the drinks.

Connor snickered quietly. "My 'thing' is electronics. Gets me into trouble. A lot. Because electricity can be dangerous."

It was an important detail, and Eden wondered why it hadn't been included in the boy's file.

Thomas nodded thoughtfully. "Guess you'd say my 'thing'," he said, biting into a cookie, "is fire."

CHAPTER TWENTY-ONE

IT HAD BEEN a gray and miserable week, with sleety rain and biting gusts that twirled around the house like a giant squid, knocking on windows and rattling doors. The wind shook the satellite dish out of alignment, too, giving the boys little to do after school but read and watch DVDs they'd already seen dozens of times. After four straight days of that, they were only too eager to head for the Double M for Thanksgiving.

A glance in the rearview mirror assured Eden that for the time being, Thomas was fine. But everyone handled grief differently. Some by putting their feelings out there every chance they got, others by not handling it at all. Thomas was one of the latter. Like a human chameleon, Thomas could mask his emotions. The night he'd run away to Nate's was a prime example. Despite having more or less forced an impromptu session on him after his father left that afternoon, he'd seemed rational to her. But then, he'd been in her care long enough to anticipate what she'd ask and deliver the expected answer. Going forward, she intended to shake things up, not only with Thomas, but with all the boys.

"Why are you doing all the work, Eden?" DeShawn asked.

It was a good question. When she'd heard that Nate's mom sprained her ankle, offering to pitch in seemed the right thing to do. If she'd known his aunts and female cousins wouldn't share in the meal preparations, she might not have been so quick to volunteer.

On second thought, she probably would have; the weather would force everyone to stay indoors, and all that time alone in the kitchen would be so much easier than making small talk with his family.

"Yeah, what's up with that?" Devon added.

"Nate's mom sprained her ankle, and his aunts and cousins…they have other stuff to do."

"We could help," Ben said.

Smiling, Eden said, "We'll see."

"So how big of a turkey does it take to feed fifty-seven people?" Greg asked.

A moment of silence was followed by Luke's explanation.

"An average-sized adult eats approximately one point five pounds of turkey," he said. "Which means the Marshall family will need to provide Eden with eighty-five point five pounds of meat to cook. The largest turkey on record weighed eighty-six pounds with his feathers on and his innards in." He pushed his glasses higher on his nose. "So the question, Greg, is how many turkeys—plural—does it take to feed fifty-seven people. And the answer, based on the fact that the average supermarket turkey weighs sixteen pounds, is three point five-six-two."

"Where does he *get* that stuff?" Cody asked.

"Same place I get it," Connor replied. "We *read*."

"I'm sure Mrs. Marshall has everything well in hand," Eden said.

DeShawn said, "She can't do much with a sprained ankle, though."

"You're right. Sometimes they're more difficult to cope with than a break."

"Yeah," Cody agreed. "You can walk on a cast."

And he would know, since he'd arrived at Latimer House wearing one.

"So you gonna do *everything*, since Miz Marshall can't stand?" Ben wanted to know.

"I'll help any way I can, and I'm sure if I need you, so will all of you."

They responded with feigned groans, and she looked into the rearview to say, "Spare me the theatrics. The Marshalls have been very good to us, and we're going to show them how grateful we are."

"Even if we aren't?"

"I'm surprised at you, Nick. Are you forgetting that Mrs. Marshall has baked chocolate cupcakes every time we've visited since she found out they're your favorite?"

"Aw, gimme a break. Everybody likes chocolate cupcakes. She didn't make 'em just for me."

She wasn't sure if he was kidding or not, but just in case, Eden said, "Let's table the attitudes, okay? It's no trouble to turn this van around and drive straight back home."

Their voices rose in protest, telling her they'd be on their best behavior at the ranch, and upon arrival, the boys quietly settled into their appointed rooms at Nate's house. Carl invited them to tag along as he inspected fences, and after they left, Eden started a big pot of chicken soup. While it simmered, she baked brownies and pies.

With her to-do list complete, Eden tucked a tablet and pen into her jacket pocket, stepped into her boots and headed out to the barn, thinking to make a list of things she could do out there tomorrow to get it ready for the guests. The sun had set and it was beginning to get dark, but she had no problem making her way down the flagstone path, thanks to patio lights that lined the walk.

Eden wouldn't have needed them, though, if she'd followed the sound of her boys' voices. She found them inside, cheerfully moving tables under Carl's supervision. But the foreman had about as much knack for decorating as Nate's horse.

"Let me help with this," she told him. "I'm sure you have better things to do than rearrange furniture."

He gave her hand a grateful squeeze. "You're a lifesaver, girl." Carl borrowed her pen and scribbled his cell number on her pad. "If you need anything, call."

She wondered if Nate had put him in charge of things like tables and helpers, or if, like herself, he'd volunteered. And where *was* he, anyway?

"Nate's on his way to Fort Collins."

Was she so transparent that he could read her face? "I thought Travis was riding home with a classmate."

"I don't write the news," Carl joked, heading for the door, "I just deliver it."

Travis was safer with Nate behind the wheel than a boy his own age. How typical of Nate to change the plans without so much as running the idea by her.

She sounded ungrateful and petty, even in her own head. If she'd grown up under the thumb of an angry, controlling man, her attitude might make sense. Except for losing her parents, her childhood had been idyllic. She blamed those tense, infuriating months with Jake for her irrational fear that Nate was trying to control her. The problem would vanish, if only she could stop comparing the two.

If wasn't as easy to dismiss other things she'd been doing—and saying—lately. She made a slow turn in the center of the barn, where recessed ceiling fixtures winked from massive ceiling beams and two-story windows glittered with a thousand tiny lights. The *Denver Post*'s coverage of Zach and Summer's wedding had shown a fun and casual hoedown reception. Readers had seen an entirely different side of the space in the *Denver Life Magazine* spread, which concentrated on the glitz and glamour of the elegant decorations. It was a bit of a letdown, stepping inside and realizing the Marshalls didn't decorate as elaborately for the Thanksgiving holiday.

Eden had an idea, and dialed Carl's number. "I hate to bother you so soon, but I was wondering…do the Marshalls hire caterers for most functions?"

"Yes'm, they do."

"What about casual family get-togethers? I'm guessing they have their own tablecloths and dinnerware for those, right?"

"Yes'm, in the kitchen. Just go through the door to the right of the stage. You should find everything you need in there. Anything else?"

"As a matter of fact, there is something I've been wondering. Where are all the Marshall women?"

He hesitated, as if searching for an explanation. "Everybody went to Denver to pick up stuff for Summer's baby shower."

"Goodness. They don't believe in waiting until the last minute, do they?"

He echoed her laugh. "Her mom threw her one in LA a month or so ago…her agent, some people she worked with back in the day. This one is for our family and friends, so I'm sure you'll get an invite."

She'd thrown a few showers for friends, and knew firsthand how much work and time was involved. Which raised the question of hired help. They brought in caterers for big bashes, yet did their own housework, cooking and laundry?

"I wonder why the Marshall women don't have maids," she said, mostly to herself.

"'Cause they're Marshalls, that's why, and Marshalls take pride in doing for themselves and for their own."

A spark of understanding flared in her mind as Carl ended the call. Nate had spent his whole life surrounded by independent women. She'd seen them together often enough to know he didn't just love them. He liked and respected their strength and grit. Before she'd allowed fear and uncertainty to shake her resolve, Nate had liked her, too. For every instance of his impatience or short temper he'd shown toward her, Eden could see a direct link to her own display of weakness.

Eden analyzed people for a living, so why hadn't she acknowledged before now that *she* was the proverbial fly in their relationship? He liked her. She liked him, so...

But who was she kidding? She didn't just like Nate. Eden had fallen in love with him, months ago.

She stepped into the barn's fully equipped kitchen, thinking, *If you'd just act like an adult and admit it...*

What was the worst that could happen, she wondered, making note of dinnerware and flatware, tablecloths and napkins, if she told him how she felt?

He could say she'd misunderstood his intentions. That he wasn't interested in anything more than friendship. How would she cope with *that*?

She peered into the double-doored fridge, saw four fat turkeys on the shelves.

"Only one way to find out," she said aloud.

EDEN KNOCKED QUIETLY, not wanting to wake Maeve.

"Come in, Eden."

She put the tray on the dresser and walked toward the double-wide windows. "I made some soup," she said, opening the blinds.

"And tea and a sandwich and fruit, I see," Maeve said. "My goodness, aren't you sweet!"

On the table were an unfinished puzzle, a paperback novel and a journal. Eden flapped one of the two napkins she'd brought and carefully covered the puzzle.

"That should keep it safe," she said.

"Oh, the books are mine, but the puzzle is Royce's. He's been working on it for months." She rolled her eyes. "Sometimes he sits there for hours, humming, whistling, sliding pieces back and forth while I'm trying to sleep." Maeve laughed. "Biggest decorating mistake I ever made was putting that table by the window."

"Is this too much light for you?"

"No, no, it's just fine." She inhaled. "Mmm, that soup smells like a little bowl of heaven."

"It's my grandmother's recipe."

"'Alice's One of a Kind Chicken Soup'?"

How could she have known?

"She shared that recipe with me years ago, and it's always a hit around here."

"I didn't realize you and Gran knew one another."

"Oh, yes. We go way back." She counted on her fingers. "Sang with the Sweet Adeline's. Volunteered at the hospital. Worked in the soup kitchen. And we were members of the same book club."

"You know, I *do* remember those things." Eden pulled out the chair nearest the window and slid a stool from the vanity for Maeve's ankle. "Gran loved to sing. And I don't remember a time when she wasn't reading a book."

Maeve threw back the covers and climbed out of bed. "So how are the Thanksgiving plans coming? Is everybody running around like headless chickens?"

"I wouldn't go that far, but they're busy."

Eden helped her limp over to the table. "You're going to sit with me while I eat, right? It'll save you the bother of coming all the way back up here later to get the tray."

"Well, I have a cake in the oven," she said, checking the timer on her phone, "but I can stay for a while."

"So tell me, Eden Quinn, how did you get into the business of saving lost boys?"

"Oh, I don't save them. They save themselves. I just make sure they have a safe nest and food in their bellies until they're ready to fly."

"That isn't the way Nate tells it, but please. Continue."

Nate had discussed her? With his mother? Eden didn't know what to think about that. "After college, I worked as a patient advocate for a while, but that didn't work out."

"I imagine it can be a stressful job, especially when you're working with families that sometimes refuse to cooperate, even to help their loved ones."

"That did happen, but it's not why I left. The guy I dated in college ended up working at the same hospital as me, in human resources. Jake's suggestion to merge that department with patient advocacy saved the hospital a lot of money, and they rewarded him with a promotion… which made him my boss."

"Ah, the old 'familiarity breeds contempt' thing, eh?"

Eden smiled. "Something like that."

"So you moved on to a job that's not only challenging and complicated, but dangerous, as well."

"Dangerous?"

"Well, it stands to reason," Maeve said. "The boys come to you because abuse and neglect

have put them on the wrong path. It's only nat-
ural they're angry and mistrustful of adults."

"I don't know what Nate told you," Eden said,
"but I've never felt as though I'm working in an
unsafe environment."

"Oh, he didn't say a word. Having grown up
in a house full of boys, then marrying into a
mostly male family, I notice things others might
not." She patted Eden's hand. "I never meant
to imply the Pinewood boys aren't good kids,
or that you aren't capable of caring for them. It
was just an observation, that's all."

There had admittedly been a few close calls—
boys getting into fistfights, making idle threats
when people gawked at them in public. But she
took pride in having defused every alterca-
tion and watched the troublemakers even more
closely to prevent future disputes. After what
she'd overheard between Connor and Thomas
the other evening, Eden knew she had to pay
extra attention to both boys. But what had
Nate's mother seen to inspire her questions?
Something that Eden hadn't?

"This is delicious, Eden! Alice must have left
out a key ingredient, because mine doesn't taste
nearly as good!"

"Just between you and me, I altered her recipe
by adding a jar of store-bought chicken gravy
and half a teaspoon of light brown sugar."

"Oh, how clever! Your secret's safe with me. And you know? I can count on one hand—and have fingers left over—the number of people willing to divulge their secret ingredients. That son of mine was right about you."

Eden stared at two puzzle pieces that looked like mates. Sure enough, they snapped together. Was there any hope she and Nate might fit together that well someday?

"Horrible thing that happened to your Mr. Burke. I've tossed and turned for days, thinking about that poor little boy seeing the whole awful thing. He'll probably have nightmares for years."

It had been fifteen years since her parents were killed, and although Eden hadn't witnessed the shooting, she still had an occasional nightmare. "He's doing as well as can be expected, but you're right. Even adults raised in loving, stable families would suffer aftereffects from something like that."

"I can't think of anyone better suited to get Thomas through this. And he seems like he's got a good head on his shoulders."

Would Maeve say the same thing if she knew about Thomas's "thing" for fire?

The image of Thomas, staring wide-eyed into a fire of his own making, sent a shiver down Eden's spine.

CHAPTER TWENTY-TWO

"I DON'T BELIEVE my eyes," Cora said. "Four-alarm Texas chili? As the main course at a Marshall family Thanksgiving? What were you thinking, girl!"

There were fifty-seven people gathered in the Marshalls' barn, and even the youngest of them was looking at Eden now.

"Well, there's turkey, too, and all the sides." *Three point five-six-two turkeys*, Eden thought, recalling Connor's math lesson. "It's just that the boys made the chili, and there was so much left over from the other—"

The room erupted in laughter, whistles and applause.

"Congratulations," Summer said, lifting her goblet of apple juice, "you've just been tricked by one of the trickiest tricksters this side of the Mississippi!"

Her gaze went instantly to Nate, whose innocent expression was meant to imply he'd had nothing to do with it. But clearly, he'd enlisted the assistance of Cora and the boys in the whole "let's razz her about serving a Lone Star dish at a Denver Thanksgiving feast," and their happy, slightly guilty faces were all the proof she needed.

Eden raised her goblet. "I read somewhere that at the conclusion of a good prank, the victim—ah, prankee—is supposed to sing the praises of the pranker. But I have a terrible voice, so…happy Thanksgiving…*Cora*!"

"Another point in her favor," Nate's mom said. "She can take a joke!"

Handshakes, hugs and kisses were followed by a volley of holiday-related jokes.

"What's the most musical part of the turkey?"

"Drumstick!"

"Why did the turkey cross the road twice?"

"To prove he wasn't chicken!"

"What kind of music did the Pilgrims listen to?"

"Plymouth Rock!"

As bowls and baskets and platters were passed from table to table, Eden smiled. She'd grown up in a happy home, but nowhere near as happy as this one. Of all the emotions swirling inside her, envy seemed strongest, because this soul-stirring cacophony had begun generations ago in the shadow of Sweet Mountain, where it took root, sprouted and spread, producing family unity, love and loyalty. What they'd built...this was what Eden had longed for since childhood.

Eden glanced up and caught Nate looking at her, blue eyes gleaming and lips slanted in a tantalizing, flirty grin. For one heart-pounding, soul-stirring instant, they were connected. When he broke eye contact, her wish drifted away like a bluebird feather sails on a calm breeze, only to fade into the morning mist.

Eden had a whole new reason to tell him how she felt.

Because if she couldn't share her dream with her hero cowboy, she'd rather not dream it at all.

ON HIS WAY back from delivering Travis to Fort Collins, Nate stopped at Pinewood to return Connor's backpack and Ben's retainer. He hadn't peeked into the bag, but based on the little he'd picked up about the newest kid, it was a pretty sure bet it contained at least one electronic device. It was just as likely that Eden had noticed something missing when Ben smiled. So why hadn't she called to see if anyone had found the appliance?

The minute Kirk opened the door, the robust scent of tomato sauce greeted Nate on the doorstep.

"Lasagna?"

"Spaghetti and meatballs." The young teacher

waved him inside. "With salad, garlic bread…" He leaned closer to whisper, "And chocolate cake for dessert."

And if he knew Eden, she'd brewed a big pitcher of old-fashioned sweet tea to wash it all down. Nate held out the retainer case and backpack. "Couple of the kids forgot stuff at the house over Thanksgiving, and since Pinewood's pretty much on my way home, I thought I'd drop them off, save you or Eden having to pick them up."

Eden breezed into the foyer. "That was nice of you," she said around a stack of bed linens. "Thanks."

"No problem. Pinewood's practically on the way," he repeated.

"If you're not in a hurry, you're more than welcome to join us for supper."

Why did it seem that 90 percent of their most pleasant interactions took place over food? He remembered his plan to lay it all out there— admit how he felt about her—and hopefully interact over a couple of kisses, instead.

"I should have it on the table in half an hour or so." Her tone was polite and friendly, but Nate noticed tension in her brow. "The kids will be thrilled to see you again so soon."

The kids, not her. Nate wondered if his disappointment showed.

"This will only take a minute. Make yourself

comfortable, and help yourself to…whatever." Eden disappeared into an upstairs room.

"It's fresh sheets day," Kirk explained, leaning on the newel post. "I'd help, but I have a class to teach. See you at supper."

Eden had fourteen beds to change, counting her own. If he helped, they'd finish in half the time. And maybe she'd have a few minutes to sit and talk when there *wasn't* a mountain of food on the table—or thirteen nosy boys sitting around it.

He took the steps two at a time and followed the sound of soft, sweet humming. He found her in a room where two sets of bunk beds dwarfed the space and knocked lightly on the open door so as not to startle her. Nate waited until she'd flapped the sheet over the mattress cover before grabbing a corner to help her tuck it in.

"You don't have to do that," she said.

"Yeah, I kinda do."

And there it was again, the arched left brow that said *back off*.

At least she let him pitch in, and as predicted, they made quick—and mostly quiet—work of the bunks. When they finished, she handed him a stack of folded sheets.

"Since you seem determined to help, could I get you to change just the top bunks in the rest of the bedrooms? That'll save me having to drag my stepstool around."

"If it'll get me to a couple minutes alone with you sooner, I'm happy to…shorty."

"Thanks, Nate," she said, ducking into the room behind her.

For a moment, he stood in the hallway, sheets pressed to his chest, wondering how things between them had gotten so far off track. They'd argued after the pizza party, but that didn't explain everything. A woman in her line of work didn't just go ballistic over a little ill-timed advice. He'd known her for months before that, and they'd connected. He licked his lips, remembering the way she'd kissed him. The way *she'd* kissed *him*. Nate shook his head and headed into the nearest room. Would he ever feel comfortable in her presence again? Did he really *want* to?

Yeah, he did. In truth, he wanted to feel a whole lot more than comfortable. He wanted to feel connected.

Forget the rules, he told himself.

DOWNSTAIRS, WHILE EDEN prepped the pasta pot, Nate set the table.

"Thanks," she said. "Can you remember a time when I didn't foist a household chore on you?"

He grinned. "You're feisty. But foisty? No way."

"Well, one of these days, I'll surprise you, invite you over and treat you like a real guest. No washing dishes, no setting the table, no making up bunk beds."

"That's the last thing I want. Helping out makes me feel like family." He laid out the last plate. "I *like* feeling like family, because—"

"Please. You've already got enough family to populate a small city." Then she surprised him by flopping into a chair at the end of the table.

"How's your mom? Still limping?"

"Nope. If I didn't know better, I'd say she only ducked into her room to get out of making Thanksgiving dinner."

"Really? But I thought you said she loved parties. The bigger, the better, you said. Everything, from the planning to the cooking and even the cleanup!"

"I have a theory about that."

"And I thought the Marshall women loved getting together to make those big parties happen. Especially family gatherings."

"I have a theory about that, too."

She got up, poured two glasses of sweet tea and carried them to the table.

"So these theories of yours," she said, sitting down and hugging her knees to her chest, "they wouldn't have anything to do with a test, would they?"

"I haven't confirmed it, but yeah, maybe."

"See, now that makes sense." Eden laughed. "All weekend, I felt like the little red hen."

Nate only vaguely remembered the children's story, and when he admitted it, Eden provided a plot summary. The hen asks for help from the rest of the barnyard animals, first for planting and harvesting grain, then to mill the wheat into flour, but each request is met with "Not I!" Until, of course, she asks who'd like to help eat the bread she bakes after all her hard work.

"On second thought," she said, "that's a terrible analogy."

"How do you figure? The hen worked alone, and so did you."

On her feet again, she poured the noodles into boiling water. "The hen asked for help," Eden said. "I didn't. I'm sure if I *had* asked for any, an army of Marshall women would have shown up."

Nate knew they would have, but their help would have been beside the point.

They hadn't asked him, but he had a feeling everyone at the Double M knew how he felt about Eden. They'd probably known before he admitted it, himself.

But a rancher's life could be hard, so they'd

put Eden through her paces to see how well she'd stand up under pressure, thinking that if she managed to pull off a traditional sit-down dinner for fifty-seven family members and friends, all by herself, with no whimpering or whining, they could rest easy, knowing Nate had chosen a woman strong enough to stand beside him, no matter what life threw at them.

Eden had passed their test, but she hadn't passed his: he wanted the old Eden back, and wouldn't settle for anything less. First chance he got, he aimed to get it all out in the open and let the chips fall where they may. If she passed *that* test, he'd ask her to marry him.

DURING THE DRIVE HOME, Nate made a decision, and the moment he reached the ranch house, he dialed Stuart's number.

"The older I get," her brother said, "the more I believe everything happens for a reason. I've been meaning to talk with you, explain a few things about Eden. Things that go back to our childhood. Can't talk now, 'cause I'm on duty. But I'm off tomorrow."

Nate couldn't help being curious. "You name the time and place."

"Tom's Diner, nine o'clock?"

He'd have to rearrange a few things, but it would work. "Nine sounds good."

"Great. And let's keep this on the down-low," Stuart said. "At least for the time being."

The following morning, Nate chose a table near the window at Tom's. Stuart was right on time, and in uniform.

"'Mornin'," he said, sliding into the booth. He got the waitress's attention. "Hey, Tammy. Could we get some coffee over here?"

"Thought you had the day off," Nate remarked.

"I did, but a buddy's wife went into labor. It'll be me in his boots someday, I hope. And you know what they say about karma." He shrugged. "Anyway, I'm glad you could meet me, 'cause I've been wondering how much Eden told you about our past."

"I know you lost your parents at a young age. That's about it."

"Really?" He sounded surprised. "She didn't tell you why I became a cop?"

"No."

"Well, I'm not surprised. Neither of us talks about it much. Except on the anniversary..."

Stuart's shoulder radio hissed and crackled, and he turned down the volume. "Don't tell Eden, but I've signed on with the Denver PD. Put a down payment on a house right next door to Pinewood. It's in foreclosure, so it'll be a while before I can move in." He held up one hand. "I know, I know," he said, "you think it's weird that I didn't tell her. I just didn't want her wigging out, you know, while I'm still assigned to District 3."

"Whoa. Rough neighborhood."

"One of the roughest. But I'm taking the detective's test soon. If I pass, I'll be reassigned. But I digress."

Their parents had been at a dinner party, Stuart explained, came home early and surprised a burglar, who killed them both. It took years for the cops to find the killer. Soon as he was old enough, he joined the Baltimore police force, hoping to help with the search. Eventually, after the killer was arrested during an armed robbery, a savvy public defender found a loophole in the case, and the guy served two years instead of the double life sentence he'd earned. Furious and frustrated, Stuart needed to get away from all of that, so he moved to Colorado and hired on with the Boulder police force…and started making risky decisions, such as volunteering to go undercover; guilt over the sleazy things he'd been forced to do caused him to turn to alcohol.

Nate had relived the accident a thousand times, awake and asleep. How often had Eden and Stuart relived *that*? "Where were you two that night?" he asked.

"Not at home, thank God. We were spending the weekend with my mom's parents."

"How long after… When did they send you to Colorado?"

Stuart shook his head. "A week, two weeks maybe, after the funerals. That part's a little fuzzy." Understandably, Nate thought.

"This diner has been our favorite place since we were kids. Our grandparents brought us here every Sunday after church. Eden and I kept meeting here, once a month or so, even after they died, so I never saw it coming when she picked me up as usual, but instead of bringing me here, she delivered me to a rehab center. Told me if I didn't go in willingly, she'd have a talk with my sergeant, and that if I didn't stay, she'd walk it up the chain of command until the department made it mandatory.

"So I put in the two months. Never gave a thought to who was paying for it. Until one of the nurses slipped and told me how lucky I was to have a sister like Eden. She'd sold the jewelry, antiques and silver our grandmother left her. And when I got out, I found out she'd called in a couple of favors so that instead of a couple months' worth of desk duty, I served two weeks."

"That's some story," Nate admitted. "I'm sorry for your loss." Eden's decision to work with troubled teens made more sense to him now. "But help me out here, Stuart. Why are you telling me all this?"

"Because she's in love with you."

"She's…" Nate swallowed. Hard. "She said that?"

"Didn't have to. I can read her like a book. And something tells me you have feelings for her, too."

He paused, then added, "Look, you seem like a decent guy." Stuart shook his head. "Okay, I *know* you're a decent guy."

"You had me checked out?"

"Yeah." He winced. "Sorry."

"Don't be. I'd do the same in your shoes."

"But here's the thing. If she keeps acting hot and cold, you're gonna walk. I'd do the same in your shoes," he said, quoting Nate. He sat back, glanced at his watch. "My sister wasn't always like this. You've got my word on that. This stuff with her boys, I'm sure you know that's just *Eden*. She's always been a person who'd go to any lengths to protect the people she cares about. And it didn't start when she took this job."

Stuart launched into a story about when he was fourteen or so, when he got it into his head to start a fire in their grandparents' backyard so they could toast marshmallows. The wind picked up, carried sparks to their grandmother's winter-dry hedge and the shed roof.

"Eden sent me inside to tell our grandparents.

When we got back out there, she was shivering in the dark, soaked to the skin thanks to the leaky hose, but the fires were out. She told them the whole thing was her idea, that she hadn't counted on the wind. They said she should have known better at her age, and grounded her for six months. I tried to tell them it was me, but she wouldn't let me get a word in edgewise."

"I don't get it. Why would she take the blame?"

"Because I was an out-of-control brat. Always in some sort of trouble, and I'd just been suspended from school. For the second time that year. Gramps was at his wits' end. He'd already shown us the stack of military academy brochures he'd sent away for. Said next time I got into trouble, he'd pack me up and deliver me to one so fast it'd make my eyeballs rattle in their sockets. Evidently, Eden believed him."

Nate got it now. Historically, she'd been the rescuer, not the rescued.

"This temperamental behavior didn't start until that jerk landlord of hers messed with her sense of stability. Eden's probably sleep-deprived, too. And I know my moods are shot when I haven't gotten enough shut-eye. All this to say I hope you'll cut her some slack."

What could he say? *Well, it's like this Stuart, I've* been *cutting her slack!* Clearly, not enough slack.

"I might be a little biased, but she's good people. I'd bet my badge that she'll pull herself together soon."

The radio crackled again, and Stuart turned it up a notch.

"Two-one-four, do you copy?"

"This is two-one-four," Stuart said.

"Respond to a 10-21 at 573 South Main."

"Ten-four, on my way." He slid from the booth. "Probably just someone punching in the wrong code on their burglar alarm." Hand extended, he added, "Good seeing you, Nate. You'll think about what I said?"

"Good to see you, too," Nate said, shaking it. "And yeah, you can count on it."

Driving back to the Double M, Nate rehashed the conversation. Stuart believed Eden had saved his life. And Nate had seen rock-solid evidence of all she'd done for those boys. What a hypocrite he'd been, judging her as moody and erratic when his own behavior hadn't exactly been rational.

He could pretend it was because he hadn't adhered to the two rules…

…or admit that he was crazy in love with her.

CHAPTER TWENTY-THREE

STUART GAVE EDEN a dual surprise: He'd taken a job with the Denver PD, and, tired of waiting for the bank to sign off on the foreclosure, he'd bought Shamus's house. The older man had decided to move into an assisted living center.

"It'll take some getting used to," she admitted, "but it'll be great having you right next door."

Nate was flattered to have been part of the secret. Flattered that Stuart had included him in the invitation to the housewarming party, too. His only question was how he'd moved in without Eden noticing—and kept Shamus quiet in the two weeks since their meeting.

After introducing everyone to his new girlfriend, Stuart took Eden's kids into the kitchen to help him cook up some frozen pizzas, and Eden said she wanted to check out the backyard where she and her brother had spent so many happy afternoons.

Nate followed her.

"Why so quiet?" he asked.

"Oh, it's nothing. Silly stuff, really." She

shrugged. "It's just hard to imagine Shamus in an assisted living center. He's always been so active and energetic. I can't believe I let myself get so wrapped up in my own problems that I didn't know about any of this. I would have loved to help him out."

"And just how would you have managed that?"

"I could have done some housework or laundry, yard work, gone shopping for him, *something*."

"When? In the middle of the night? You already have too much on your plate. Shamus knows that, and so does Stuart."

Nate wasn't sure, but when she looked up at him, he thought he noticed the hint of a wistful smile.

"Makes me a little homesick, being here. This place is like a time capsule. My grandparents had the same beautiful old fixtures as Shamus before the Hansons ruined them."

Taking her hand, he led her to the porch swing.

"What does this remind you of?" he asked as she sat beside him.

"That my grandfather made one just like it at Pinewood. Both of these houses will probably fall down before this swing comes apart."

"The boys told me that he hung the swing right here on the porch so that your grandmother could enjoy her roses, even in the rain."

"And the rest of the flower beds," Eden said. "We worked day and night for weeks, Gran and I, gathering these football-sized rocks to line all the beds."

Eden continued listing memories—Shamus's shed, designed and built by her grandfather, hand-painted ceramic gnomes and toads her grandmother had fired in her kiln, the hanging basket she'd crocheted when Shamus turned fifty.

When it seemed she'd run out of them, Nate said, "Those memories aren't like glass doorknobs or brass light fixtures. They're etched into your heart, and no matter where life takes you, that's right where you'll find them."

A silent second passed, and then she aimed a mischievous grin his way.

"Gosh. I never would have figured you for the poetic type."

"There's a lot you haven't figured out about me, Eden."

"I'm sure you're right."

Her voice, barely a whisper, changed. Was she crying? Nate leaned forward, and sure enough, tears glistened on her long lashes.

"Eden," he said, turning slightly, "I didn't mean to upset you. The opposite, actually."

She gave his hand a reassuring pat. "I know. These are happy tears."

Happy tears. Nate sighed. He'd been surrounded by women of all ages for his whole life, but he didn't think he'd ever understand that line.

"Your hands are cold." He wrapped them in his own. "You want to go in?"

"Not yet." She sighed, then added, "Promise me something, Nate."

"Anything, anytime." And he meant it.

"Next time I start feeling sorry for myself, will you remind me of everything you just said?"

"Even the poetic stuff?"

"Especially the poetic stuff."

And then she kissed him like she meant it.

He thought about taking a breath, just long enough to tell her that he loved her. But he had a feeling he'd recite those words a thousand times in the years to come.

So he returned the kiss, instead.

CHAPTER TWENTY-FOUR

"I KNOW YOU'VE been busy," Nate said, waving Eden out to his porch, "so I got you a little surprise."

Her gaze traveled from the bottom to the top of a Douglas fir. "A *little* surprise? That tree is at least eight feet tall!"

"I'll throw it into the back of the truck and follow you back to Pinewood," he said as if he hadn't heard her. "Do you like it?"

He seemed so pleased with himself that Eden didn't have the heart to tell him it would never fit in the Pinewood family room. Not without slicing two feet from the bottom and moving the recliner to the parlor.

"It's perfect. And smells like the forest."

"I cut it down myself, just this afternoon, so it should last all through the season."

Eden noticed two big shopping bags beside the tree. "What's that?"

"Garland, lights, ornaments, a wreath, even an angel tree-topper."

"But I have all of those things up in the attic."

"I know. But Travis told me they're all old, and barely covered your six-foot artificial tree. What would you say about putting that one in the parlor and this one in your family room, so the boys can enjoy it while they're watching TV and stuff? If they all pitch in, we could have the outside lights strung and the wreath hung before dark. It's supposed to rain, so we can take care of the inside tomorrow."

"A poet *and* a Christmas addict, are you?"

"Actually," he said, "I've never been keen on the holiday. Too noisy and messy, gaudy colors, commercialism…what's to like? At least, that's how I felt before…"

"Before what?"

"Before Memorial Day."

Eden instantly got his meaning. Smiling, heart drumming, she said, "We'll need to rearrange the furniture a bit to make room for it, but I think it'll look great near the patio doors."

"Aw, man, you're right. It's way too big for your place. I came *this* close to getting a blue spruce, instead. They look just as good, but they're skinnier." He started down the steps. "I'll go back."

"But it'll be dark in a few minutes!"

"Relax. I have a flashlight. Besides, I know those woods like the back of my hand."

"Really, Nate, a little fine-tuning, and this one will—"

Standing beside his pickup, he said, "Tell you what. You and the boys get the pizzas ready and figure out which movie you want to watch while I hunt for something smaller. I'll text you some pictures. It'll be like shopping at an on-line Christmas tree lot, only better." He slid in behind the steering wheel.

"I wish you wouldn't. I really *like* this tree!"

"It's no trouble. Honest. I'll be back before you can say Rudolph the Red-Nosed Reindeer."

He backed down the drive as DeShawn joined her on the porch.

"Is that for us?" he said, pointing at the tree.

Grinning, she picked up the bags and headed inside. "Yup."

"Man," he said, "this'll be interesting. I've never decorated a redwood before."

"Be nice," Eden said, laughing. "He meant well."

"Where's Nate going in such a hurry?" Carlos asked.

"He thinks this tree is too big for our family room, so he's going back to cut down a smaller one."

"He's right." Carlos looked toward the top. "We could put King Kong up there instead of a star."

Squealing tires and the blare of a car horn silenced their laughter. Eden whirled around as Nate leaped from his truck without taking time to slam the door.

"Where are the rest of the boys?"

"Inside. Why?"

"Keep them there." Walking backward, he pointed at the orange glow, visible beyond the bunkhouse roof.

"Fire in the barn?" DeShawn whispered. His voice was shaking when he yelled, "The horses! Let me help you get the horses out of there, Nate!"

"No way!" he bellowed. "Stay put." He pointed at Eden. "Call 911, then call my folks and tell 'em what's going on. They'll spread the word to the rest of the family."

With that, he turned and disappeared into the darkness.

Like a robot, Eden followed his orders.

"I didn't smell anything, did you?" DeShawn asked.

Nick said, "Nope."

"Maybe that's a sign the fire hasn't gotten out of control," Carlos suggested.

But the glow was brighter now, and that could mean only one thing. After reporting the fire to 911, Eden dialed Stuart's number. Maybe he knew people who could move things along faster. She got his voicemail and left a message, her voice sounding wooden and strange in her own ears.

By now, all of the boys had gathered on Nate's deck.

"I think we should get over there," DeShawn said. "I know he said he doesn't need help, but you know how he is."

"The dispatcher said the fire department is on its way. So stay put," Eden ordered.

"Are you kidding? It'll take them half an hour to get here. He can't put out that fire all by himself!"

Good point, Eden thought, hugging herself to fend off the chill. "Let's hope they get here sooner than that." *Lots sooner.* "But for the time being, let's do what Nate asked us to, okay?"

They formed a semicircle around her. "It's freezing out here. Get your coats and gloves, then come back out. No matter what, nobody leaves this deck, got it?"

Thankfully, they complied without complaint.

"While you're inside, find Thomas. He's probably in Nate's office, looking something up on the computer. Let him know what's going on and tell him I said to come out here."

While they darted inside, Eden shrugged into her coat. Had Nate been wearing one? She couldn't be sure, so she grabbed the gray duster at the end of the rack.

The heat intensified as she moved closer to the barn. If Nate hadn't worn a coat, he sure wouldn't need one!

Twenty yards from the entrance, she heard the boys running up behind her.

"I told you to stay on the deck!"

"We're not going into the barn," Carlos said. "We just wanted to make sure Nate doesn't need help getting the horses into the back corral. Plus, you shouldn't be by yourself."

Her heart squeezed at their compassion, but she couldn't let her boys put themselves in danger. "If he needs our help, he'll ask for it. Now step back up, I mean it, or I'll send the lot of you inside."

She did a mental head count, heart beating harder when she didn't see Thomas. "Didn't you tell Thomas—"

"I looked everywhere for him," Devon said. "When I couldn't find him, I figured he slipped past me and was already out here with you."

By now her heart was hammering. She didn't want to think about what his absence likely meant.

"Try again. He has to be somewhere in the house," she said, though she knew deep down that the boys wouldn't find Thomas inside.

"Look," Ben said, pointing at the corral.

Nate was in there with some of the horses.

"I wish they'd stand still," Devon said. "I can't count 'em!"

"They're scared," Connor explained. "Soon as they figure out they're safe, they'll calm down."

"He's right," Luke agreed. "Carl told me about a field fire that happened when Nate was a youngster. A bad one that killed a couple of his father's best horses. Carl said that's why when Nate built his barn, he installed double doors at the back and a split-rail alleyway that leads into the corral."

Normally, when these two spouted facts and figures, the others responded with good-natured ribbing. Tonight, their encyclopedic knowledge was strangely comforting to them all.

"Once all the horses are out of the barn," Connor continued, "Nate will close off the corral gate, so they can't turn around and run back toward the barn." By now, the fire had doubled in size and intensity. One look at the flames clawing the sky like malicious witch fingers, and Eden wished she *was* a robot, because machines couldn't feel fear. Or heartache. Or dread.

Earlier, when the boys voted to watch a science-fiction movie, Thomas had cursed at them. When she read him the riot act for his language, he'd cursed her, too. So she'd sent him into the seldom-used living room to calm down. Could he be in there?

"Thomas loves fire," Connor pointed out.

And when the others perked up at the statement, he added, "He told me it fascinates him. So it's highly unlikely he's inside. Either he's at a window, watching, or—"

"Listen," Ben said, "sirens!"

DeShawn harrumphed. "Took 'em long enough."

Eden held out her arms and the boys joined her in a group hug. "I know you want to help—and I love you for it—but you need to stay here, stay *safe*. I have to let Nate know that Thomas might be in there." She nodded toward the barn.

"We ain't goin' nowhere," Carlos said. "Promise."

Nate had just secured the slide bolt on the corral gate when she ran up. Sweat-streaked soot coated his haggard face and hands as he stomped toward the fence that separated them.

"Didn't I tell you to stay in the house?"

She held out his jacket. "Put this on. It's freezing out here and you're soaked to the skin."

He hesitated, but only for a moment. "Thanks," he managed before a coughing jag stopped him.

"Wish I'd thought to bring a bottle of water. You need—"

"What I need is for you to get back to the house," he choked out, "and take those kids with you."

"I will, but..." Eden gripped his forearm. "Nate, Thomas is missing."

He blinked once, twice, and her heart beat double-time as he turned on his heel and disappeared into the rolling black smoke.

As the fire roared, sirens screamed and the blast of a fire engine's air horn shook the ground. Strobe lights crisscrossed the sky as emergency vehicles raced up the drive—two white-and-gold pumpers, one EMT unit, three police squad cars.

Eden ran up to the first firefighter. "Nate Marshall is in there," she shouted over the clamor of motors, men shouting, the growl of the inferno, "along with a teenage boy, Thomas Burke."

He nodded and, voice muffled by his face mask, said, "Where?"

Nate had been in and out of the stall area and would have seen Thomas, if that's where he'd hidden.

"He's probably in the loft."

He signaled his comrades, who charged forward, shouldering axes, pry bars and hoses. "You're safer in the house," he said, "and so are those kids, because there could be propane or other combustibles in there."

Eden jogged back to the boys, whose voices blended in a myriad of questions. Once they'd settled around Nate's kitchen table, she passed out bottled water and did her best to answer them. Not an easy feat, she admitted, sliding a bag of popcorn into the microwave, since she knew little to nothing, herself.

"Thomas did it, didn't he?"

"Luke! Why would you ask such a thing?"

"Because when I went in the living room to see if he still had my tablet, he said something about his father and paybacks and justice. I don't mean to sound cruel, but his ranting was rather difficult to process."

The boys didn't talk and barely moved, not even to sip water. The scent of charred wood and popcorn mingled with thin strands of smoke that floated near the overhead light. Outside, firefighters' shouts merged with the rumble of diesel engines. Inside, just the popcorn popping and the clock counting out the seconds.

The microwave timer dinged, making them all jump.

Eden shook the popcorn into a too-small bowl and put it in the middle of the table. "When did you last see Thomas, Luke?"

"I can't answer, not with any great accuracy, at any rate." He glanced at the clock and shrugged. "Thirty to forty-five minutes ago, perhaps?"

More than long enough for Thomas to sneak outside, make his way to the barn and—

A deafening blast rattled dishes in the cupboards, sent a few kernels cascading from the bowl and onto the table. The boys looked from Eden to one another, then to the window wall, eyes wide as they saw the plume of fire, pulsing and roiling above the barn before it merged with existing flames.

Chairs squealed as the boys shoved back from the table.

One silhouette, backlit by the fire, staggered away from the barn. Nate, cradling an unconscious Thomas in his arms.

"If any of you takes a step off this deck, you'll be grounded until you're eighteen. I mean it!" she shouted.

And then she ran for all she was worth toward him. She'd just reached him when Nate dropped to his knees. One paramedic took Thomas to a waiting rescue vehicle as another knelt beside Nate.

"Got a problem here," said the second.

A firefighter stepped up, threw his gloves and helmet to the ground. "What the…" He knelt on the other side of Nate, who met Eden's eyes.

"Don't look so scared, kiddo," he said through clenched teeth. "Thomas is gonna be okay."

Eyelids fluttering, he slumped forward. If not for the burly men holding tight to his upper arms, he would have landed face-first in the gravel.

When they finally eased him to the ground,

Eden stifled a gasp at the sight of a foot-long shard of wood sticking out of his back.

THE BOYS OPTED to stay with the Marshalls while Eden went to the radiology unit with Thomas.

He'd carried on something fierce, nearly knocking down one nurse, and Eden had to sign a form giving them permission to sedate him.

"The X-rays show that he inhaled a lot of smoke," the doctor began. And then he rattled off so much information—carbonaceous sputum, elevated carbon monoxide levels, the potential for acute respiratory distress—that Eden had a hard time processing it.

"He has a few minor burns, but our main concern is the smoke inhalation. We'll need to keep him, at least overnight, to monitor his symptoms, to ensure we aren't dealing with anything more serious. We'll keep him on oxygen and a low dose of benzodiazepine for now, and if his condition doesn't improve by morning, we may have to treat with corticosteroids." He patted Eden's hand. "I know it's easier said than done, but relax. He's being monitored closely, and he'll be fine."

After scribbling something on Thomas's chart, he added, "You might as well get some rest and come back in the morning. He's going to be out of it for quite a while." Sliding his ballpoint into his lab coat pocket, he lowered his voice and frowned. "The police have already said they want to talk with him, soon as he comes to, find out what he knows about that fire. You might want to be here when they do, so make sure the nurses have your cell number."

With that, he left her standing beside Thomas's bed. He looked so peaceful lying there, so young and angelic that it was hard to believe he could have set that fire. And the sad fact was, he probably didn't understand why any better than she did.

Eden leaned in and pressed a kiss to his forehead. "Rest well," she said, while you can.

When she joined the boys and the Marshalls in the surgical waiting room, Devon grabbed her hand.

"Nate's been in surgery for two hours," he whispered. "Nobody has told anybody anything. What do you think is going on in there?"

"Waiting is hard," she said, leading him to the bank of chairs across the room. "I wish I could tell you something, but I'm not family…"

She glanced around the room, at Zach, staring at some unknown spot on the carpet between his boots. At Hank, leafing through a magazine so quickly that the pages created a draft that mussed her bangs. At Carl, who paced like a caged tiger, and the ranch hands who cracked their knuckles. And Nate's parents, who flinched every time a door opened.

"…I'm not family, so I don't want to upset them by asking questions."

She pictured her maternal grandparents on the night her parents were shot. She and Stuart had clung to one another that night, and they'd done the same thing when Gramps had his stroke, and yet again after Gran's heart attack.

Surely the medical team realized that facts— even vague ones—would be easier for the family to cope with than *nothing*. How severe were Nate's internal injuries that they felt the need to shield the Marshalls from the truth? The possibilities were endless, and the longer they waited, the more anxious Eden became.

"How's Thomas?" DeShawn asked.

Eden explained the situation as best she could without providing too many details.

"They gonna put him in jail?" Carlos wanted to know.

"Why would they do that?" Devon ground out.

"It's a legitimate question," Luke said in his customary calm-and-informed manner. "Arson is against the law. The authorities may go easier on him, considering he's a minor and all, but—"

Mercifully, a doctor entered the waiting area and interrupted Luke's recitation of the legalities.

"Mr. and Mrs. Marshall?" he said.

Maeve and Royce stood, crossed the room and met him near the hallway doors.

"Barry Tremayne." He shook their hands. "They're wrapping up in there, and your son will head into Recovery in a few minutes. Things went better than anticipated, and because he's young and healthy, he should come through this very well."

Should? That wasn't good enough for Eden, but it wasn't her place to speak up.

"Your son has a mild concussion, a broken jaw and some cracked teeth, probably sustained when he lost his footing on the loft ladder."

Had he guessed at that, Eden wondered, or had Nate been able to speak before surgery?

"We repaired the punctured lung, but as you likely know, there isn't much we can do about broken ribs."

"Broken ribs, too?" Maeve echoed. "How many?"

"Three. And according to the paramedics, it could have been a lot worse. Their report indicates he walked quite a distance, carrying a boy?"

Maeve hid behind her hands.

"Shock and adrenaline," the doctor said, "pure and simple. No way he could have accomplished that otherwise."

He glanced at Nate's chart, then took a deep breath and continued. "The most severe injuries were to his left leg—lacerations, torn meniscus and tendons—and to his left arm. He lost a lot of blood, but we've taken care of all that. We don't anticipate any complications, but if any of you are A-negative, you might want to have a word with his nurse." He paused, glanced at every worried face in the room and stopped when he saw Eden. "Any questions?"

"How long will he be in recovery?" she asked.

"Oh, another hour or so. I'd say he's facing five, six days here, at least, followed by several weeks of physical therapy."

"And restrictions once he's released?" she pressed.

"Well, he won't be competing in any rodeos for a good long while, that's for sure. He'll need to avoid stairs, lifting, bending…" He winked. "But don't worry. We'll send him home with a detailed list of dos and don'ts."

He took a step backward. "Well, if that's all, I'll see if they've moved him into Recovery. A nurse will let you know when he's awake. For now, you might as well grab a bite to eat." He promised to update them when he made his morning rounds, and left.

Half an hour later, Eden's phone buzzed. She stepped into the hall to take the call from

Thomas's doctor, informing her that they'd moved him to the psych ward. "And for his own safety, we had to increase the dose of benzodiazepine."

She knew what that meant: Thomas had come to enough to fight the IVs, and they'd been forced to restrain him.

After thanking the doctor, she sat down beside Zach. "I heard the boys' stomachs rumbling. With all the...the excitement, they missed supper. They're tired and scared, too."

Zach nodded. "Can't say as I blame 'em."

"If I try to send them to the cafeteria, they'll say no. But if you ask them..."

He smiled and gave her hand a gentle squeeze. "My folks are in the same boat, so maybe I can kill two birds with one stone."

"If it's all right with you, I'll stay...in case Nate wakes up before they expect him to. Because it'd be awful if no one was there when—"

"You don't need to explain yourself to me, Eden. I get it." He gave her hand another squeeze. "And I approve."

Within minutes, she sat alone in the waiting room, watching news headlines crawl across the bottom of the silent TV screen. Eden switched seats and put her back to it. She had no interest in any announcement, except to hear that Nate was awake.

"Eden Quinn?"

She turned and met the gaze of a middle-aged nurse. Her pink cheeks almost matched her scrubs.

"Mr. Marshall is asking for you."

CHAPTER TWENTY-FIVE

THE NURSE WARNED her that Nate would be in rough shape. She hadn't exaggerated.

A gauze skullcap hid his beautiful golden waves, and his left arm, wrapped in an L-shaped cast, rested on his chest. A canvas sling elevated his left leg. The steady *beep-beep-beep* of the heart monitor was oddly comforting. The bulging bag that held blood, on the other hand, was not.

"Eden?"

His voice was raspy, no doubt a combination of smoke inhalation and the breathing tubes they'd used during surgery.

She leaned on the safety rail of his bed. "How are you feeling?" The minute the words were out, she felt like an idiot. "Sorry. Just call me the mistress of dumb questions."

"Knock it off," he said through wired-shut teeth, "it hurts to smile."

"How much do you remember?"

"Everything. They say I have a concussion, though, so…"

"Are you in much pain?"

One corner of his mouth lifted in a weak grin. "Let's just say I've felt better." Then, "How's Thomas?"

Eden gave him a quick rundown of the boy's condition, but thought it best not to tell him that Thomas was in the psych ward, drugged, to keep him quiet and still.

"Is my whole family's here?"

"Pretty much." She rattled off the names. "Zach was going to take your parents to the cafeteria, then drive Summer home. Swollen ankles, you know?"

"The boys are down there, too?"

"Of course." Eden found his hand, and patted it gently. "I can't believe I'm the first person you asked for."

His eyes twinkled. "Yes, you can."

His long-lashed eyelids fluttered and slowly closed. Soft, steady breaths told her he'd fallen asleep.

"Good," she whispered. "You rest, because—"

A sob choked off the rest of her sentence. Nate was in bad shape, but he was alive. Dropping onto the dusty-pink seat of the plastic recliner beside his bed.

"I love you," she whispered. Then she rested her forehead on his fingertips and let the grateful tears come.

Nate remembered this sensation, and he didn't like it, like riding a roller coaster underwater.

He felt woozy and dry-mouthed and a little afraid. Nate blamed the concussion. The pain. And the meds dulled his senses, but not the constant ache of his injuries. *How is this even possible*, he wondered, in an age when people could connect electronically from just about any place in the world and astronauts were training for a trip to Mars.

It was the way he'd felt after another accident, years ago. In the morning, when the doc made his rounds, he'd find out how long they'd keep him here. A week, give or take a day, Nate guessed, followed by a couple of months of physical therapy. Older and wiser—and tougher—he wouldn't slide into that chasm of self-pity and self-recrimination like he did last time, because *this* time, he had a lifeline.

Had she really stood to his right and whispered "I love you"? Or had he dreamed that? Whether she had or hadn't, *he* intended to say it. He'd come close to dying, again. Life was fleeting and precious, and Nate refused to waste one more second of it waiting for things to get perfect.

They'd get past all the misunderstandings, and figure out ways to prevent them in the future. That's what people who were meant to be together did, right?

While he slept, Eden had surrounded the window of his hospital room with the LED mini-lights he'd delivered on the night of the fire. She'd hung a fat, artificial wreath on the bulletin board, and lined the windowsill with get-well and Christmas cards. A tiny reindeer and sleigh decorated his rolling food tray. A menorah sat on the night table and a fat snowman on the radiator. And the handmade banner that was tacked to the ceiling tiles read Warning: This Patient Is a Christmas Addict; Candy Canes Prohibited. Maybe he ought to give the fentanyl more credit, because he hadn't heard a thing.

"Merry Christmas Eve," said his nurse. She glanced at all the decorations. "You know, yours is our favorite room on the entire floor." She adjusted his IV drip, then typed a bunch of stuff into the computer near the wall.

"Because it's so very merry, you mean."

"Well, yeah, there's that. But mostly, it's the goodies." Winking, she added, "That sweet little wife of yours sure can cook. We're trying to figure out how you both stay so fit and trim eating brownies and chocolate chip cookies and cheesecake."

Nate felt more alert today than he had since arriving, but he was still having trouble concentrating. Goodies? And...*wife*? It had a nice ring to it, but still…why hadn't anyone corrected the staff?

"You want me to give you a shave so you'll look handsome for the party?"

Party… Nothing registered. "Did my, ah, wife bring my electric razor? I could do it myself, save you some time."

She opened a drawer, removed the appliance and placed it at the foot of his bed. "Let's get this mirror adjusted first. We don't want you growing one of those nasty little soul patches, now, do we?"

Nate chuckled, then winced.

"You need to laugh more," she said.

"What are you, a sadist? It hurts when I laugh!"

"But every time you do, it'll hurt a little less than the time before." Another wink, and then, "Try it. You'll see I'm right. Besides, you're as handsome as a movie star when you do!" Her soft-soled shoes squeaked as she made her way to the door. "And you know what they say…"

"Laughter is the best medicine," they said together.

Nate laughed, and wished he hadn't. But the discomfort was quickly forgotten when Eden padded into the room.

"*That's* probably the best thing I've heard all week."

"That old saw? You need to get out more."

He almost tacked on "...wife" but thought better of it. "What's in the bag?" he asked through his wired-shut teeth.

"That's for me to know and you to find out."

And before he could press her for more information, his parents joined them. They, too, carried a bag.

His mom pressed a light kiss to his forehead. "There's a little color in your cheeks today!"

Kirk arrived next, with all of the boys in tow. Then, Zach and Summer.

"Better close the door," Nate advised. "For some strange reason, the hospital frowns on mobs."

"Time to get this party started," Eden said. "Who's hungry? I made mini-sandwiches and mini-quiches and mini-cheesecakes!"

Amazing, he thought, watching the lively interaction. He'd loved half of them since birth, and though he'd come to know the other half only recently, his growing fondness for the boys was just as genuine.

And then there was Eden, who'd hung the funny sign above his bed and decked out his room, organized this little bash and kept the staff happy so they'd spoil him rotten.

Eden, his very own slice of paradise.

HE'D BEEN OUT cold when the phone rang, dreaming that he and Patches were moving full tilt along the tree line. Blinking, he groped for his phone and muttered a groggy hello.

"Took you long enough. What happened? Lose the phone in the sofa cushions again?"

Big mistake, Nate thought, telling Sam that until he could maneuver the stairs, all on his own, he was stuck here on his folks' couch. He'd been deflecting mama's boy references for more than a week now, and running out of smart-aleck comebacks. "Better watch it, cousin. I know where all of your bodies are buried."

Sam laughed. "Ah, there's the old spit and vinegar I know and love. And by the way? You talk pretty good with your mouth wired shut!"

"If nothing else, I try." Nate sat up straighter, and grunted with the effort.

"Ah, they weaned you off the feel-good juice, did they?"

"Didn't have to," Nate said, smirking, "'cause I wouldn't let 'em hook me up in the first place." At least, not since his release from the hospital.

"Liar."

The cousins shared a moment of quiet, companionable laughter.

"But seriously, how are you?"

"Same as last time you called. Stiff, sore, bruised, grouchy, dopey…"

"Well, when Snow White comes back to fluff your pillows, have her call the doc. Maybe he can give you a little something to make you sleepy."

"That's mean, making a guy laugh with three broken ribs."

"Sorry."

"Liar," Nate copied. "So what's new in Nashville? Have you jammed with any big country stars lately?"

"*Now* who's mean? I haven't had time to tune the old Yamaha, let alone take her on a pub crawl."

Seemed a shame that a guy with as much talent as Sam hadn't caught a break. It couldn't have been easy, moving cross-country to pursue a dream, only to discover there were ten thousand equally talented musicians in line ahead of him. A lesser man would have come home, or let the situation turn him into a self-pitying drunk. Instead, Sam had turned his second-biggest dream into a reality, and signed on with the Nashville Fire Department.

"You're being careful down there, right?"

"You know it."

"Okay, out with it. What's the real reason you called?"

"To see how you're doing."

"Uh-huh. What's her name?"

"Can't get anything past you, can—"

A blaring alarm interrupted Sam's sentence, the call to duty.

"Gotta go," he said. "Call you tonight."

"Be careful, Sam."

"You know it," he said, and hung up.

Nate winced as he reached over to put the phone back in its charger. He didn't know how Sam did it day in and day out—leaving the firehouse without knowing what he'd find at the scene...or if he and his colleagues would return unharmed.

He flipped through the TV channels, and then gave in to drowsiness. He didn't know how much time had passed before he opened his eyes. Was he dreaming? He blinked a few times to sharpen his focus.

"You look so much better today," Eden said.

"Uh-huh." He ran a hand through his hair, then scrubbed it over his stubbly chin. "How'd you get in here?"

She wiggled her fingers.

"Hello, yourself."

"You need to watch more cops-and-robbers shows," she said, wiggling them again.

"I know that fingers thing means hello or goodbye in every language. And that it's how safecrackers warm up their—"

"Your mother let me in."

"Ah. So tell me, what brings you out on this snowy winter day?"

"Oh, just..." Eden shrugged. "Stuart says hi."

He started to sit up, but she stopped him.

"Your mom told me the physical therapy session took a lot out of you today. She also said you're talking too much, and that's why your poor jaw is all swollen still." She glanced around, at sports magazines, newspapers and a novel or two. "Can I get you anything?"

He wanted to say, "A kiss would be nice." Instead, Nate fished his water bottle out of the crevice between the sofa cushions, took the straw from his pocket and said, "All set. But thanks. How's Thomas?"

"Better. But he's a long way from coming back to Pinewood."

"How do the boys feel about that?"

"They're confused, and that's understandable. They're also angry with him."

"Why? It was my barn he destroyed."

"They think the world of you, that's why, and they nearly lost you, thanks to Thomas."

"So dramatic." He paused, happy to lie there and just look at her. "Talk to Shamus lately?"

"As a matter of fact, I did. Guess who moved in across the hall from him at the assisted living center?"

"I stink at guessing games."

"Cora."

He grinned. "No kiddin'. So they're…a couple?"

"I should say so. They've even set a date."

"Well, I'll be."

"Nate?" She knelt beside the couch, rested a hand on his forearm. "The real reason I'm here is to apologize."

"What? Why!"

"For dumping all my problems in your lap, then punishing you for having the wherewithal to offer to help me."

"Ooh, *wherewithal*. This sounds serious."

She rolled her eyes. "All right. The abbreviated version, then. I didn't do a very good job of showing my appreciation after your generous donation to Pinewood. You deserved better, so I'm sorry."

"Sorry that you didn't behave well? Or sorry that I deserve better? There's a big difference, you know." He forgot himself and shrugged, and paid for it with a sharp pain in his side. Eden's eyes widened, and she rose slightly. To do what, he couldn't say, but Nate felt bad for scaring her. "I'm fine. Honest. So relax." He paused a beat. "You were saying?"

She got the joke, and clucked her tongue. "You're impossible."

"Yeah, I know."

"But only sometimes."

Oh, how he loved that face. Whatever problems cropped up, they'd solve them. He'd help her with the boys—until they had a few of their own—and then he'd help her with them.

"Better not smile that way around any EPA offices," he said. "They're liable to cite you as a contributing factor in global warming."

She blushed. "They call it climate change these days."

"Oh, yeah. I forgot."

Eden sat back on her heels, head tilted as she studied his face.

"What? Is there spinach stuck in my jaw wires?"

"You shouldn't suck spinach through a straw. Your jaw will never heal."

"Point made and taken."

"There are a lot of things to like about you, Nate Marshall."

He raised his eyebrows. "Oh?"

She counted on her fingers. "You're a man of your word, and good to your family. Generous, kind, patient. The boys have learned a lot from you. They need you, you know." She stopped counting. "*I* need you, and if you'll let me, I'll spend the rest of my days proving how much I appreciate you."

Nate slid his arm around her and pulled her closer. "Was that...was that a *proposal*?"

In place of an answer, Eden leaned in and pressed a gentle kiss to the corner of his mouth.

When she sat back on her heels, he tucked a curl behind her ear.

"I love you, Eden."

"I love you, too, Nate."

He winked, which was about the only thing he could do that didn't hurt.

"In that case," he said, "the answer is yes."

* * * * *

LARGER-PRINT BOOKS!

GET 2 FREE LARGER-PRINT NOVELS PLUS 2 FREE MYSTERY GIFTS

Love Inspired®

Larger-print novels are now available...

YES! Please send me 2 FREE LARGER-PRINT Love Inspired® novels and my 2 FREE mystery gifts (gifts are worth about $10). After receiving them, if I don't wish to receive any more books, I can return the shipping statement marked "cancel." If I don't cancel, I will receive 6 brand-new novels every month and be billed just $5.49 per book in the U.S. or $5.99 per book in Canada. That's a savings of at least 19% off the cover price. It's quite a bargain! Shipping and handling is just 50¢ per book in the U.S. and 75¢ per book in Canada.* I understand that accepting the 2 free books and gifts places me under no obligation to buy anything. I can always return a shipment and cancel at any time. Even if I never buy another book, the two free books and gifts are mine to keep forever.

122/322 IDN GH6D

Name	(PLEASE PRINT)
Address	Apt. #
City	State/Prov.	Zip/Postal Code

Signature (if under 18, a parent or guardian must sign)

Mail to the **Reader Service:**
IN U.S.A.: P.O. Box 1867, Buffalo, NY 14240-1867
IN CANADA: P.O. Box 609, Fort Erie, Ontario L2A 5X3

**Are you a current subscriber to Love Inspired® books
and want to receive the larger-print edition?
Call 1-800-873-8635 or visit www.ReaderService.com.**

* Terms and prices subject to change without notice. Prices do not include applicable taxes. Sales tax applicable in N.Y. Canadian residents will be charged applicable taxes. Offer not valid in Quebec. This offer is limited to one order per household. Not valid to current subscribers to Love Inspired Larger-Print books. All orders subject to credit approval. Credit or debit balances in a customer's account(s) may be offset by any other outstanding balance owed by or to the customer. Please allow 4 to 6 weeks for delivery. Offer available while quantities last.

Your Privacy—The Reader Service is committed to protecting your privacy. Our Privacy Policy is available online at www.ReaderService.com or upon request from the Reader Service.

We make a portion of our mailing list available to reputable third parties that offer products we believe may interest you. If you prefer that we not exchange your name with third parties, or if you wish to clarify or modify your communication preferences, please visit us at www.ReaderService.com/consumerschoice or write to us at Reader Service Preference Service, P.O. Box 9062, Buffalo, NY 14240-9062. Include your complete name and address.

LILP15

YES! Please send me **The Montana Mavericks Collection** in Larger Print. This collection begins with 3 FREE books and 2 FREE gifts (gifts valued at approx. $20.00 retail) in the first shipment, along with the other first 4 books from the collection! If I do not cancel, I will receive 8 monthly shipments until I have the entire 51-book Montana Mavericks collection. I will receive 2 or 3 FREE books in each shipment and I will pay just $4.99 US/ $5.89 CDN for each of the other four books in each shipment, plus $2.99 for shipping and handling per shipment.*If I decide to keep the entire collection, I'll have paid for only 32 books, because 19 books are FREE! I understand that accepting the 3 free books and gifts places me under no obligation to buy anything. I can always return a shipment and cancel at any time. My free books and gifts are mine to keep no matter what I decide.

263 HCN 2404   463 HCN 2404

Name	(PLEASE PRINT)	
Address		Apt. #
City	State/Prov.	Zip/Postal Code

Signature (if under 18, a parent or guardian must sign)

Mail to the **Reader Service:**
IN U.S.A.: P.O. Box 1867, Buffalo, NY 14240-1867
IN CANADA: P.O. Box 609, Fort Erie, Ontario L2A 5X3

* Terms and prices subject to change without notice. Prices do not include applicable taxes. Sales tax applicable in N.Y. Canadian residents will be charged applicable taxes. This offer is limited to one order per household. All orders subject to approval. Credit or debit balances in a customer's account(s) may be offset by any other outstanding balance owed by or to the customer. Please allow 4 to 6 weeks for delivery. Offer available while quantities last. Offer not available to Quebec residents.

Your Privacy—The Reader Service is committed to protecting your privacy. Our Privacy Policy is available online at www.ReaderService.com or upon request from the Reader Service.

We make a portion of our mailing list available to reputable third parties that offer products we believe may interest you. If you prefer that we not exchange your name with third parties, or if you wish to clarify or modify your communication preferences, please visit us at www.ReaderService.com/consumerschoice or write to us at Reader Service Preference Service, P.O. Box 9062, Buffalo, NY 14269. Include your complete name and address.

MMLPBPA15